PENGUIN CANADA

THE HORSE'S SHADOW

LAWRENCE SCANLAN is the author of nine books, including *Wild About Horses, Big Ben, Horses Forever, Little Horse of Iron* and *Grace Under Fire*. He worked closely with Monty Roberts on *The Man Who Listens to Horses*, which spent over a year on *The New York Times* bestseller list. His most recent book was *Harvest of a Quiet Eye*. He lives with his wife and son in Kingston, Ontario.

Also by Lawrence Scanlan

Riding High: Ian Millar's World of Show Jumping
(with Ian Millar)

Big Ben

*Heading Home: On Starting a New Life
in a Country Place*

Horses Forever

*Wild About Horses:
Our Timeless Passion for the Horse*

The Man Who Listens to Horses
(with Monty Roberts)

*Little Horse of Iron:
A Quest for the Canadian Horse*

*Grace Under Fire:
The State of Our Sweet and Savage Game*

*Harvest of a Quiet Eye:
The Cabin as Sanctuary*

The HORSE'S SHADOW

Lawrence Scanlan

PENGUIN
CANADA

PENGUIN CANADA

Published by the Penguin Group

Penguin Group (Canada), 90 Eglinton Avenue East, Suite 700, Toronto, Ontario, Canada
M4P 2Y3 (a division of Pearson Penguin Canada Inc.)

Penguin Group (USA) Inc., 375 Hudson Street, New York, New York 10014, U.S.A.
Penguin Books Ltd, 80 Strand, London WC2R 0RL, England
Penguin Ireland, 25 St Stephen's Green, Dublin 2, Ireland (a division of Penguin Books Ltd)
Penguin Group (Australia), 250 Camberwell Road, Camberwell, Victoria 3124, Australia
(a division of Pearson Australia Group Pty Ltd)
Penguin Books India Pvt Ltd, 11 Community Centre, Panchsheel Park, New Delhi – 110 017,
India
Penguin Group (NZ), cnr Airborne and Rosedale Roads, Albany, Auckland 1310, New Zealand
(a division of Pearson New Zealand Ltd)
Penguin Books (South Africa) (Pty) Ltd, 24 Sturdee Avenue, Rosebank, Johannesburg 2196,
South Africa

Penguin Books Ltd, Registered Offices: 80 Strand, London WC2R 0RL, England

First published 2005

1 2 3 4 5 6 7 8 9 10   (WEB)

Copyright © Lawrence Scanlan, 2005
Map on page ix copyright © ArtPlus, 2005

All rights reserved. Without limiting the rights under copyright reserved above, no part
of this publication may be reproduced, stored in or introduced into a retrieval system,
or transmitted in any form or by any means (electronic, mechanical, photocopying,
recording or otherwise), without the prior written permission of both the
copyright owner and the above publisher of this book.

*Publisher's note: This book is a work of fiction. Names, characters, places and incidents
either are the product of the author's imagination or are used fictitiously, and any
resemblance to actual persons living or dead, events, or locales is entirely coincidental.*

Manufactured in Canada.

LIBRARY AND ARCHIVES CANADA CATALOGUING IN PUBLICATION

Scanlan, Lawrence
The horse's shadow / Lawrence Scanlan.

ISBN 0-14-301715-2

1. Acadians—Juvenile fiction. 2. Horses—Juvenile fiction.
3. United States—History—Civil War, 1861-1865—Juvenile fiction. I. Title.

PS8637.C35H67   2005   jC813'.6   C2005-902718-5

Visit the Penguin Group (Canada) website at **www.penguin.ca**

for Dal

CONTENTS

A DAY AT THE RACES   1

THE STONE HORSE   23

A BAILIFF'S WAGON   29

THE MAPLE LOCKET   49

POKER FACE   62

RUNAWAY   74

THE CROSSING   89

TWO HORSES HEADING HOME   104

FROM CLAIRE TO CLINT   118

ARMY LIFE   134

THE STORY OF MOSES   150

THE LONG ROAD SOUTH   172

SEEING THE ELEPHANT   198

CROSSING THE RIVER   220

GODSPEED   243

AUTHOR'S NOTE   273

ACKNOWLEDGMENTS   276

Claire Vigere's Journey, 1864

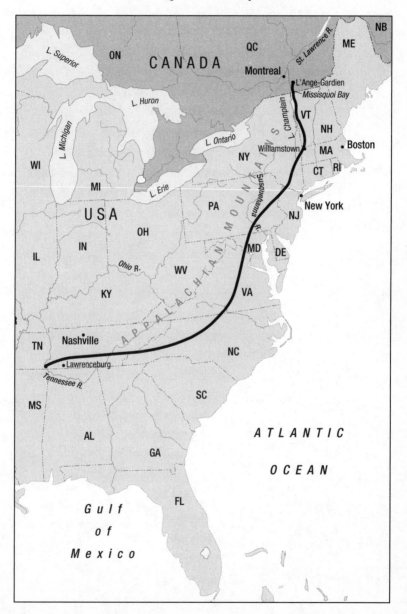

CHAPTER 1

A Day at the Races

"Salut, mon vieux."

It was the greeting that Claire Vigere always gave Beau Albert, and she never failed to deliver it with genuine feeling.

"Hello, old man." There was music in the girl's phrasing, each word lower on the scale than the one above. The greeting made no sense, for Beau Albert was neither old nor human, but Claire liked the expression. It was, of course, one of her grandfather's, and the horse had come to expect it. He bowed his great black head and curling mane and offered his ears to be scratched, leaning into Claire's touch like a cat.

Now the brushing began. Claire loved the grooming ritual, especially on a day like this when the bright winter sun sent shafts of light into the barn to illuminate the dust that now rose from her horse's flanks. Sometimes she paused in her brushing to watch the particles float and dance in the sunbeams. The faster she brushed, the faster they danced. The dust moved in circles, following the rhythm and motion of her brush. All this lively brushing meant that horse's dust invaded the girl's ears, her nose, it lay on her skin, her hair, her clothes.

Claire didn't mind a bit, for it meant that the smell of Beau Albert was in her and on her. Where it belonged.

And always, Claire talked to her horse, as her grandfather, Ambrose Vigere, had taught her. All horses, she knew, love ritual, so she often told Albert the same things, in the same chatty voice, in the same order. She told him how truly handsome he was, which seemed to please him.

"*Que tu es vraiment BEAU!*" Claire would say with enthusiasm, especially the last word, which she uttered with a pop, and he would slowly blink once in response. As if he knew it to be true yet was glad of the reminder.

Claire wondered aloud where he had found the burrs in his mane and tail, but her complaint as she plucked them was friendly, and, again, Beau Albert knew it. The grooming ended, as always, with Claire behind Beau Albert, rubbing each flank in wide circles with her two bare hands. This was ecstasy for the horse, who would press into each hand as it rubbed. He would shift left, then right, as if he were slowly dancing on the spot.

"*Tu aimes ça?*" Claire asked him. "You like that?" By the softness in his brown eyes, by the low set of his head, she knew that he did. Then she delivered the news she was most delighted to tell him. About the race coming up in a week's time, and the little trial run planned for that morning.

"*Vite, vite,*" she said softly. "Quick, quick." And the black horse pricked an ear and eyed Claire hopefully.

Beau Albert knew almost as much English as French (he was like Claire in that way). He knew *walk* and *trot* and *canter,* he knew *stand* and *halt, grass* and *apple* and much more. But it was French words he warmed to most. English he heeded, but French gave him comfort, for it told him all was well with his world. He welcomed it as he would the shade on a hot summer day. *"Doucement"* meant "softly, easy, boy." *"Juste comme ça"* meant he should continue doing whatever he was doing. *"Attend,"* Albert knew, meant he should wait. *"Vas-y"* was like *"marche donc"* or *"vite, vite."* "Giddyup, let's go."

In the old days, Ambrose had told Claire, they used to call the Canadian horse by the nickname of *marche donc.* A Swedish traveller to Canada in the mid-1700s marvelled at the stout little horses he saw, their broad feet tailor-made for deep snow. In his book, the Swede described a British officer stabling his pureblood horse during a snowstorm and carrying on with a Canadian horse—the only horse thought capable of navigating the land's notoriously bad roads in winter.

When Claire looked into the eye of Beau Albert on that frosty morning in early December of 1863, she thought she could see into history. At thirteen ("and a half," she told anyone who asked), she well knew the story of this breed that stretched back to the 1600s and Louis XIV, King of France. King Louis claimed that celestial blood flowed in his veins. He was *le Roi Soleil.* The Sun King.

"Would I have had to bow to him?" Claire had asked her grandfather when she first heard the story. She was proud too, and disliked the idea of bowing to anyone.

"Not if you didn't want to keep your head," Ambrose replied with a smile.

"Those who hung about the palace," he continued, "were like flies drawn to honey. They thought it a great honour to watch the King eat his supper, to see him retire to his canopied four-poster bed and to observe him rise in the morning. They paid him the same due that ancient tribes paid the sun. When the King put on his hat, the fancy lords and ladies right away took theirs off. But they had to pay attention! For when the King removed his hat, everyone had to put theirs back on!"

Claire had giggled as she imagined the scene. Hats on, hats off, hats on, hats off. It was even, she was shocked to learn, considered an offence for a mere mortal to turn his or her back on a *portrait* of the King. As for his horses, they were a blend of the best of the day: Arab horses from Africa, French horses from Breton and Normandy, Friesians from Holland, Barbs from Spain.

The first horses came to Acadia (what we now call Nova Scotia) in 1610, Ambrose explained. They arrived from the royal stables in France with a brand on the left haunch: an *L* (for Louis) and over that a king's crown. It was the Sun King's personal stamp, a stamp of quality.

More followed in the middle of that century, and their journey across the ocean was even more terrible than the one that Ambrose's ancestors would later endure. Horses were held in the air in crude hammocks, with slings at their bellies, and many of them perished. Of the two stallions and twenty mares the Sun King sent to New France in 1665, eight mares died on the crossing. Even coming ashore was an adventure. In the young colony there were no docks, and the horses were lowered into the cold waters of the St. Lawrence River and forced to swim for shore.

Claire could imagine what they must have looked like after the crossing. Ribs showing, matted manes and tails, only a faint light in their eyes. Nothing like Beau Albert, now snoozing in his stall, his left hind foot tipped up in relaxation, his coat shining.

"You like the cold, don't you?" Claire whispered into Albert's ear. Claire knew that her horse had no way of fending off the bugs of summer—horseflies, deer flies, mosquitoes—but that protection against winter cold was a simple matter of growing fur. Albert's coat was now thick, so thick the snow would land on his back and just sit there, as if he were a cedar-rail fence or a tall rock in the forest. Albert's ancestors, at least the ones who had survived the brutal winters of New France—and many had not—had produced somewhat smaller offspring. As if by becoming small they had hoped to hide behind the trees and avoid the cutting winds that blew in off the St. Lawrence River all winter long.

Neither the bluebloods of New France for whom the royal horses were intended nor the *habitants* who happily bred them were prepared for horses in the seventeenth century. There were no barns to shelter them, and almost no grain or hay for them.

But the little horse of iron, *le petit cheval de fer* as he came to be called, learned to cope. The horses would forage in the forest, turn their tails to the wind, and grow thick coats as the buffalo did. Over time, the harsh climate worked its magic on the horses, and they grew ever more hardy and immune to both cold and disease. The sturdy horses would somehow look plump and healthy in the spring. The breed flourished, and stories were told of the horses' uncommon speed, stamina and grit. Claire knew all the legends, even the ones that weren't entirely true.

But this much was fact. The little horse of iron had the best feet in all of horsedom. "No foot, no horse," was the first bit of horse wisdom that Claire had ever learned. She thought of it now as she asked Albert to lift each foot to be cleaned of stones and dirt. *"Le pied,"* she said to him softly. "The foot." And he paused in his napping to oblige her.

Claire ran her hand down Albert's legs, feeling for bumps and swellings, or heat that would signal injury. She could do it with her eyes closed and detect anything unusual. Claire thought of all the horses that had come before Albert, a line that stretched back unbroken for more than two hundred years.

During the Sun King's reign, horses sent to New France were viewed as royal property but they could be rented for a price: anyone, nobleman or farmer, could either pay the King one hundred pounds a year for each horse or return one foal to the King's treasury. Of course, no farmer had a hundred pounds. And even the King couldn't afford to go on sending horses across the ocean, not with wars in Europe and losing so many horses along the way. So, the *habitants* bred horses.

Black was a favoured colour, though there were lots of dark bays, greys and chestnuts, too. Claire had no idea how many there were. She knew only that every farm in Canada East had these stocky little horses who could work or trot all day.

And a good thing, too, she thought. Without good horses, how would her father get his goods to market or his family to church, plough his fields or bring venison and firewood home from the forest? Every child she knew had his or her own horse, and while the Vigere string of twelve horses was unusual, it was not thought excessive.

Claire tried to imagine a life without horses, and could not. In winter, the horses pulled *carrioles* (these "cutters," as the English called them, were carriages with steel runners for going over snow). *Berlines* were heavy sleds used to transport people, blocks of ice, wood, game from the forest and farm supplies. Finally, there was the *berlot,* an open sled with poles on the sides that three standing passengers could hold on to. The Vigere farm, of course, had all three winter vehicles.

Spring through fall, the *calèche,* or wheeled carriage, was the vehicle of choice. As she brushed Beau Albert, Claire thought of all the times she had travelled with her grandfather in their old *calèche,* even from the time she was a baby. He would rise early on a Sunday morning, then brush and rub Albert to make him handsome for "the promenade"—a stroll around the village after Mass.

Inevitably they would stop at a farm, where little Claire would play with other children or Ambrose would gab with old friends. Some candy would perhaps come her way, Ambrose might get a small glass of rum, and even Albert could count on a carrot. Indeed, he came to expect it and would snap his tail left and right all the way home if denied.

The slow passage of a gaily ribboned *calèche* on a wedding day (with guests trailing behind on foot), the solemn walk of a horse on a funeral march, the easy trot of a rider along a forest path: they were all part of Claire's life.

But so, too, was the gallop over fields on horseback with the summer wind at her back and another horse in hot pursuit. And racing on the glare ice of a bay with the cold cutting into her cheeks as her horse gained on the one just ahead. The *habitants* loved to race, Claire Vigere more than most.

"Do you like the speed?" old Vinet Leblanc had once asked her, trying to fathom her love of racing.

"A horse," she told him, "can never go fast enough for me."

———∞∞———

Now, with Albert groomed and ready to go, Claire called for her grandfather, and soon they were standing side by side in the *berlot* behind Beau Albert heading south and west, covering the twelve miles to Missisquoi Bay on Lake Champlain. The route was one that girl, man and horse knew well. The old map-maker, Samuel de Champlain, the man they called the Father of New France, had been the first European to see and explore the lake in 1609. Just five miles down the lake was an invisible line, what the Yankees called "the Canadian Line." For those in Canada East (that was the new name for Lower Canada), that line marked the American border. The state of Vermont lay to the south.

Every now and again Claire looked over at Ambrose. He had his eyes closed and a faint smile on his lips. What Claire saw was an aged man with a good heart and a full head of curly white hair, a man who seemed always on the edge of a grin. He was not an imposing man, but for Claire much about him seemed large: his hands, his ears, his nose. Yet he was surprisingly loose and nimble for a man his age, and Claire marvelled at the way he ate dinner sitting in his chair with his feet tucked beneath him. Such a pose naturally put him higher than everyone else at mealtimes, and Claire thought he rather liked the view from up there.

She loved how her grandfather cut his own path. He took midday naps with a towel over his head to shut out the light (no matter who was visiting), he peeled fruit with the small jackknife he carried in his pocket, he dunked toast in his tea at breakfast, he smoked one pipe a day—no more, no less. Like his horses, he took comfort in his rituals. His eyes were soft and watery and blue, the colour of the sky on a midsummer's morning. He had the look of someone who was up to something, and often he was. If he was smiling now, thought Claire, he must be back in the old days—he had won many races on this great expanse of ice.

For the upcoming race Ambrose had made certain arrangements, ones that no one else in the family would have approved of, so he had kept his plan to himself. More or less. Only Claire and Beau Albert were in on the secret.

Scheming, Ambrose had told Claire, is like a horse race: timing is everything. Actually, he had not used the words "scheme" or "lie" to his granddaughter. He called what they were planning to do "a little theatre" based on "*un petit mensonge*. A fib."

———

After Mass one Sunday late that November, the Vigere family had sat down to the noon meal (the centrepiece a partridge that Claire's father, Jean, had hunted in the forest). Ambrose had waited until there was a pause. He had waited until Claire's youngest brother, Jérôme—who was fourteen yet retained the innocence and wide eyes of a boy half his age—stopped asking questions about the new priest's sermon that morning ("Where is Hell?" "If I'm bad, will I go there?" "Do they put boys in Hell?" "How much does it hurt?"). Ambrose had waited until Claudine, his daughter-in-law, and Magrette, his wife, had finished their exchange on the merits of the new priest ("He seems so young," Magrette complained mildly, though Claudine didn't seem to mind). As for Jean, he said little. He was a quiet and mostly contented man. And he seemed grateful that on this day, at least, there was plenty to eat, the cabin was warm and his family was well.

"I see," Ambrose said, carefully picking his moment, "there's a race on the ice at the bay next week. Vinet Leblanc was telling me." This was a kind of truth Ambrose was speaking, for he had known about the race for months.

"Will you race?" Claire asked. It seemed a genuine question, but she, too, was playing a role, and playing it well.

"You know, *ma petite,* your old *Père-père* is too old for the races. But I know that Beau Albert is still the fastest trotter on our bay—or any bay, for that matter." Now Ambrose aimed his story at his own son. "Vinet says there's a young lad on the other side of Farnham, named Vincent Beaupierre, who drives almost as well as our Claire." And he turned to Claire and gave her a wink.

Claire's other brothers—André and Léo, then fifteen and sixteen years of age—found this of only passing interest, for they did not share their sister's passion for horses. They would happily go to the race—after all, it was a chance to be with friends—but the outcome hardly mattered. Jérôme, for his part, was eager to return to the matter of Hell. "The priest," he said, "told us sinners are in Hell for eternally. How long is eternally?"

"*Eternity,*" Claudine corrected him. "It means forever, and that means a very long time. But don't worry, Jérôme, my sweet boy. You're not going there."

Unconvinced, Jérôme frowned and fell quiet. Dinner table conversation then resumed its usual rhythms, with André and Léo laughing and poking at each other while the women spoke easily, as women do, about everything and anything. Ambrose and Claire looked content. Only Jean was not himself. He knew everyone for miles around and he had never heard of Vincent Beaupierre. But he kept his suspicions to himself, took out his clay pipe and went to sit by the fire.

───≈≋≈───

As Claire, Ambrose and Beau Albert took the *berlot* towards the village that Saturday before the race, no suspicion was aroused.

Those three were always taking trips to the village and the hills beyond. No one would be surprised that they were going to L'Ange-Gardien (Guardian Angel), the village twenty-five miles southeast of Montreal where the Vigere family and all their neighbours bought supplies, attended church and posted letters.

But once in the village, Claire headed south and west, towards Missisquoi Bay. Her heart beat faster the closer they got, and Beau Albert likewise put some pepper into his trot as the bay swung into view. Once out on the ice, Ambrose held up his hand and Claire eased Beau Albert into a halt.

"*Ecoute, ma petite*. Listen, my little one," he told her. Then he stepped out from the *berlot*, stooped down low, set his hands on her shoulders and looked her straight in the eye.

"Your job," he told Claire, "is to keep this fine horse out of trouble. He's relying on you, and so am I. Today, we work him lightly. I want you both to focus on one old and important lesson: that you are in charge. The driver decides, not the horse. In a race, you decide the pace, when to stay back, when to take the lead. You know how Albert is. He would just charge to the front, and we don't want that, do we?"

Claire nodded, her eyes fixed on her grandfather, who now continued.

"But neither do I want you hauling on his mouth to keep him back. You know this, I'm just reminding you. Everything has to be soft and easy. Today, just cross the bay and come back. Work on pace and changing speeds. Get Albert listening to you. The ice excites him and he needs to know you're there. All horses want a worthy leader, Claire. Tell him again what a good and clever driver you are."

And off they went, Claire standing in the *berlot* with her legs slightly apart for balance. She fancied herself a young captain at the wheel of a sailing ship with a steady wind blowing from behind. She could feel in her hands the power in Albert's trot, the pride in his bearing, how keen he was to run. Claire wouldn't trade him for any three horses in the whole region.

The races on the ice of Missisquoi Bay were usually occasions for the Vigere family to celebrate, for their horses rarely lost. But the races were sometimes sad events, too, for horses would go down on the slick ice and not rise again. More recently, winners endured another fate: sold to the highest bidder.

The carriage trade around Boston had discovered Canadian horses, and breeders in Kentucky had for years been snapping them up, aiming to inject size and vigour into their racing stock. Canadian blood was like a tonic for any herd. Whenever you tossed one in, whether on the stallion side or the mare side, the foals who followed were bigger, quicker, tougher.

Civil war, too, was now raging below the border, and in war, there were never enough horses. In Canada East, meanwhile, there was never enough money. The Vigere family was poor, but selling off his most cherished horses—Beau Albert, Tibeau, Minon—was not something Ambrose cared to dwell on.

Out on the frozen lake now, Claire had no markers—trees whizzing past, a fence post, a barn—to measure her speed. Only the wind in her eyes told her they were moving along at a brisk pace. Claire's eyes began to water, but she made no attempt to wipe them. The wind that created the tears also took them away in tiny streams at her cheeks. Besides, both hands were busy. She let Beau Albert out, by softening her hands and easing her grip on the reins. That and the words *"Vas-y,"* said quietly. Beau Albert replied instantly.

Claire loved that surge, how it came with no loss of balance or form. The black horse stayed smooth, his ears forward and fixed on the far shore, though now and again the left ear would swivel back to take in whatever Claire was saying. Beau Albert's black mane and tail were lifting and falling, the feathers of hair on his legs were trembling, and the far shore of the bay drew closer with every stride. The only noise was the wind, the sound of the *berlot*'s iron runners skimming across the ice and snow and Albert's hooves drumming the ice with a steady beat. *Kik-kik kik-kik kik-kik kik-kik,* Claire heard as she sped on and on across the bay.

Now she brought Beau Albert back with a *"doucement"* and a slight tug on the reins. The *kik-kik* tempo eased and Claire smiled as she heard, and felt, the shift. Beau Albert had a sensitive mouth, and if he wanted to run and his driver wanted to hold him back, his driver would have to ask nicely and properly. This horse was big on manners. And his driver could never touch him with the whip. One could show it, or crack it over his head, but to make contact was to invite disaster.

All this Claire knew. In the race, she would be by far the youngest driver of the thirty. And though she surely had the fastest horse, she would also have to keep him out of danger. The strategy in each race would be the same. Hold Albert back and let the others waste themselves early in the going.

The day of the race was bright and cold. High winds in the night had swept most of the snow off the bay, and now there was only a whispering wind. A perfect day for racing.

Someone standing on the shore that morning, with the Vigere family and the *habitants* from miles around, would have seen Ambrose with his arm around his driver. Vincent Beaupierre was about Claire's height and wore a coat much like hers, with a bold blue sash at his waist. His red toque was pulled low, and a black scarf covered his mouth. Jean Vigere almost remarked on all this protection ("What's he going to do when the real cold comes?"). But he said nothing.

Finally, he asked Claudine. "You said Claire was coming along later?"

"Yes," she replied. "With friends. Ambrose arranged it."

"Hmmm," said Jean. Now he knew.

The *berlots*, dozens of them, were lining up along the eastern shore of the wide Missisquoi Bay as noon approached. The horses, Canadians every one, knew what was up and most of them looked anxious. Not Beau Albert. You might have thought that he was just following Claire into the barn at the end of a hot summer day in his pasture. His head was low, his walk laboured, his eyes half shut. A proud horse was sending a message to his competitors: *You pose no threat. I think I'll have a nap.*

Two *habitants* now took a long rope and held it waist-high along the shoreline while the ten *berlots* and ten horses went about arranging themselves behind it. Ten horses would race west across the bay, circle a flag on a mast stuck in the ice, then head for home. Then another ten would race, and another. The fastest three from each race would meet later in the day to decide that day's champion.

A horse knows when a race is in the works, and it made no sense that a thin rope could contain them. Yet it did. Some horses, the younger ones especially, were pawing the ground and dancing on their toes. The wiser ones, like Albert, were saving their energy for the race.

Ambrose and others now gave last-minute instructions to their drivers. The old man had his arm around the boy and he was pointing with his free hand to a spot out on the bay. *There,* he seemed to say, *there* is where the race is won. Not before, not after. The boy appeared to nod. He took up the reins with great deliberation, bent slightly at the knees, cocked his elbows and waited for the rope to drop.

Spectators let out a great yell when the rope touched the ice. It was nearly a mile to the far shore. A lot could happen in two miles when you had ten horses and ten sleds and the footing was glare ice as thick and hard as oak.

If Beau Albert was confident, so was Claire. When the rope came down, the shouting began, but inside the girl's head it was almost quiet. Ambrose had come up with an idea, and though Claire had thought this precaution unnecessary, she had stuffed her ears with cotton anyway. "It will get loud out there," he had warned her. "Men shouting, horses pounding on ice ..."

Claire didn't want Ambrose to worry. She had plugged her ears for the same reason she always pretended not to have heard the many stories he told her a hundred times before. Because he was her grandfather.

In no time at all, Claire and Beau Albert were last. But Claire kept a steady distance—about ten horse lengths—between her and the leader. She watched from behind as the race widened, like a fan. All those horses and drivers were fighting for the same thing: the lead, a lead clear of trouble.

No one wanted to be last, for that position was in some ways the most perilous. The trailing horse would have to pass nine others to grab the lead. Collisions and sideswipes, a simple trip: all could break a leg, end a life. Halfway across the bay, some drivers grew impatient for the lead, and they smacked their horses' flanks with their whips.

Suddenly a grey fled from the whip, fled hard to the right; the *berlot* went hard to the left and then tipped, sending the driver tumbling and sliding across the ice. Out of the corner of her eye, Claire watched the driver rise from the ice and shake a fist at the horse as the creature galloped for home dragging a tipped *berlot* behind him.

Now it was a nine-horse race. Then, just as quickly, eight. The horses were approaching the far shore, and one horse—a pretty, little chestnut mare—slipped and fell hard to her side. As Claire and Beau Albert went wide to avoid her, Claire saw the horse's head rise but not the body. The horse's legs were bent at the knees in a pose that suggested rest. Claire knew otherwise, and she thought she could feel in her bones that horse's shock and astonishment. After they rounded the flag at the far shore and passed the downed horse once more, the driver kneeling on the ice at the horse's head, she thought she could even feel the mare's pain.

But she put that horse's plight behind her and focused on the horses ahead. Claire picked them off delicately, never rushing, choosing paths as they opened. Seen from a distance, a race unfolds casually—almost in slow motion. To be in the thick of it is another matter, and the winner of a race is often the driver who can stay calm.

Then, out of nowhere, a driver came up alongside Claire, not more than three feet away, and told Vincent Beaupierre to get back and out of the way. He used words that the new priest in L'Ange-Gardien would not have liked. Claire ignored him, showed Albert the whip and left the rude man and his horse behind, then cut in front of him and showered him in a swirl of snow and chips of ice. She couldn't help herself: she turned to look back at the man, and smiled.

Beau Albert had done all this so many times and now he had his eye on the finish line—the long black rope that lay on the ice, a rope that Claire could also now see. She glanced to the left, to the right, and there was no one. Claire (or Vincent Beaupierre, whose praises Ambrose was now singing on the shore) smiled again and even let out a yell as her horse crossed first over the black rope.

The last race of the day, held just before the sun went down on the bay, asked the most of Albert. This race gathered the fastest nine, some of them seasoned racers with their own notions of victory. Ambrose watched the race develop from the shore and he grew worried as the nine passed the halfway mark, kept on for the near shore, and still, Claire held Albert back. She was last by ten horse lengths with just over a quarter mile to go.

Later, Ambrose took her aside and asked her about that moment.

"Oh!" she said, her voice high and loud. "It was *tellement bien,* so *fantastique!*"

"*Ma petite,*" Ambrose said, "why don't you choose one language to tell your story instead of mixing French and English?"

Just then a man approached them and said, in English, "I wouldn't mind hearing this story myself." Then he thrust out his hand. "Tip Weldon," he said, shaking hands with Ambrose, who introduced both himself and young Vincent Beaupierre. "I'm a Yank," the man said to Ambrose before turning to the boy, "and I'm here to buy some horses. But go ahead, young fellow, tell your story."

Claire paused and looked to Ambrose for assurance. He nodded, and so she picked up her tale. But only after she had assessed the American. He was impossibly tall, much past six feet, and his oilskin greatcoat went from his wide shoulders all the way down to his knees. Tip Weldon was imposing in every way, yet there was a bearish warmth and an air of relaxation about him, too. Besides, Ambrose seemed to have accepted him, and Claire took her cue from that as well.

"*Bien,*" she began. "*Je me souviens que—*"

"Monsieur Weldon," said Ambrose, "needs your best English ..."

"Sorry," Claire said, slowing down her words and trying hard to play the role of Vincent Beaupierre. Were Claire a horse, you might have said she trotted in English and cantered in French. "The wind out on the bay and the speed of our horses were making my eyes all wet. This race was faster than the others and I couldn't see very well. And all the men were shouting '*Plus vite! Plus vite!*' That means, Monsieur Weldon, 'Faster! faster!'" She did not mention the cotton in her ears, for she was embarrassed by this, and had removed the balls of cotton as soon as the race was over.

Monsieur Weldon seemed to look down at her from a great height, his felt hat pulled low. But there was softness in his brown eyes, and he smiled ever so slightly at her courtesy.

"But Beau Albert," Claire continued, "he hears very very well though my voice is small. He could even hear me say the word I use to make him go faster."

"What's the word, young fellow?" Tip Weldon asked, genuinely curious.

"I say *'whooosh,'*" said Claire, "and Beau Albert goes like the wind. I don't show him the whip or yell *'vite! vite!'*" I just say *'whoosh.'* *'Vite'* means fast, but *'whoosh'*—that means really fast! I only use the word when I have to."

Ambrose interjected. "You waited until very late in the race to say the magic word, didn't you?"

"Yes," Claire conceded. She gave Ambrose a knowing look, one that seemed to beg forgiveness, but her mouth was curling at the edges. That smile again. Claire did not want to come out and say so, but she had delayed saying *"whoosh"* out of mischief and cockiness. She knew they would not lose and just thought to inject a little drama into the race. Ambrose frowned ever so slightly, and then laughed while shaking his head.

"And then," Claire continued, "the other horses and *berlots* were behind us and the race was over and the men on the shore were all patting Beau Albert on the neck and saying how smart they were to bet on him again this year. And that, *enfin*, I mean finally, is my story," said Claire, wondering how much longer she was supposed to pretend she was Vincent Beaupierre.

"How much did you win?" the Yankee asked Ambrose.

"Ten dollars, *monsieur*," the elderly man replied, "and the right to say that my ten-year-old gelding is still the fastest horse on Missisquoi Bay."

"Does Beau Albert have a younger brother?" Weldon asked Ambrose.

Ambrose immediately knew where this was going, and he would wish later that Claire had not heard his answer or what followed. There was a hard edge to his words, as if he were discussing an antique chair he had a mind to sell and not horses he loved. But it was too late. He had already put on his horse dealer's hat.

He told the American that Beau Albert was just gelded last year, that over the course of seven years he had sired many fine sons and daughters. Indeed, his son, the four-year-old Tibeau, short for Petit Beau, had all the gifts of his sire and then some. Ambrose called Tibeau the finest horse he had ever bred, indeed, had ever seen. A small farm can only accommodate one stud (two stallions in a pasture would fight to the death), and so Ambrose had been forced to choose between Albert and Tibeau, between father and son. Young Tibeau got the nod as farm sire; poor Albert was gelded and was thus deprived of a private, precious part of his anatomy, but he had lost none of his bearing or speed.

"Father and son," Ambrose said, "make for a mighty pair."

"I'm sure they do," said Monsieur Weldon, though his tone made him sound indifferent to this news.

Claire said nothing, but she, too, had caught the drift of what was happening here. She fell back, and leaned on Beau Albert, as if she could, by folding her body into his, protect them both from this unspeakable danger.

"I'll give you five hundred dollars for the pair," Weldon said finally. "That's top dollar, Monsieur Vigere, and I'm sure you know that. And I'm sure you know that I'm buying horses for the American government. The war at home between the southern and northern states has been going on for close to three years, and the North has need of horses. I imagine a cavalry

officer would be well pleased with Beau Albert or his son.
Think about it. I'm staying in Farnham, at La Grande Auberge.
Find me there if you're interested in selling those horses."

Sell.

The word made Claire feel ill. For the longest time on the
way home she said nothing, and neither did Ambrose. Even
Beau Albert seemed subdued on a day when there should have
been victory in the air and singing all the way home. Instead
there was silence. For the first time in their lives, grandfather
and granddaughter had nothing to say to each other.

Before the race (though never during the race), Claire had
imagined all sorts of possibilities for how the day might end.
Beau Albert might lose, of course, for even great champions—
as this horse surely was—cannot win every time out. Claire
had imagined, though only briefly for it was too sad a
thought, Albert going down as the chestnut mare had gone
down. Almost every race day on the bay had its casualties.
Claire had imagined winning, too, and she had that image in
her head every time the rope hit the ice.

But Claire had never thought of this possibility. Beau Albert
and Tibeau were family. You do not sell family, or even
consider it, at any price. She was shocked that her grandfather
had not dismissed the idea outright. Claire gritted her teeth at
the thought, then anger—an emotion she almost never felt—
rose in her. Beau Albert trotted on through the night along
that narrow snowy road with tall pines and spruce on either
side, and for a long time the *berlot* was quiet.

"*Ma petite,*" said Ambrose, who could not stand the silence
any longer, "have I told you the story of the stone horse?"

Claire said nothing. It had always been her offering to him, to pretend his tales were fresh and new. What a small thing it seemed to her, and what joy it brought to him. Claire's gift was to listen. There were tears in her eyes as she stared straight ahead at the trotting Beau Albert and shook her head.

In truth, Ambrose had no heart for the story either, but neither had he the stomach for the awful quiet that lay between them. He would warm to his tale. He always did.

CHAPTER 2

The Stone Horse

"On the day you were born," said Ambrose, "I knew you would have the gift."

Beau Albert was pulling them north along a snowy road towards L'Ange-Gardien, and the old man had an audience of countless stars overhead. They filled the sky, every black inch of it, right down to the treetops. The old man looked up, as if addressing the Milky Way itself. Claire stood beside him in the *berlot,* the reins in her hands. She was there, but she was not there, and she heard her *Père-père* only faintly, as if the cotton were back in her ears. As if her grandfather's voice had strangely grown faint.

"I was digging in the side of a hill to make a root cellar," he began. It would be a place to store the carrots and apples he divided—almost evenly, Magrette always teased him— between his family and his horses. "I was wearing, for luck, my red cloth belt. You know the one. And I sang as I dug that day in 1850."

Ambrose began humming the tune, and Beau Albert cocked an ear to take it in. His song, he told Claire and the stars, was a lively old reel, something about always coming in the back door. *"La porte en arrière"* was a phrase from the chorus, and Ambrose said he was humming the refrain as he dug on the day that Claire was born.

He had started at dawn, before the cicadas commenced singing their songs in praise of the summer day's heat. Early on in his work, he heard a thunk. The sound of metal striking rock. "I tried digging around it, Claire. I tried to the left, to the right, down the hill, up the hill. *Thunk,* the hill kept saying to me." It wasn't rocks Ambrose was hitting, but one huge rock that shrugged off the pokes of his shovel, as if the earth and the hill itself were mere skin on some great animal. He was certain that the rock's shape, if recognizable, would have meaning. He would take it as an omen.

"On the day a child is born, *ma petite,* you watch for signs." Claire persisted in not looking at him as he spoke, and Ambrose persisted in looking at her as he told his tale. They were a stubborn pair.

Like many *habitants,* Ambrose was superstitious, which is another way of saying that he was open to possibility. He didn't necessarily believe in all the myths and legends of his day, but neither did he dismiss them. Like the legend of *la chasse-galerie,* a flying canoe that would take you where you wanted—if you were prepared to sell your soul to the devil. Ambrose had never actually seen a flying canoe, but his mother had said she saw flying fish on the ocean when they crossed to the new land from Ireland. So if fish could fly, he figured, maybe canoes could too.

Many people believed in ghosts. Some claimed to have heard strange sounds (bones rattling, the clanging of metal) coming at night from the iron cage that hung from a pole near the Plains of Abraham at Quebec City. Inside the cage, awful to say, were the bones of Marie-Josephte Corriveau—a woman hung in 1763 for murdering her husband with an axe. Every *habitant* knew the legend of La Corriveau, especially after her body was placed in that iron cage as a warning to all.

Ambrose believed that the world offers signs of what is to come. If you paid attention on days that mattered (like the day a child is born), you could learn things. Other men might have cursed their luck that day. Who wants to hit rock while digging? Bad luck, some might have said. Not Ambrose Vigere.

"I know all about luck," he said to the brisk night air. Beau Albert was pulling the *berlot* ever closer to the village and he would soon have to wrap up his story. But the old man continued at his own pace, and Claire listened, though she knew every detail by heart.

On the day she was born, she knew, her father was off in the woods hunting deer. Having babies was women's work, and Magrette, Claire's grandmother, had delivered many babies in her time. "After three boys," she told Claire's mother, "you're going to have a girl." Magrette, a tiny woman with a booming voice, was almost as superstitious as Ambrose, and all signs, she said, pointed to a girl: the way Claudine carried this child so high in her belly, the fullness of the August moon and its peach colour, the call of a certain chickadee from the woods at dawn. *Chicka dee-dee-dee*, the bird would call from the same tree every morning. *Chicka dee-dee-dee*.

"Call her Claire," Magrette suggested, and Claudine liked the name. From that day, every time she heard a chickadee she thought of Claire.

"Magrette," said Ambrose—who had indeed warmed to

his tale—"was right. I remember the door of the cabin flying open and your grandmother yelling to me—I had taken a break from the digging and was sitting under the hickory tree—'It's a girl! Ambrose, get us some water. *Vite! Vite!'*"

The old man ran to the well as fast as his seventy-year-old legs could take him that day, the fifteenth day of July. He turned the name Claire Vigere over and over in his head—now quickly, now less so, now slowly.

Claire-Vigere.

Claire Vigere.

Claire … Vigere.

He liked the sound of it. There was music in that name.

Next morning, at dawn, Ambrose returned to the task of the root cellar. This time he tried a different hill, one closer to the creek that ran behind the cabin. But he had hardly moved three shovelfuls of earth before some powerful urge sent him back to that first hill. It made no sense that he would expend so much energy, shovel all that dirt, just to view the rock below, but Ambrose Vigere had whims. Moments of pure instinct.

He was a man who could invent a bedtime story for a grandchild, making it up as he went. The stories had a beginning, a middle and, always, a funny end. Ambrose would laugh, and they would laugh, too: Jérôme, André and Léo. Jérôme was then one, André was two, Léo was three and they had come into the world, respectively, in spring, winter and fall. Now Claudine had her summer baby. Four seasons, four children. *Quatre saisons, quatre petits enfants.*

As the newborn Claire Vigere sucked on her mother's breast inside the cabin, her grandfather spent that morning digging to see what he could see. His dog, a golden mix of husky, terrier and border collie called Babette, had ambled over to check on things. With her one eye—the right one had been lost in a scrap with a raccoon—she would peer down into the hole, look up at her master, then groan as she dropped heavily to the ground alongside him.

For Claire's benefit—though she gave no hint that she was even listening as she stood beside him in the *berlot*—Ambrose re-created that conversation between him and his dog on the day that Claire was born.

"'Babette, look at that! It's a horse's head. *C'est bizarre, ça.* This is strange.'"

Ambrose paused in his labours that day to examine the horse's head—from above, from the sides. He could see the horse's eye (a pit in the rock), he admired the throat, the fine nose, the outline of heavy mane.

"'Babette, you think there's more to this horse?'"

Ambrose remembered that Babette turned her head to one side, trying to fathom his words. She had no idea what he was saying but she hoped he was talking about food.

Ambrose picked up his shovel and began to dig once more, methodically now. By noon, he had removed the few inches of earth and the horse's head gave way to shoulders and back and rump, legs and feet—as if a life-sized stone horse had walked the earth thousands of years ago and chosen this place to fold his legs, drop onto his side and sleep the sleep of the ancient dead. But no, the stone horse was the work, plain and simple, of glaciers and sand, of pure chance and the slow passage of time. Nature had sculpted him.

"For me," said Ambrose, winding up his tale just as Beau Albert pulled the *berlot* into the Vigere farmyard, "the stone horse was an omen. I knew that baby in the cabin"—and here he touched Claire's red toque with the palm of his right hand—"would one day charm horses, as they would charm her. I told myself that tiny Claire Catherine Vigere had a lot to learn, and that old Ambrose Léonard Vigere had a lot to teach."

For the first time in all the time they had been travelling home, Claire turned and looked at her grandfather. It was as if she were looking right through him, and still she said nothing. Ambrose was deeply unsettled by that look, for he could not decipher it, and he was a man who prided himself on his ability to read both humans and horses. Suddenly the little girl born under the sign of the stone horse seemed older, and more complicated, than he had ever imagined.

CHAPTER 3

A Bailiff's Wagon

Claire put Albert away as she always did after a race. She went to the root cellar and found two carrots and cut them up, did the same with an apple, and put everything in Albert's bucket in the little barn by the creek. She watched him run his lips over the delicacies before taking them in.

A great malaise had begun to consume Claire, making her anxious and tense. She was a naturally bright and cheerful girl. Now sadness gripped her like a belt two notches too tight. But watching Albert attack his food seemed to dull the pain and help her forget it, for a while anyway. No horse in the barn valued mealtime more than this fellow, and Claire delighted in watching him eat.

"You earned your prize," she said, stroking his neck as he noisily chewed. Even Tibeau, who had done nothing more than snooze away the afternoon, got some of his father's booty. "You don't know, do you?" Claire said as she hovered over the young horse and touched his velvet black ears.

She moved slowly, as if she were sleepwalking. She had no desire to leave the barn, her safe haven. The world of adults, even her grandfather, seemed now to possess a treachery beyond her imagining.

Sell Beau Albert? Sell Tibeau? Ambrose had sold horses in the past, and that had always made Claire sad, for she loved them all. Every mare, every foal, every colt and filly. But Albert, Albert was like one of the family, and Tibeau, too. And besides, you don't sell your best horses! Even to think of such a thing made her head spin and her stomach turn. Claire had not eaten all day, yet she had no desire for food. Breathing itself had become a chore.

A full moon rose over the cabin and a deep frost settled over the land. There was no sound, or almost none. Just the odd rustling and snorting of horses, Minon the chestnut mare snoring, the occasional loud crack as if a board in the barn were complaining of the plummeting temperature. But then would come a long period of quiet. In cold such as this, Claire knew, it was best either to keep moving or to stay perfectly still. She chose stillness.

Shunning the warmth of the cabin, Claire hunkered down in the straw beside Beau Albert, sat on her haunches and leaned against his stall wall. She thought of what some of the men had said back at the bay about Monsieur Weldon, how quickly he made up his mind about a horse. "He once bought a horse at a hundred yards!" one old man had recalled, shaking his head as he said it. As if he still had trouble believing it.

The *habitant,* Claire knew, was a cautious soul, made so by decade after decade of hard times. Buying a horse was serious business, not something done quickly or instinctively. Buying a horse at a glance put Tip Weldon in a separate category, like a Wild West sharpshooter or a magician in a travelling circus. He was, people in the village said, *"pas comme nous autres.* Not like us. Not like us at all."

Last year Monsieur Weldon had bought several hundred horses from towns and villages all around Farnham and used a small crew of Yankee riders to herd them south across the ice of Lake Champlain. He himself had brought up the rear, like some lord of the hunt, insisting that the men and horses go no faster than the easy pace of his wagon.

Tip Weldon was not alone in his quest. Other buyers from below the border, or their agents, were showing up at every farm—even the far-flung ones—looking for horses to buy. Some farmers regretted the loss of favourite horses, but most were happy to find a buyer for so common a resource. Times like this, you sold what you had to sell. Horses were like crops: you sold at market in the fall, then planted again in the spring.

Just then the barn door opened and Jean Vigere walked in. Claire had always found her father to be more serious than Ambrose, and quieter, too. As if he knew from the time he was a child that no one could be as light and playful and as funny as his father, and the son had no interest in competing with him. Yet there was also about Jean a solid quality. With his blond hair and formidable nose, he was neither handsome nor plain, neither spirited nor dull, but content to exist in the middle of those extremes. Jean was as reliable as the west wind, and many women in the village envied Claudine her steady husband. Just as many girls around L'Ange-Gardien wished for a father like Jean.

He seemed to know where his daughter would be, and though he sat down beside her, he said nothing. The two of them just stared into the darkness of the barn, the moon coming in through the window offering the only light. Finally, he reached into his pocket and produced some bread, with meat inside, wrapped in cloth.

"You must be hungry, Vincent Beaupierre," Jean said with a straight face.

But Claire wasn't interested in the food, and she was not about to laugh at the joke that was meant to lighten the mood. She just shook her head and fought back tears.

"Claire," said Jean, "maybe we sell Beau Albert and Tibeau. Maybe we don't. It's something we must at least discuss, Ambrose and Magrette, your mother and me. One day you will understand why. I will not burden you now with the details, but you must realize, we are poor and getting poorer. Yet we will not make a decision about these horses lightly."

Claire said nothing. She felt a great sadness for her father, for she knew without being told what his circumstances were. There are no secrets in a log cabin. Besides, children can sense trouble on the home front. They can smell it, hear it, feel it in their bones. A mother and father can fool another adult more easily than they can fool their own child.

When Claire was only two, she once stopped eating for days when she heard her father and mother squabbling over something. Jean and Claudine thought they had kept the matter from their children, but the boys knew something was up, and little Claire did too. Like a horse balking at rank water, the child sniffed the air and knew that something was not right. The trouble passed, but the worry returned and Claire sensed it. Whispers in the far corner of the cabin. Moments of stony silence over dinner. Someone crying in the dark.

Later, when Claire was older, she was able to make the connections. It was never a lack of love that stirred the whispers, as it did in some cabins she knew of around L'Ange-Gardien.

Nor was it illness or death that stalked them, as some *habitant* families were stalked, leaving a mother or father alone to tend the broken survivors. No, it was money.

Like many farmers throughout the Canadas, Jean Vigere had borrowed money to finance his modest farm. To buy seed and replace old ploughs, to buy horses, pigs and chickens. And he had been optimistic that the farm would fly, that his father's genius with horses would mean eager buyers, that hunting would be fine and the crops finer. And some years, all of that happened, and other years, almost none of it did. The interest on the debt got paid most years, but never the debt itself. It hung over the farm like crows in a tree at dawn. Loud and dark and threatening.

The sale of Beau Albert and Tibeau would banish the crows, kill the debt. Worry would not find them, at least not for a long while. Small wonder the Vigere family were tempted, and tempted more than Jean had let on to his daughter in their brief talk. He left Claire to seek comfort from the horses in that cold barn, and he returned to the cabin.

Claire sat in Beau Albert's stall and thought of what to do. The future was much in her mind, but so, too, was the past. She called up her earliest memories, her childhood, her life with horses. How, she asked herself, had it come to this?

"A wilful child," Magrette used to say, sighing as she did so, "is an intelligent child." She was speaking of baby Claire.

The child's eyes were blue, of a light and haunting hue. With her long black hair falling in ringlets about her fair skin, she was the sort of child to draw stares. And the sort to stare right back. Claire walked at the age of one and talked at the age of two, as her brothers had done before her. But she had a presence and bearing far beyond her years. Her brothers learned to respect her and her sense of territory. Were Léo or André or Jérôme to pick up one of her toys—her cloth doll, say, or the hobby horse that Ambrose had made for her—she would fill the cabin with her scream. It was so piercing, so loud, that she never had to scream for long. And she seemed to have the good sense not to use her weapon recklessly.

Claudine, of course, loved her daughter, and delighted in her. Claudine's hair was fine and gleaming red and it hung down to her waist. On the day that Claire was born, she lay on her pillow with her hair spread out behind her, as if she were underwater. Claudine was, the villagers agreed, a striking woman. And she had given birth to a striking daughter.

Sometimes Claire would look up and catch her mother staring at her. And the child would put out her arms. "*Chick*-a-dee," Claudine would say. "*Chick*-a-dee," Claire would reply. And they would run to each other for a hug. For years when Claire was growing up, it was their ritual. A greeting after an absence, a peace offering after a squabble, or simply because one or the other needed to say the word. A bird's song became another name for the love between them.

When she was little more than an infant, Claire adopted a favourite blanket, a patchwork quilt with blue edging, which she would cuddle for comfort as she drifted off to sleep. "*Ma couverture bleue*," she called it when the words came. "My blue blanket." Bedtime was unthinkable without that blanket in her grasp. She would hug the blanket with every part of her: between her knees, with her hands, the side of her face.

The first time Claudine took it away for washing, or tried to, she offered her daughter a similar blanket in the darkness of her room. Claire took one sniff and knew she had been tricked. Like an animal who knows its own smell, the infant knew her own scent. The child liked how the blue blanket was home to her mother's spilt milk, her baby drool and other signature smells. She kicked up such a fuss that no attempt was ever made to wash that blanket again.

Sometimes Ambrose would bounce her on his knee and sing a nonsensical ditty that his Irish mother had sung to him when he was a child. "Diddle-dee-eye dee-dee," it began. He would say it over and over, slowly at first, then rapidly, playing with the phrasing, his knee keeping pace with the song's rhythm. Claire would scream with joy as she rode his bouncing knee, her tiny outstretched hands engulfed in his huge hands, her blue eyes locked on his blue eyes. The baby called him *Père-père*, and would do so all her life.

Sometimes, Ambrose would turn baby Claire upside down, grab her bare feet and tickle them on his whiskers. "Booga," he would say. "Boo-booga-boo!" The cabin would resound with her ecstasy.

Claudine would look at her child and marvel at her outbursts of joy. Her boys had all been so even as babies; this one seemed blessed with the most extraordinary sense of wonder. Claire would play by herself in a corner of the cabin, putting a lid on a mason jar, taking it off, putting it on, taking it off. She took such delight in this game. Or she would find the ray of light that fell on the cabin floor from the window and there she would sing to herself, talk to herself, often loudly. The words made no sense, but whatever the language, it was a grammar of pure glee.

When she was older, Claire realized how like her grandfather she was in so many ways. "You have more than his nose," her mother would tease her, though clearly Claudine was pleased by the similarities. And so was Claire.

Claire saw, too, that she had inherited the optimism that lay at her grandfather's core and that shielded him from the hard things in life. She knew his peasant roots and bloodlines. Ambrose Vigere was the son of an old *habitant* from Trois-Pistoles on the south shore of the St. Lawrence River, where it was seven miles to the other shore and the water was as much salt as fresh; his mother was an Irish woman named Flynn who had come from Calumet, on the north side of the Ottawa River. Ambrose had big rivers in his veins and would, if he could, pass whole afternoons staring from a shoreline. Water—the sound, the feel, the sight of it, even the smell of it—made him content.

These periods of solitude seemed to stoke the stories in him, and, as often as not, they were horse stories. Tales in which the horses had names such as Fablo and Duc, Corbeau and Capitaine. Each horse in his stories had a distinct character and a central role in the telling, and Claire was far and away his best audience. She listened, spellbound, as he told her about being lost in the blizzard of 1842 and trusting his horse to get him home. Or of winning races when he had bet more than he should have on his own horse. If her grandfather's stories had a hero, the hero—more often than not—was a horse.

Claire's *Père-père* was the one people went to with their problem horses, their questions about shoeing and feeding and foaling, about tack and training and every horse ailment under the sun. All this only raised him higher in Claire's eyes.

She thought her old grandfather was special, because he

spoke all the important languages—French, English and Horse. She knew that he dreamed and sang and conversed in both English and French, effortlessly shifting from one language to the other like a horse changing leads on the fly. On a warm day, Claire might hear him say as he worked, *"Qu'il fait chaud, mon Dieu, qu'il fait chaud!"* in the manner of his father, Pascal Vigere. Then he would follow with the same phrase in English, "Oh my Lord but it's hot!" as his mother, Loretta Flynn, might have put it.

On the day that Claire was born, the day he found the stone horse, Ambrose took out his white clay pipe, tenderly stuffed it with tobacco and found the shade of the shagbark hickory just west of the family cabin. He sat on the ground, leaned into his favourite tree and sighed as he lit the pipe. He thought of all the hickory that had gone into the building of that cabin. Hickory was rock hard, and cutting it with cross-saws was a trial, but that cabin would be there long after Ambrose was in the ground. He wanted to be buried in a plain pine box at the foot of that shagbark hickory.

"Will you talk to me here when I'm gone?" he would ask Claire several times a year. "Will you sit by that hickory and tell me stories?"

"Of course, *Père-père*," she would say.

"Long stories?" he would prod her.

"Yes," she would reply, impatiently now but still speaking with a smile. "I said I would, and I will!"

"Ben," he would say, sounding satisfied at last. "Fine."

⁂

Claire knew the story of the cabin. The tale was one of Ambrose's favourites, and it never changed in the telling. He and his neighbours had felled the trees nearby, peeled the bark and squared the timbers. Friends and relations from miles around all pitched in, and when the roof rafters were finally in place, Ambrose, then a young man, was the first to reach the peak. Custom declared that the first up was to swing a bottle three times around his head, and if the bottle landed on the ground without breaking, this was taken as a good omen for the house. Prosperity would surely follow. The bottle that Ambrose launched that day landed softly in some low cedars, then slid into the undergrowth, and he clapped his hands with delight.

So did Claire every time he got to that point in the story. The clump of white cedars was still there, but now they were four times her height.

Ambrose and the others then laid down a bark roof on the cabin, chinked the spaces between the logs with clay and installed one lone window looking south. The government had given his mother's folks—fresh off a dark and reeking boat from Ireland—tiny encouragement in the form of building supplies: fourteen pounds of nails, one pound of putty, nine panes of glass. They were numbers that Claire would keep in her head all her life. Fourteen, one and nine. What the numbers told her was this: as hard as their life was now, it had been even harder for her grandparents and great-grandparents.

The nine panes of glass were still there, and Claire couldn't help but count them each time she glanced at the window. It would have meant the worst luck to break even one. When she was small, she would sit in Ambrose's lap and stare out that window at the clouds.

Père-père would talk about his own mother looking out that window and drawing a picture of their grim Atlantic crossing. The foul water they were forced to drink. The poor and the sick, the old and the young, living almost atop one another like wooden matches in a box. She remembered the bodies of the dead wrapped in torn sailcloth and dropped into the sea while the women wailed in lament. She called up the lashing storms, the howling winds, the dreadful roll and pitch of the ship, the nausea that assailed them for days on end. Claire's great-grandmother would close her eyes and breathe deeply when she said the word "storms." She had learned of an old proverb that put it well: "Whoever would learn to pray to God must go upon the sea."

<hr />

Claire had no idea how long she had been sitting in Beau Albert's stall. She had kept her eyes open all that time yet somehow she had missed the horse changing his position. Now he was lying down, his head so close to her that she could reach out and rub his ears.

"*Salut, mon vieux,*" she said. "*Salut.*"

The stout black horse looked at Claire, his eyes and ears fixed on her. No doubt he was wondering what his mistress was doing in his stall so long into the night. This was a break with custom, and therefore suspect. There was worry in his eyes, a small tension in him, but at last he relaxed. Albert softened his eye and issued a great sigh.

Claire had a habit of sighing right after he did, as if in sympathy, but there was a hint of mockery in the custom. "Woe is me," the horse seemed to say by his sigh. "Oh, it's not so bad," the girl would reply.

Claire's thoughts drifted back, once again, to the more than thirteen years she had spent on this hard patch of ground. A cabin in the woods, there and then, was not without happiness. Music, especially and most commonly music from a fiddle, brightened the *habitants'* days, as did weddings and saints' days and festivals. Even deaths were an occasion for fellowship and kinship. But that other "ship," hardship, was a constant. Even as a child Claire knew this.

Crops would fail. One year it was wheat, the next year potatoes. There was too much rain, causing flooding, or too little, dooming the harvest. Spring came late or winter too early. Forest fires swept through their region, and only chance—a shift in the wind, a heavy rain—halted them. Some years, insect plagues wiped out precious crops meant to take families through the always harsh winters. Claire had witnessed each of these hardships at least once; Ambrose had seen them countless times.

Worse, land became more and more precious. Each *habitant* was forced to divide his land into smaller plots as it fell to his sons, and their sons, on and on. Claire heard Ambrose and Jean talking in the fields about how all three sons might have to find land of their own elsewhere. Too much was asked of the soil and the soil grew weary. And what good land remained—if, by some miracle, the *habitant* could afford to buy it—had long ago been grabbed by the English after their victory on the Plains of Abraham in 1759.

Ambrose and Magrette had taught Claire the family history and the hard blows their ancestors had taken. She knew, for example, that immigrant ships from Ireland—like the one that had brought Claire's maternal great-grandparents to this country—also brought cholera. Several epidemics had ripped through Montreal and Quebec and the surrounding countryside in the 1830s, and thousands had died. Great numbers of the *habitants,* tired of it all, pulled up stakes and sought new beginnings in the south and west on both sides of the border.

And if the men worked hard, the women worked harder. *I remember,* thought Claire, as she stroked the fine head of Beau Albert that night in the stall, *the year I turned seven.* That year had marked a turning point. She had suddenly stopped being the baby of the family. There was still time for play, but suddenly there was work—gathering firewood, helping in the kitchen and garden, trying to lighten the family's load.

Claire's mother had endless tasks, and the range of her skills was enviable: Claudine could seed the garden in the spring, weed it all summer long and put away the vegetables in the fall. She could make preserves of jams and beets, pickles and pears; she could milk cows, raise calves and pigs, chickens and sheep. Claudine could care for bees, paddle a canoe, ride or drive a horse to market. She baked bread, made butter and cheese, cured meat, turned sap into maple syrup, lye into soap, wax into candles, and sewed clothes for her family. Older women like Magrette taught younger women like Claudine how to be midwives at births, to tend the sick and see to the dead. From cradle to coffin, from dawn to dusk, and then some, women in the Canadas worked. Sometimes they worked themselves to death. Some went blind sewing by candlelight in the small hours of the morning, while the family slept.

The soil around L'Ange-Gardien was black and rich—rich in nutrients, rich in rocks. Every spring, the frost would heave up a new round and each family would have to collect the boulders and, with the help of horses, toss them onto wagons and then into the forest. Ambrose called these sessions "bees," though Claire could never figure out why. She thought it was an Irish expression, one meant to make work sound cheery and light, even fun. But of all the duties that came Claire's way, and she was not one to grumble, clearing rocks from the fields every spring was the one she looked forward to least.

The Yamaska River flowed lazily through the village of L'Ange-Gardien, and on the river's banks grew pitcher plants, wild yellow lilies and marsh marigolds. The birch tree, Claire's favourite, was everywhere, and so were certain birds—kildeer, marsh wrens and loons. The land around L'Ange-Gardien was as flat as a plate, though mountains rose up to the west, north and east. As if the village had guardian angels of its own.

Claire thought of the cemetery in the village. Ambrose had taken her for walks there when she was a child and introduced her to the dead. Claire liked the dignified first names on the gravestones: Nazaire, Philomène and Salomée, Alphonsine, Eudoxe and Flavien. The last names on the stones, Claire noticed, were mostly French—Viens, Gagné, Dion, Vadnais, Mercure—but the English and Irish were there, too. The Stuarts, the O'Havillands, the Briens.

This, thought Claire that night in the frigid barn, *is my world. I was born here.* And a new thought came: *Will I die here? Will I one day join Ambrose under that old hickory tree?* Suddenly Claire's world seemed small and predictable. What she loved about horses was how unpredictable they sometimes were.

Claire's bottom was getting sore after all this time in the stall, and she began to pace back and forth. She was weighing things, and counting all the good things in her life. There was Magrette's *tarte au sucre* (sugar pie), how her father kept a warm fire all winter long, how her mother doted on her and rarely lost patience with her.

Her older brothers were a nuisance but they were play-mates, too, and usually included her in their games. And there was *Père-père,* whom she adored, and his horses, whom she likewise adored. For Claire, the apple smell of a horse's breath, the velvety skin on a horse's muzzle, the peace that came over her when she watched the horses graze in the fields: all this made life feel soft and secure.

But as she paced, she saw dark as well as light. She consid-ered how few were their clothes, how plain were their meals, how cold was the cabin in its further reaches, how hard they all worked to keep the Vigere farm afloat. Claire was unusual in many ways, but she was still, and at heart, a *habitant*. She was supposed to be grateful when the little she asked for in life came her way. Others were not so fortunate.

Claire looked down at Beau Albert, who had now nodded off to sleep, and she thought of her first dark memory.

∼∞∼

She was travelling with her grandfather to the farm owned by the Charettes, six miles to the south and east. Claire was five, coming on six, as horse people say. It was a bright, cool day in early June, when the new leaves of spring still bore their light-green tint and the rivers were still high and fast from the winter melt.

Ambrose had tacked up the then young Beau Albert, and Claire was watching him as she rode in the buggy. On the rough roads, the *calèche* offered a rattling ride but Claire delighted in the bumps. "*Père-père,* make butterflies in my belly!" she begged her grandfather, and, of course, he complied. As they approached a hill, he raised his whip and the three-year-old stallion kicked into a canter. The *calèche* hit the peak of the hill on the fly and dropped like a stone down the other side. "Whee!" said Claire, who got her butterflies.

One thing Claire never was, was afraid. Her brothers had learned the hard way to keep their palms flat when feeding the horses their carrots. Each boy had been nipped or startled or stepped on by a horse, and though they were not fearful around horses, neither were they fearless. Claire was.

Ambrose had her on the back of a horse when she was still an infant, and he never ceased to talk about horses. The constant talk of horses had a double effect: his chatter calmed the horse, who took comfort, as horses do, in human prattle; and his words educated Claire, who listened attentively to what *Père-père* had to say.

Claire remembered everything about that trip to the Charette farm, even their conversation along the way.

"You see Albert's ears there, Claire? See how they're moving forward, then backward? That tells you where his mind is. Backward means he's paying attention to me; forward means he's wondering what's ahead. Sometimes his brain is divided, with one ear forward and one back. And see how low he carries his head? That's a sign of his calm. If you can get a horse to keep his head low even when he's worried about something else, then you've got his trust. He's your pal, and a horse, my little Claire, is the best pal there is."

Claire seemed to ponder her grandfather's words. She watched Beau Albert, watched his black tail lifting in the wind and the blue ribbons gaily flying on either side of his bridle, just below his ears. She heard the bells on his harness jingle as they went and she took in the smell of him. Leather and sweat and horse—the sweetest perfume in the world, Ambrose told her.

They finally arrived at the Charette farm. Ambrose had become more silent the closer they got, and Claire had noticed. She was learning to read humans as well as horses.

"I hate the sight of a bailiff's wagon," he told her, his tone uncharacteristically sour.

"*Père-père,* what is a *bay-lift*?" Claire asked.

"Bailiff," the old man gently corrected her. "He's a kind of sheriff who takes away the things of the poor when they can't pay what they owe."

The normally peaceful farm was all business now, with men darting into the cabin like ants raiding another colony's supply of eggs. The Charette farm was even humbler than the Vigere place, the cabin smaller and lower. Two wagons, with a single horse in front of each one, stood outside the cabin while its contents were shouldered to one or the other wagon. Madame Charette sat in one wagon, looking straight ahead. She had no tears left to shed. Her children—there were five, all older than Claire—had taken their cue from their mother. They sat silent and rigid in the back of the wagon, resigned to whatever lay ahead.

The children had for company in the wagon a small cupboard, a few pots and wooden stools, some blankets and patchwork quilts, several axes and saws and two family portraits. This is what the bailiff had left them. The bailiff's own wagon bore the lion's share of the Charette household: a tall cupboard, a handsome rocking chair, a four-poster bed painted a proud sea green and, glinting in the sun, a pewter teapot and a small clock with the timepiece above and a nun's portrait below. The heavier pieces had all been roped to the wagon, for the cargo was precious and would fetch a good price in a Montreal market.

Suddenly, there was shouting from within.

"Claire," said Ambrose, "hold the reins. If Albert moves at all—and he won't—just say 'Hoah.'" And then he got down and went inside the cabin. The shouting grew even louder then, but an almost eerie silence followed. Ambrose came out with his arm around Monsieur Charette's shoulder. The bailiff—a small, stiff man with his bloodied nose in the air—followed. That's what Claire would always remember of the day: how broken was Monsieur Charette, how hard was the face of the bailiff. Monsieur Charette's fist had found the bailiff's nose, but the blow had brought the *habitant* no comfort.

Ambrose then reached into the back of his own *calèche* and grabbed two sacks, giving one to Monsieur Charette, the other to the children. Preserves for the shattered mother, fruit for the shaken children, tobacco for the stricken father. And, with a heart as heavy as theirs, Ambrose wished his old neighbours Godspeed on their journey.

On the way home, Claire was full of questions. "Why were they so sad?" "How come they're leaving their farm?" "Why did that man take their things?" "Where will they go?" "Why did you say 'Godspeed'?"

"Claire, the *habitant* is poor. And sometimes he has no luck. Monsieur Charette worked hard, and so did Madame Charette. Last year, he lost his potato crop when the creek overflowed, and he borrowed money to get them through the winter. He thought he would have calves to sell in the spring, but he lost two during that bitter cold in January. The man who lent him the money does not care about drowned fields or dead calves; he wants his money, and the law backs him. And when there is no money, he takes what little the *habitant* possesses. It's why

I hate to see a bailiff's wagon. It means another poor family is going down the road, and we will not see them again. The Charette family will stay with Madame Charette's sister in Saint-Alphonse, but after that, I don't know. As for 'Godspeed,' it's what you wish for those going on a journey—that God will guide them and see them safely to their destination."

Ambrose then muttered something under his breath. He wouldn't tell Claire what he had said.

"Never swear," he told her. "The horses—especially Beau Albert—don't approve."

Claire would remember that. She and Ambrose said nothing for a while and then she put this question to her grandfather.

"*Père-père,* are you afraid of the bailiff man?"

"I am afraid," he replied. "I am afraid of many things. I am afraid a foal will die in the night, I am afraid your father will put an axe through his foot (you know how quickly he splits wood), and some day I might be afraid for you. But these are things beyond my control, *ma petite.* The French of France, they have an expression, '*C'est comme ça.*' It means 'That's how it is. Nothing to be done.'

"But am I afraid of the bailiff?" Ambrose laughed, then went on. "Some people fear those who have schooling or power or wealth. I am not impressed by those things, Claire, nor should you be. I'll tell you my secret."

And though they were miles from a living soul, Ambrose halted Albert. He bent low to his granddaughter and whispered, "Can you keep a secret?" And he put his forefinger to his lips.

Claire was thrilled to be part of this, or any, conspiracy. "Oh yes, *Père-père!*" she cried.

"Shhhhh," said Ambrose, pretending alarm. Then he looked around, to make sure no one was about, and paused for effect. He waved Claire in closer with his hand, and she did as she was asked before cupping her right ear to take in his whispered wisdom.

"When I meet someone who thinks he's above me," said Ambrose in a hushed voice, "I imagine him"—and here again he paused for effect before letting his voice rise—"without a stitch of clothing, and in diapers!!!" Then Ambrose slapped his knee and guffawed out loud. And Claire did the same.

The dark shadow of the bailiff seemed to pass with their laughter, and the rest of the journey home was, as always with Ambrose, most pleasant. Not at all like the dreadful trip home from Missisquoi Bay.

The races, meeting Monsieur Weldon, talk of selling her beloved horses: all had set something in motion. *But what?* thought Claire. *And where will it take me?*

CHAPTER 4

The Maple Locket

The girl who sat in the stall with her horse in that cold, dark barn was just over five feet tall. *"Ma petite,"* Ambrose always called her, and she was indeed small. Her hair was thick and black and curly, as curly as the long manes of the horses in the Vigere herd. Her wide blue eyes were balanced by a sculpted mouth with lips always slightly apart, as if in anticipation. She had flawless milky skin and bright teeth that were revealed every time she smiled, and Claire was a girl who smiled a lot. Laughter came harder, for she could seem serious at times, but when it did come it came rolling in like a wave. Her nose was a tad too large for her face (Magrette called it a strong nose and insisted it came from Ambrose's side of the family), but even this seemed to suit young Claire. She was not delicate or lovely or pretty in the usual way, but she was striking nonetheless.

Claire had a scar on her right cheek, barely noticeable. The blemish, no wider than the nail on her small finger and turned up at the edges like a smile, lent character to that handsome face.

Claire had just turned ten and she was harnessing Minon for a trip into the village. She was bending low by the *berline* to adjust one of the traces when a hunter's shot rang out in the forest. Minon had been napping but instantly shot forward (it was a divine mystery how a creature so large could move so quickly from a standstill). Pure instinct had launched the mare; years of schooling braked her (another divine mystery, that such a rush of energy could be so suddenly arrested). But the damage was done. Claire's cheek opened like a red flower.

Claire never blamed Minon. She expected to pay a price for a life with horses: broken bones, bruises, cuts like this. Claire counted them a small cost for all that horses bestowed, and she wore her tiny scar with pride.

Even the way she walked, like a filly sure of her own pedigree, spoke of her dignity. And part of that came from a love of knowledge. Unlike most cabins in the parish served by the church in L'Ange-Gardien, hers had books inside. Not many, but some, and they were treated with respect. The parish was then home to two thousand souls, and of the four hundred children between five and sixteen, only half ever went to school. Claire went to the village school when her duties at home allowed it, but she was lucky in that both her parents and grandparents had more schooling than most and passed on their knowledge to her.

Claire had friends in the village, and she was especially fond of Lisette Brodeur, the grocer's daughter. They were the same age, shared a love for horses, and laughed at the same things (like the funny faces and noises that Luc Gendron made in class). Where Claire was short and fine, Lisette was tall and bulky: a slender pony had befriended a draft horse. Sometimes the two girls would walk home in the snow, Claire on Lisette's sturdy back, the two of them shrieking with laughter. But farm labour and the distance between them made such contact infrequent. After Mass, weddings, funerals, baptisms: these were the times that children could enjoy each other's company. Work at home came first, then school, with play a distant third.

Claire soon learned that at the Vigere farm, home was school—at least where language was concerned. Her grandfather would rise at dawn, as always, and sometimes announce to the family that "Today is an English day!" and everyone was supposed to converse in that language until bedtime. French days needed no such introduction. If Ambrose took his morning tea from Magrette and said *"C'est bon, ça,"* then the cabin took its cue. Today would be a French day, and everyone—the boys, especially—was secretly relieved.

The routine achieved what Ambrose intended. Claire, for one, could read and write and speak well enough in both English and French, and that was most unusual in her day.

She was also a naturally confident girl, and working with horses only made her more so. And while her grandfather continued to pass on his considerable knowledge of horses, she seemed to possess her own instincts. Claire seemed to know when to be still on a horse's back, when to prod, how much to ask of a horse on any given day.

She had a way with them. Almost without thinking, she could calm a troubled horse. Sometimes it was a stern word, or a fearlessness in the face of one horse's fury or panic. Sometimes it was a word of encouragement, or something in her body language that told the horse she would wait it out, no matter what. Her grandfather had an expression, a pearl of wisdom about getting a horse on side and the virtue of patience: "Act with a horse like you have all day and then some, it takes only minutes. Act like you have only minutes, it takes all day and then some."

Claire was especially fond of Tibeau, Beau Albert's four-year-old son, without question the sparkiest horse in the bunch. He was, at more than sixteen hands, taller than his father and slimmer. Haughtier, too, with his black eyes and tail in the air when he wanted to show off. Claire had come off him several times at a sudden noise in the bush or when the wind got high and loud. To a young horse the wind is a doubled-edged sword: it robs him of his senses of smell and hearing, his key defences against danger. When in doubt, a young horse knows, you run. So Claire came off him as Tibeau darted hard left, hard right, or sideways—came off him in the time it takes to spit out an apple seed.

This colt, for whatever reason, was terrified of chipmunks. Tibeau would stiffen at the sound of them, flee at the sight of them, and sometimes Claire rode out these little tempests and sometimes she found herself spilled on the ground. But she would laugh, circle him till he calmed, and get back on, talking all the while of the weather and what a good boy he really was, down deep.

Like many good riders, Claire got an early start. When she was five, she was riding bareback. Ambrose would put her on Minon, an older mare, and they would circle in a field thick with clover and hay. Ambrose had the mare on the end of a long rope, and he would keep her in a walk, then cluck her into a trot and, finally, into a rolling canter.

"Keep your hands outstretched, *ma petite*, and don't grip with your legs," Ambrose would say. "Just feel the horse's rhythm underneath you and go with him. Go with him. And if you fall off, roll when you land." And sometimes Claire would fall off, though Minon was so short and the clover so dense that little harm was done. Claire would laugh, Ambrose would set her back on the horse, and they would continue.

Eventually, Ambrose took away the rope and gave Claire the reins. The circle got bigger, the pace quicker. She stopped falling off Minon and graduated to taller geldings, and even the boss of the herd, Beau Albert. By the age of ten, Claire was an accomplished rider, with soft hands and fine balance. She was fearless at the gallop and over fences and expected her horse to be likewise.

One day, Albert, perhaps sore from a long ride the day before, stopped at a low fence not far from the Vigere cabin, and Claire's nose almost met the topmost cedar rail. She dismounted, gave Albert a smack on the chest, said "*Fais pas ça!* Don't do that!" and got back on before retaking the fence. Ambrose happened to witness the incident and lectured her afterwards.

"The horse," he said, clearly disappointed in her, "is entitled to his moments of doubt. Your job is to anticipate those moments. And you never strike your horse in anger." Then he walked away from her.

Claire rarely saw her *Père-père* express displeasure at something she had done, especially something to do with horses. That small rebuke, the memory of the tears that followed, the sense of deep regret: all would stay with her the rest of her life.

Later she realized how right her grandfather had been. On the way home that day, Albert had not been himself. Claire actually had to use a little leg on him; usually he responded to the lightest touch. She should have foreseen that moment at the fence.

"On the other hand," said Ambrose, and Claire's spirit lifted at his change in tone, "you never share your fear with the horse. You give him your confidence, and that, *ma petite,* you have in spades."

Now Claire lay down in the stall, rested her head on Beau Albert's chest and folded her arms across her body. She wasn't finished her thinking, wasn't yet sure how to proceed if the horses were sold to Monsieur Weldon.

The night silence was broken just then by a great thrashing in the trees near the barn. She could hear the flapping of powerful wings, the sound of snow dropping heavily to the ground and a hawk's shrill complaint. By the racket, you would have thought a band of monkeys were chasing each other through the trees. But this was no jungle, this was a farm on a cold winter's night in 1863. Claire wondered if an owl had been pursuing a nighthawk, and she knew instantly where her allegiance lay. With the prey, never the predator—even though the pursued animal in this case was itself a predator. The chase finally ended, and silence was restored.

Claire thought of all she knew about animals and where that knowledge had come from. From Ambrose, always from Ambrose. But where had *he* learned it? she wondered.

It was from a traveller, while he was still a young man, that Ambrose had learned about "secret societies" in England. He listened with fascination when a blacksmith from Liverpool told him about the charms horsemen would use to acquire magical powers over horses. The recipe would be passed from one generation to the next, but it never much varied. You took the bones of a frog or a toad, said certain words over the bones, buried them in an anthill, then cooked them. A man who possessed such bones had complete mastery over horses, or so it was believed.

One day, when Claire was seven, Ambrose told her the same story.

"Is it true, *Père-père*?" she asked him, wide-eyed.

"Well," he replied, "I'm curious to know myself. Let's try it."

That morning, he found a frog and prepared it as the story prescribed. Later, he and Claire put the frog's bones in Magrette's oven when she wasn't looking (and later blamed the foul smell on a mouse that had found its way into the cabin and perished in the stove).

"But what words should we say over the bones?" Claire asked.

Ambrose thought for a second, and some Latin an old priest had taught him was pressed into service. He closed his eyes and began, *"Semper paratus, semper paratus, semper paratus ..."* He said it over and over, and had Claire manage it as well and say it with him. The next day Ambrose carved a locket of maple with a sliding cover, placed the bones inside and insisted she wear it when she was riding Minon.

"Do you notice a difference?" he asked after she had been in the saddle a while.

"I can't believe it!" Claire replied. "There's nothing she won't do for me."

"Well, I have learned something today," Ambrose said, nodding once as he said so, and he promised Claire he would tell all his friends.

The next day, he looked on again as Claire rode Minon.

"Is that locket still working its magic?" Ambrose asked her from the ground. And she assured him it was.

"Stop your horse," he suddenly said. "I need to see the locket." There was urgency in his voice. Claire brought Minon to a halt and leaned low so Ambrose could lift the locket off her neck.

"Claire, let me show you something." When he opened the locket she stared inside. It was empty.

"I took the bones out this morning," he said. "I wanted to make a point. There is no magic in frog bones buried in anthills and cooked in ovens. The magic with horses is in your hands and your heart, Claire. I'm sorry I deceived you, but I wanted you to understand. You have a gift for horses, and you should use that gift wisely. Approach every horse with confidence, as if you wore a magic locket around your neck. But your magic is inside you, Claire, and every horse knows that."

Later, Claire asked him about the Latin.

"It was a Latin motto," he said, grinning as he spoke. "It did sound solemn, didn't it? I was saying, 'Always prepared, always prepared ...'"

Grandfather and granddaughter walked hand in hand back to the cabin, and when Magrette asked them what they were smiling about, they both burst out laughing. And for weeks thereafter, one of them had only to say *"semper"* or *"paratus"* and the other would grin.

The barn at the Vigere farm was a separate world for Claire. She seemed to move more freely there than in the cabin. The barn's lively fragrances, its dawn and dusk routines and, especially, its creatures all sustained her. She knew every horse in the herd of twelve, knew that one place—up by the withers, under the jaw, behind the ears—that each horse longed to have scratched.

One horse liked Claire to tap with her fingers on his lower set of teeth, and then he would gently mouth her knuckle. Another liked to have his face rubbed, but only after he had made a show of being a nasty boy—ears back, teeth threatening. It was a game they played. Claire had spent many hours learning all this—what each one liked and didn't like. This gelding wanted his gums massaged. That mare delighted in having her nostrils worked. Another older mare just wanted Claire to hug her and she would lay her head on Claire's chest and close her eyes while the girl stroked her face and ears and told her what she wanted to hear: that she—the horse, that is—was an angel.

Not everyone delighted in Claire's savvy with horses. Magrette, for one, did not approve. And when Claire was ten, Magrette embarked on a campaign to bring Claire out of the barn and into the kitchen. Where girls belonged.

Ambrose and Magrette—who usually agreed on things that mattered—never openly sparred about the fate of their grand-daughter. They were too clever, too kind, too devoted to one another for that. Instead, they threw praise Claire's way, hoping she would take the hint. They were like an old couple sitting on a porch tossing seed on the ground and waiting to see whose seed the bird would peck first.

Claire shook her head and smiled as she thought of what she had long called "*la guerre Vigere.*" The Vigere war. She stepped out of Beau Albert's stall and lugged a flake of hay inside so she could sit more comfortably. The gelding, of course, was delighted to see breakfast coming before dawn. The chair wouldn't last nearly as long as *la guerre Vigere.*

Magrette, or *Mamie* as her granddaughter called her, gave Claire instruction in herding cows, seeding the garden, light-ing the morning fire, emptying chamber pots into the privy outside, stacking wood, sweeping floors. Magrette also taught Claire to sew and knit, and fussed over her simple creations, which grew ever more elaborate. She taught Claire to cook, showed her how to make *tarte au sucre* and pork pie, which the French called *tourtière.*

"Claire," she would say, "one day you will have children of your own and you will pass on these skills. You are a smart little girl and I'm very proud that you learn so quickly." When she was pleased, Magrette would gather in her right fist the shawl she always wore—summer and winter—and lift her shoulders.

Ambrose had his own plan. He gave Claire a bound and blank book and instructed her to write down everything he told her about horses, to list her notes according to the alphabet, and all of it in English.

"One of these days," he told her, "you will deal in horses, you will breed and train them, and not all your customers will be the *habitants*. More and more the English come for our horses. Yankees from below the border, people from Canada West—though it'll always be Upper Canada to me—buyers from the east coast. They're all English-speakers. So think in French, *ma petite*, but write your horse book in English."

And so she did. In her neat penmanship, as her mother had taught her, Claire made precise notes under each letter of the alphabet.

B for Bridle, and how to protect the leather of saddle and harness and her own leather boots with saddle soap and Ambrose's special blend of beeswax and neatsfoot oil.

H for Hoof, how to clean the hoof and calm young horses wary of having their feet picked up, how to trim and shoe, how to treat problems like sandcracks and foot rot.

P for Poisonous Plants that horses should avoid, such as ragwort with its bright yellow flowers, and others with pretty names—foxglove, meadow saffron, buttercup.

T for Teeth, how to file (or "float") them, how to remove bad teeth and wolf teeth, how teeth tell the age of a horse.

V for Veterinary Care, with recipes for all the ointments and oils that Ambrose would prepare for sore muscles and against ringworm, colic and much else.

Over the years, the book filled, and Claire would start another and yet another, until she had a set of nine volumes. Claudine jokingly called it the *Encyclopedia Ambrosia,* and almost everything Ambrose knew about training, breeding and racing horses found its way into those volumes. Some pages were graced with Claire's drawings—of a prized foal or colt or filly, a promising yearling, a good-hearted mare, an aging but still proud stallion. Over time, the books became more decorative than useful. They occupied the shelf on the wall over Claire's bed, but she rarely had to consult them, for the contents existed as fully in her brain as they did on the page.

Ambrose knew he had a dedicated student of the horse. And he told her so.

"The luckiest horses in the world—do you know who they are?" he would ask her.

"No, *Père-père,*" Claire would reply, pretending not to know the answer.

"The luckiest horses in the world," he would say, "are those who belong to Claire Vigere."

Claire's misfortune, she knew, was to be the prize pupil of both Ambrose and Magrette. *Mamie* thought Claire would make the perfect wife and mother; *Père-père* thought Claire was God's gift to the world of horses. The war over Claire spread, with allegiances divided in surprising ways.

Jean Vigere was naturally proud of Claire's accomplishments in the barn and pasture. But in the end he took Magrette's side and wished his only daughter would forget about horses and focus on her other duties around the farm.

Claudine threw her lot in with Ambrose, for she dreamed of a future for her daughter other than the one that Canada East was then offering its girls. Ceaseless farm labour, early marriage, many children—some of whom would die in childbirth. The seasons passing until one day you were lowered into the ground in a plain box and your children mourned your passing. Word of Claire's horsemanship had spread in the region, and there was enough of the dreamer left in Claudine that her daughter's ambition—vague as it was—made her feel young again.

Claire was acutely aware of the divisions she was causing in the family, and she tried desperately to please both sides. She would sew a shirt for one of her brothers, then cook a meal of venison stew; she would spend an afternoon working with the colts and oil tack in the evening. Claire worked as hard as any horse in the field and would fall into her straw-and-feather bed, the remnants of her blue blanket under her pillow, exhausted at the end of such days.

The day was coming when she would have to choose a path to follow. Talk of selling her favourite horses had simply brought that day a lot closer.

───⊗∞⊗───

There was a faint light now showing on the eastern horizon, and Claire realized she had spent the entire night in the stall with Beau Albert. The horse was up again, maybe in hopes of more hay. Claire went to the back of the barn and got some, but the others caught wind of this, and soon they were all nickering for their breakfast. There was a pause in Claire's thinking as she performed this chore, but she soon enough returned to her spot in the stall. As if all memory was rooted there. As if she had to keep looking back in order to know the way forward.

An idea began to form in her head, an idea as outrageous as the one of selling Beau Albert and Tibeau. In her mind, she was back at the bay, watching Tip Weldon ease his large frame into a long, oversized wagon. It was like the *berline,* with wide wooden runners for rolling over snow, but this wagon was much taller and wider. The back formed a kind of low, closed-in cupboard with a hinged cover. Claire imagined it full of bits and bridles, saddles and lead ropes—all that a man would need on a horse-buying mission ...

Claire finally left the stall just as the sun peered over the pines. She passed her grandfather between the cabin and the barn and he looked at her expectantly, waiting for her to speak first.

"Bonjour, Père-père," she said, as cheerfully and as naturally as she could, her voice rising at the end. In fact, it wasn't hard to say those words with a smile. She knew her warmth would cheer and relieve the poor man. But she had another reason to feel good. The long night had been well spent. By the time dawn broke she had made her decision about what she would do if Beau Albert and Tibeau were sold off and signed on for Tip Weldon's war.

CHAPTER 5

Poker Face

Nothing more was said about the selling of horses, for a while. Christmas was close and the focus of the Vigere farm shifted to that event. Jérôme, André and Léo seemed unaffected by the talk of selling horses. All they could think about was Christmas, and the huge meal they would eat after midnight Mass, the best meal of the year. Called *le réveillon,* it featured—in good years—meat pies, fowl, suet puddings and cakes. There was also the prospect of what *Père Noël* might bring. Maple candy? A carving knife? Woollen mittens? A book?

Magrette took to her baking, Claudine knitted into the night, and Ambrose and Jean seemed not to be about very much. The adults in the cabin wore slightly smug smiles, as if they were all up to mischief.

Claire likewise seemed preoccupied but, unlike the adults and siblings around her, quite unmoved by the whole business of Christmas. She had always cherished its rituals and cere-monies—the gift-giving, the special foods, the singing of carols—but the joy seemed to have been sapped from her. Ambrose watched her with ever-growing alarm. Claire seemed as vocal as usual at mealtimes and did her chores, but there was a reserve about her now.

"She'll soon be fourteen," Magrette reassured Ambrose. "Almost a woman. Everything is changing for her: her body, her mind. You don't know everything," she said, and gave him a poke with her elbow.

But he was not reassured. "She never laughs any more," he complained. "And when I ask her what's troubling her, she insists all is well." But all was not well with his granddaughter, and the old man could sense it. He himself had taught her to play poker, how to reveal nothing with your eyes, your mouth, the set of your shoulders. Whether you had four aces in your hand or a pair of deuces, you offered no clue to your opponents.

"Pick a face, any face," Ambrose had told her as they played cards one night. "Sad, silly, happy. Then make that your face, and stick with it."

Claire's face these days was vacant, as if she were staring into a fire, intent on emptying her brain of all thoughts. In fact, her brain was as busy as an anthill. She was plotting her next move, waiting for the other poker players in the Vigere cabin to show their hands.

⁊⊛⊛⊘

Christmas came and went. Everyone got something, almost everything made by the hands of someone else in the family. Jérôme got a wooden flute, maybe not the wisest choice, because the simple-hearted lad played it badly and incessantly— but joyfully. The ever playful André got a cup-and-ball game. A wooden ball was tied to a long string and attached to the thin handle of a wooden cup. You tossed the ball in the air and tried to land it in the cup. Léo, a skilled hunter and fisherman, got a wooden duck that Ambrose had carved and painted for use as a decoy in the spring and fall hunt.

Jean got a knitted sweater, and he seemed especially pleased by the colour—a deep and brilliant blue made from the flower of an herb called wild indigo. Claudine and Magrette knew all about making dyes, and so Claudine's apron was the same lively red-brown as sumach seedpods in the fall. Magrette's apron, which so delighted her she wore it to bed, was golden-rod yellow. Ambrose got a new clay pipe ("You can never have too many pipes," he beamed) and a good supply of tobacco. Even old Babette the dog was not forgotten, and she settled down to enjoy a huge hambone.

Claire got a book, but no ordinary book. Ambrose had spotted it at an outdoor *marché* during a rare visit to Montreal and he had bargained hard with the market vendor for it. The book was a collection of hand-coloured prints, and as elegant as anything Claire had ever seen. Every page was edged in gold, with a gold lock fixed to the book's sturdy leather cover—as if the book were a family Bible or a girl's private diary. Inside were tiny landscapes.

Each one, four inches wide and two inches high, had been slipped into a thick cardboard sleeve. It created the most amazing effect. Claire likened it to looking through church windows, each one offering a view of a different landscape and a different season. People called such books *carte de visite* or calling card books, for the art was about the size of a calling card in those days. A lawyer or banker or politician would carry such a card, on which was inscribed his name, address and business.

Ambrose knew he had chosen well, for Claire seemed to go into a daze as she flipped the pages. She had never heard of the painter, someone named Cornelius Krieghoff, but the scenes were instantly recognizable to her. There was one of Lake Memphremagog, just east of the village, and the birch trees and sky looked as familiar as her own hand.

"Not terribly practical," Ambrose said to her, "but I thought you'd like the pictures."

Claire said nothing. She just went to him and threw her arms around him and stayed in his grasp for a long time.

"*Merci, Père-père,*" she said. "*Merci beaucoup.*"

Claire knew the second she saw those images, with all that white space around and behind them, how these pages might serve her. But she dared not share that secret. The fate of the horses, Beau Albert and Tibeau, had yet to be decided. In Claire's mind, their fate and hers had become intertwined, like strands in a horse's lead rope. Like braids in a young girl's hair.

The glow from Christmas hung around the cabin, as it did around the village of L'Ange-Gardien, for several days into the New Year of 1864. But all that changed, for Claire at least, when Jean Vigere approached her one morning by the barn and said they should go for a walk.

He put one arm on his daughter's shoulder and was leading her towards the well-trod path into the forest when she broke away. Claire knew by the look on her father's face what news he bore. Reading a man, reading a horse: it was the same. She saw the set of his shoulders, tight. Saw the downcast look in his eyes, the guilt and worry. No, there was no need for a father-daughter walk in the woods.

Another girl might have fled for a corner of the cabin, let the tears come, pounded fists into a pillow. Not Claire. She swallowed hard, raised her chin and fought for composure. She took a deep breath and, though her mind and heart raced, tried to prepare herself for what was to come. That night in the stall with Beau Albert, she had hatched a plan, one she hoped she would not have to execute. That hope was now dashed.

"*Papa*, I know," she said. "And I understand. You will sell Beau Albert and Tibeau?"

Jean nodded, and though saddened by the grief he was causing his daughter, he seemed relieved at her bravery and proud of her.

"Monsieur Weldon is coming by tonight to pick up the horses. And, if it's any consolation, Claire, he's paying a very high price—five hundred dollars for each horse. It's twice what he originally offered. Ambrose and Monsieur Weldon have been bargaining hard, but they both know how fine Beau Albert and Tibeau are. We are all very sad, especially your grandfather—and we knew you would be saddest of all—to see these horses go down that road. But for our family, that money means a great deal. We owe Albert and Tibeau a lot. There are other stallions close by, good ones, and we still have our other horses, and Minon—who, God willing, will bring us a son or daughter of Tibeau in the spring—so there will be more young ones in days to come."

"I'd like to spend some time with them today," said Claire. "I need to say farewell."

"Of course," said her father. "Of course."

<hr />

"You see," Magrette was saying to Ambrose that afternoon over tea. "I told you she had good sense." She was staring out the window, watching as Claire headed off into the forest riding Beau Albert bareback. The girl was leaning over the horse's neck, as if the two were deep in conversation—which, in fact, they were.

Jean, too, was drawn to the window. He admired how comfortably Claire sat the horse, how her legs hung low and loose. Like a scene from a picture book he once saw of Sioux warriors on their little Plains ponies, with small leather bridles and pieces of hide for saddles. Rider and horse seemed all of a piece. That was how Claire struck Jean as she disappeared from view, past a clump of alder.

Ambrose and Claudine had formed another camp, near the fire. They seemed bothered by Claire's cool response to the news of the horse sale; they didn't trust it. Ambrose fell into silence, smoking his new pipe and staring into the flames, while Claudine half-heartedly pored over the paintings in the Krieghoff book.

Ambrose, in fact, seemed almost surprised to see Claire riding towards the barn on Beau Albert an hour later. He'd even wondered if she would just keep on going, following some sort of compass of the heart and never looking back. But there she was, leading the gelding into the barn. A minute later, she was headed back to the forest, this time leading Tibeau—as if to give each horse one last tour of the old home-stead. The young black horse was as sparky as Albert had been calm. But Claire smartly turned him a few times, spoke to him until his head came down, then led him into the woods along the tracks the older horse had made.

$$\text{\textemdash}\otimes\text{\textemdash}$$

When she returned to the cabin later that afternoon, Claire's cheeks were as red as apples. It was what Ambrose would best remember of her that day. How healthy she looked, how calm. He wondered if the young Napoleon had that look before battle, a look that said, "Come what may. I am ready."

Other details of that day would grow fuzzy with time, no matter how Ambrose struggled to recall them. What did they have for dinner that evening? Was Claire at the table with them, or not? What time was it when someone finally decided to look for her—and found the note on her bed?

Ambrose would try to tell the story, yet this born storyteller fumbled the tale. He would get the chronology twisted, forget an important detail, and, sometimes, he would grow silent. It would fall to Jean or Claudine to tell of their daughter's disappearance. They would describe the arrival of Tip Weldon and his wagon just after nightfall. It would have been rude not to offer him tea, and so they did. They all liked him, for, as horse dealers went, he was as nice as they came.

And when it was time for Monsieur Weldon to tie Beau Albert and Tibeau behind his buckboard and head off into the night, Claudine called for Claire. "It's time," she called out to the barn, but there was no answer and it was assumed that the young girl had no stomach for seeing those horses leave the farm. Everyone sympathized and understood. She had gone for a walk.

Only later in the evening did questions arise. Claudine reached into her sewing basket to find her scissors—she had the night before finished knitting a pair of mittens for herself and she had saved for tonight the little ceremony of cutting the line of wool that linked the mitten to the woollen ball. She thought of the umbilical cord that had linked her and all her babies. But the blue mittens were gone, the scissors too. And no one but Claudine ever peeked into that basket.

The list of missing items grew as she searched the cabin, and had Jean and Ambrose and Magrette join her. Gone was a loaf of bread baked that morning. Some venison. Apples and carrots from the root cellar. Especially mysterious was the disappearance of other items: a hand mirror, Ambrose's goatskin, Léo's fur hat and, missing from the fireplace mantel, the maple locket. It was approaching midnight and there was still no sign of Claire, her deerskin boots or the long, white woollen coat with the band of red at the shoulders, knees and neck. Everyone had assumed she had gone walking in the woods to be alone in her sadness; now other possibilities occurred to them.

Her snowshoes were missing from their usual spot just outside the cabin. Had she gone walking too close to the river and fallen in? Might she have encountered wolves? Consumed by grief, had she walked too far and become lost in the dark? But why was the Krieghoff book also missing? And the twelve dollars she kept in a jar under her bed, all the money she had earned over the years cleaning stables for people in the village. No, Claire was not lost. Claire had run away.

Panic had Claudine by the throat when she went to Claire's bed and lifted the pillow. Gone was the tattered corner of Claire's old blue blanket. She always went to sleep with that thing in her hands and stored it beneath her pillow; if it was gone, so was she. Still, Claudine ripped off the covers as well, as if she half expected to find her daughter curled up underneath. And there it lay, the note. A page had been ripped from the Krieghoff book, and what stared up at Claudine was a painting of an Indian hunter wearing a long coat much like Claire's, a gun slung over his shoulder, the metal of the rifle wrapped in blue cloth against the snow and the damp. Claudine stared at the painting. The hunter was handsome in his red hat, and the feathers gathered at the peak gave him an almost dapper look. He was on snowshoes, following animal tracks, and while he looked somewhat grim he seemed to know exactly where he was going.

Then Claudine spotted the arrow someone had drawn beneath the painting, inviting the finder of the painting to turn the page over. *"Mon Dieu!"* she said softly, and Jean, Magrette and Ambrose moved closer to her. Claudine simply pointed to the painting, as if she herself could not bear to follow that arrow.

Jean slowly reached down to the bed, and gently flipped the page. The writing, so neat a schoolteacher might have penned it, was Claire's.

"Chère Maman ..." Claire had written.

Dear Maman:

Forgive me for the pain I am causing you. And for the items I have borrowed. I promise to return them. Tell Père-père and Mamie I will miss them, tell Papa I forgive him for selling Beau Albert and Tibeau, and tell the boys not to touch my things while I'm gone.

My head tells me I should stay but my heart tells me to go. It is perhaps a foolish idea, but I hope to train horses in a place where they are valued. Please do not worry, though I know you will. I promise, I promise, to write every week.

My love to you all,
Claire

The ripped page looked so small lying on the bed, the four adults gathered around it. But the letter shattered everyone. It was like a fist in the face or a death in the family, and when the initial shock had subsided a great darkness settled over them all.

Magrette alone seemed certain that the runaway Claire would be home soon, much sooner than anyone else thought. The old woman composed herself, dried her tears and addressed the family.

"A night in the bush will make her see sense," Magrette insisted. "Hunger and frost will bring her back to us." It sounded like a harsh judgment, but it wasn't. A grandmother had lost her only granddaughter and thought she saw an ally in long, cold nights and hunger pains.

Ambrose knew better, or thought he did. He was aware of the deep feeling Claire had for those horses. He knew, too, what courage and pluck she possessed. A part of him felt awe at her resolve and spirit; he wondered if he, at the age of thirteen, would have walked out on a winter's night to protest a family decision. Claire had left that particular painting on her bed for a reason: she was that hunter.

But, like Magrette, Ambrose struggled to find hope amid the despair that now gripped the cabin. "If I were Claire," he told the others, "I would strike for familiar territory. I'll bet she's gone to Calumet and the Ottawa River, the English side. You remember how many times I took her there when she was young to visit the Flynns? She's gone north and west, I'm sure of it."

Claudine bore the news of her daughter's departure the hardest. She sat by the fire, Claire's note in her hand, and stared into the flames. In her mind, she blamed herself for not anticipating this. She felt she should have foreseen Claire's reaction and spoken louder against the sale of the horses.

Claudine felt numb with despair and wondered how she would ever move again. The thought of chores in the morning filled her with dread. But neither could she sleep. Finally what came to her was her daughter's name, Claire Catherine Vigere, and she began to say it in her head like a prayer.

Jean was the calmest. He pondered Ambrose's notion and decided, finally, that it had merit. He grabbed a candle from a box on the mantel, lit it with an ember from the fire and went outside. He bent low, looking for signs in the snow. Sure enough, a fresh set of snowshoe tracks followed a course north and west.

"It's too dark now," he told the others, "and we have to get at least some sleep. In the morning, I'll saddle Minon and follow those tracks. She won't get far on foot." It seemed the wisest course, and no one had a better idea. So they found their beds, and such was their exhaustion that they even slept, though dawn came hard and quick.

The morning brought only a dull light and, worse, falling snow. Whatever tracks Claire had made through the forest would rapidly fill in, so the option of riding hard and over-taking her was now lost. Still, Jean had no other option. He and Minon rode northwest, while Magrette and Claudine and Ambrose fielded hundreds of questions from Jérôme. *Ah well,* thought Ambrose, ever the optimist, *at least he's not playing the damned wooden flute.*

"Where did Claire go?" Jérôme wanted to know.

"Why?"

"What will she eat in the forest?"

"When is she coming home?"

"Is she going to Hell for running away?"

"Can I sleep in her bed while she's gone?"

For the first time since Claire's disappearance, Ambrose cracked a smile. Meanwhile, they would all wait for Jean to come back with news. It was a week's ride to Calumet, a week to return—if the weather was kind.

CHAPTER 6

Runaway

The truth was, Jean Vigere had no hope of finding his daughter by riding north and west. When Tip Weldon's wagon, pulled by a stately grey, eased out of the Vigere farmyard with Beau Albert and Tibeau trotting along behind at the end of long lead ropes, Weldon was unaware of the small passenger hidden in that long, low cupboard behind him. Rocking in the dark like a sack of potatoes, Claire Catherine Vigere was heading south.

She was leaving the only home she had ever known, a family she cherished, all that was safe and familiar. But if Claire had fears about surviving cold and hunger and loneliness and all the other dangers she could only guess at, those fears, for the moment, seemed small.

She thought of days in summer when she would push off from shore in her father's canoe and let the river's current take her. Such trips paled beside this one; this was a bold journey, with no map to guide her and no destination in mind. But her precious horses were only a few feet from her, and that fact gave her a mighty lift. In the darkness of the box, Claire took a deep breath and smiled.

Though Monsieur Weldon's wagon would occasionally roll over bumps on the snow-covered road, the falling snow was making travel a soft and almost luxurious affair. Like all wagons in those days, Tip Weldon's was pulled by a horse with bells on his bridle—a simple safety device meant to warn the drivers of horse-drawn wagons about oncoming traffic on hilltops and tight corners. In the darkness of her box, then, Claire heard music. The *she-she she-she she-she she-she* sound of the bells that matched the grey's even trot, the soft rush of the wagon's skis gliding over fresh snow, the familiar sound of Beau Albert and Tibeau blowing air through their noses as they settled into their trot-all-night pace, and, sometimes, Claire thought she could hear Tip Weldon whistling. Three horses, a man and a girl, all on the move through a dark and silent land. They were all, in their way, pleased to be going wherever it was they were going.

Claire wrestled with guilt, for she knew what anguish her disappearance would cause her family. She felt guilty about tricking them: the snowshoe tracks led nowhere. Weeks later, Ambrose would find the snowshoes, stacked neatly against a tall white pine not a hundred yards from the cabin. Claire felt guilt, too, knowing that the farm now had one less set of hands for all the work. Nor would Jérôme be pleased to find his pants missing. But the girl felt other things as well, and they were sweeter. Delight, for example, at knowing that *la guerre Vigere* was finally over. She had chosen a life with horses over a life of domestic drudgery—and won't it be nice, she thought to herself, not to peel vegetables, sweep floors and haul water for the next little while? Or will it, Claire wondered, be a long while? Wherever this new path would take her, whatever its dangers and outcome, there was no denying that she had embarked on an adventure. She was a runaway now, and she felt a sense of excitement and anticipation stronger than anything she had ever experienced.

Though Claire's dark bed was cramped, it was filled with horse blankets and surprisingly soft. The blankets, and the saddles and bridles buried below them, gave off that honest smell she knew so well—of horse and toil and leather. As the horse-drawn wagon continued on its way and the distance grew between her and home, she fell into a deep sleep, that blue blanket remnant clutched in her hand.

Claire had thought through her plan as best she could. By eavesdropping on conversations in the cabin and around the village on the days leading up to this one, Claire had learned that Tip Weldon's horses—some two hundred had been gathered near the border awaiting his arrival—were bound for war in the not-so-united states of America. In the village store, Claire had heard stories of the American war. Some called it a "civil" war, but that made no sense.

"Be civil to your brothers," Magrette would scold her when they fought. Claire took it to mean she should be kind to them. Was the American Civil War a kind war? She didn't think so.

For three savage years, the northern states had battled the southern ones, and both sides were now desperate for horses. "War eats up horses," she had heard someone in the village say, "chews 'em up, spits 'em out." That image, of war as a horse-devouring monster, had frightened her. But it had also hardened her resolve to go with her horses: they would face the monster together.

Claire's scheme—hatched during that long night in the stall—was simple. Stay hidden in Tip Weldon's wagon for as long as possible. If discovered, say nothing (for her slightly accented English might lead someone to send her back home).

First, she would have to cut off her hair. A runaway girl would surely be sent home; a boy might have a better chance. While Monsieur Weldon and the Vigere family sipped tea, that old hospitality between horse-seller and horse-buyer, Claire slipped out behind the barn and began her rough barbering. Her long black hair, curls and all, fell on the snow. Black on white, like a bruise on fair skin. By the light of a candle, she watched while a girl disappeared before her eyes as she snipped and snipped with her mother's scissors. When she put on her brother's fur hat and looked in the hand mirror, she saw a boy.

The boy, Claire decided, would present himself to the world below the border as deaf and mute. The idea had come to her in a dream. It was one she often had, in which she was communicating with a horse using her hands, her eyes, her whole body. In the dream she would twirl her body like a dancer, and the horse would take it as a cue to circle her. She would hold her hands out at her sides and slowly lower them, and the horse would know to drop to the ground. The dream was of a dance between a girl and a horse, all performed in pure silence. In the morning, recalling the dream, it had come to her: the idea that this runaway would be silent. As a horse is silent.

As for the runaway drawing undue attention, Claire had no worries. Runaway boys in a land ravaged by war were as common as sparrows. Fathers killed in bloody battle, mothers left at home to feed large families, older children striking out to ease the family burden and make for one less mouth to feed. Claire knew she would be just one more child on the loose, looking for a meal and a bed, and money in her—no, *his*—pocket.

As far as Beau Albert and Tibeau were concerned, her hope—and here the plan got fuzzier—was simply to keep them in her sights. Claire knew that both horses would be more than a handful for any rider who treated them roughly. The world, she also knew, was full of rough riders, and she had a hunch that men in war were rougher than most. Claire hoped that by offering her services as a groom, she could "kill two birds with one stone" (as Ambrose liked to say): save her horses from harm, and earn herself a wage along the way.

It was still dark outside when Claire woke and slowly, carefully, lifted the lid on the wagon's box. The cold hit her like a slap; she had been snug and warm under all those horse blankets. Her own body had heated the cavity, just as the bodies of horses will warm a stable.

She looked in every direction, once, twice, three times, and, when she was satisfied that no one was about, slipped down off the wagon and into the trees nearby. The snow was deep, hip-deep, and she had to trample it and sweep some away with her boots before she could do her business. Otherwise, it would mean cold snow on her warm bottom and she didn't want that. What a relief it was to pee in that little clearing. Claire also took the time to stretch her legs and arms, and that, too, felt good.

The snow had ceased to fall, the clouds had passed on, and a thin crescent moon and sprinkling of stars afforded a little light. But it took a while before her eyes adjusted and she could make sense of her situation. The wagon had been left not far from an inn bigger than any she had ever seen, with stairs leading to a wide second-storey porch; a lantern in one window beckoned to her, but there was no going in there. Then came the sound of horses moving in the dark. Many, many horses, to judge from all the snorting and shuffling for position.

The inn—about halfway between the village of L'Ange-Gardien and the border—was perched on a hilltop with a splendid view of the valley below. Claire could just make out a makeshift corral down there, with a dozen men on horseback posted around the perimeter. By the slump of their shoulders and the chin-to-chest set of their heads, they looked to be sleeping or napping.

So, this was the fruit of all Monsieur Weldon's travels into the bush farms beyond the towns of Quebec and Sherbrooke and Trois-Rivières. Claire couldn't see Beau Albert or Tibeau, but she knew they were there. Two whistles—one long, one short—would have brought both of them charging over those fences and up the hill to where she stood. She had trained them both to come to that call, and they would have been relieved and delighted to find their young pal in this strange place. As for those corral fences, they were nothing: Claire and the two black horses had jumped higher.

But no, Claire pocketed that trick, pocketed it like a hard candy she craved but decided to save for later. *I will need all my tricks,* she told herself, *every one.* Then she slipped back into the box of the wagon and waited for what dawn would bring.

———

Claire knew it was day by the crack of light along the wooden cupboard's lid. Night had offered at least some protection, and now she felt exposed. Were someone to come to the wagon for a saddle or bridle, she would be at his mercy.

What if she were exposed even further, not just as a runaway boy but as a runaway girl? Claire had lived a sheltered life, but she was nevertheless aware that not all men were like Ambrose and Jean or Père Boivin at the parish church. Magrette had dropped hints that there existed other kinds of men, with designs on girls and women. Just what these men did or wanted was unclear, but girls and women apparently had to beware of them. They were dangerous, like matches in a child's hands.

Claire was grateful that no one came to the wagon or lifted the lid. She could hear the sounds of the grey being brought to the front of the wagon, the harness attached and the tongue of the wagon being lifted, the bridle looped over the horse's head and the light clink of metal on tooth as the horse accepted the bit. Claire could see it all in her mind's eye, for she had done the same with Ambrose's horses a thousand times.

She could hear the words she would say to calm and reassure the horses, like an old song they knew the words to. "*Doucement*," she would say, "*doucement*. Easy, easy." Then, "*Ça y est, ça y est*. Everything's fine, just fine."

Claire was nibbling on some venison and bread when Tip Weldon's wagon rocked forward and they were under way once more. Unlike that first night when they had left the farm, when Claire was cradled by soft sounds and drifted off into sleep, she was now fully awake and alert. That first leg of the trip had seemed almost private and solitary. Now they were part of a caravan, and Claire was aware of many riders and a great herd of horses pressing forward.

She strained to hear the familiar whinnies of Tibeau and Beau Albert, but if they were calling, their message was lost amid all the others. Horses, Claire knew, are herd animals who arrange themselves according to rank. There is a precise top and bottom and middle in every herd, so that the order of eating and drinking, who gets cover in winter or shade in summer, are matters decided according to that hierarchy. The order is constantly being tested, but it usually takes only a look of the eye, a pinning of the ear, to reestablish it. Each horse knows his or her place in the herd, and takes comfort in it. A horse at the top may eat first, but he shoulders the responsibility of looking out for danger; the horse at the bottom may eat last, but he naps knowing that everyone else is looking out for his welfare.

Almost every horse in the herd has a special friend, and those two horses will gently groom each other with their teeth or stand head to tail to swish flies from each other's face. But almost every horse also knows of others in the herd who might deliver a kick or a bite for sport or spite. And every time a new horse is introduced into a herd, the whole puzzle has to be rearranged. A new pecking order comes into play as the new horse finds his or her place in the mob.

Tip Weldon's herd was not too large for horse society to arrange into smaller herds, but it would take time. And there was no time. There was only the push south, which meant that friends in the herd—old friends or friends just made (and horses can bond in minutes)—were constantly having to cope with separation. Horses were whinnying to mates, or squealing at strangers, or jostling for position. Some wanted to lead, others to follow. Some got excited and wanted to race. Others dragged their heels—for horses find comfort in routine and the familiar, and they distrust the new and unusual. The men had a job of it keeping the herd together, and the noise early in the day was steady. Like distant thunder. But after several hours, the herd fell into a rhythm.

Sometimes a rider would come up alongside Tip Weldon's wagon and they would chat. About the road ahead, the lake crossing, their destination, the war that was raging in the south.

Already there were casualties in the herd, and they had yet to cross the border.

"We lost two horses last night, Captain," a man said to Monsieur Weldon. And Claire's heart skipped a beat.

"Two mares," he went on. Claire felt relief, and then sadness at the fate of the two horses.

"What did they look like?" Monsieur Weldon asked.

"The older mare was a liver chestnut, with blue eyes," came the reply. "The younger one was a dark bay, with four white socks."

"Hmmm," said Weldon. Claire wondered if Monsieur Weldon had a memory of every horse he had bought on the trip into Canada East. Ambrose had said he was that kind of man, that every horse he looked at—never mind bought—was recorded in a large book he kept in his head.

Both horses had been kicked in the confines of that corral. They had, in fact, kicked each other and inflicted great damage. Two headstrong mares, they had both refused to back down.

Claire had witnessed such a battle herself several years ago. She had watched in horror as two of Ambrose's mares had slowly and methodically backed towards each other and begun to let fly with their deadly hind hooves. The older mare was much bigger than her young opponent, but the young one stood her ground. Bucking and kicking at close range, both horses landed blows, the two of them screaming as they fought. All this because the younger horse had challenged the queen of the herd—who was not about to surrender her throne to a young upstart. Finally, Beau Albert had had enough and the stallion intervened, sending the two mares off in different directions. Claire loved horses, but she liked Magrette's expression: "The only thing worse than a scream-ing mare is two screaming mares."

Now two brave mares in Tip Weldon's herd were dead. No mention was made of how the chestnut and the bay were dealt with. Claire wondered if the two were kept behind as the herd moved on and passed over a hill. Someone would have had to tie them to a tree, for even a horse with a broken leg will try to follow the herd. Then that someone assigned to the task would have used his rifle.

"A bullet now, a bullet later," Tip Weldon sighed. It struck Claire that there was a sadness about this man, that he was a shrewd judge of horseflesh but regretted the fate that awaited most of these horses. This became even more apparent to Claire as the two men talked of the war.

Once they had travelled the length of Lake Champlain and south through Vermont, Monsieur Weldon said, they would gather at a place in Massachusetts at the Vermont border and then veer to the southeast and make for Boston. At least that was the plan for now; in war, Claire suspected, plans changed like the weather. The 1st Massachusetts Cavalry badly needed horses, and they relied almost exclusively on Canadian horses.

Claire closed her eyes—she had grown weary of looking at that thin line of light at the cupboard's lid—and thought about Beau Albert and Tibeau trotting on somewhere out there. They were not war horses, they were family horses meant for ploughing fields and hauling logs, for trips to the village and long rides on cool summer mornings or racing on wide pans of ice.

But no, they were also meant for war. Their ancestors were war horses, bred in the royal stable of the Sun King. The first horses sent to New France, Ambrose had always insisted, were fine horses. War horses, some stout, some refined, and all descendants of chargers that had once taken French knights into battle and fought in the Crusades. Ambrose said he had once seen in a book a painting of the Sun King on a black horse who could have been Beau Albert's father, just heavier and taller. The same curly mane and powerful neck, the same high cheekbones and feathered legs. Now their offspring across the sea would haul cannons, carry officers with sabres raised, take urgent messages from regiment to regiment.

As Claire lay in that wagon, she listened and a canvas formed in her mind. It was not at all like sitting in Ambrose's lap when she was a child as he told her stories of his childhood. He was always, as he put it, "pulling her leg"—telling her a wild tale to see if she would challenge it. Claire was skeptical from an early age, for she learned that her mother and grandfather were allies in the telling of tall tales. If Claire wanted to know whether frogs really turned into princes or cows jumped over the moon (as her mother and grandfather were suggesting), she would check with her father or grandmother.

But the stories she was hearing now in the wagon seemed of another kind. They were tall tales, yet true. Horribly true. Claire didn't think that Tip Weldon and the other rider were the kind to pull legs.

The two men talked of the Civil War and its appetite for
horses. It seemed, as the villager had said, that this war did
indeed devour horses. A cavalry officer, Claire heard, needed
a new horse every two months. In that time the old one would
either be killed in battle or die of exhaustion. Claire shuddered
at the thought, but she also learned that horses belonging to
generals had an easier time of it. Such horses fought more on
the edges of war, and, if a general was far more likely than a
foot soldier to get a hot bath at the end of the day, so too was
the general's horse more likely to get a hot bran mash than a
fistful of hay. Claire found hope in that thought. Of course,
she said to herself, Tibeau and Beau Albert were horses for
high and mighty colonels and generals. Not for mere captains
or ordinary troopers.

Certainly her horses (funny, Claire thought to herself, they
were *her* horses now, not Ambrose's) would not pull cannons.
The rider trotting alongside Tip Weldon's wagon seemed to
know a lot about this aspect of the war. His name was Jacob
and he had a cousin fighting in the war on the northern side.
The cousin had sent a letter home last spring after a particu-
larly grim battle at Chancellorsville, Virginia, in which some
seven thousand horses were killed.

Claire stiffened at that number. She felt quite ill, and put
away her venison and bread. The men outside talked on but
she no longer heard them. She thought of the mighty herd
trotting on just ahead of her, and fought with the arithmetic.
Ten times that herd was still only two thousand horses. Twenty
times that herd was four thousand horses. Thirty times that
number was six thousand. Trying to imagine that sea of horses
somehow was easier on her head than trying to imagine that
number of horses struck down in battle.

As Jacob and Monsieur Weldon talked of horses and war, Claire continued drawing pictures in her mind. Soldiers or cavalry officers dressed in blue (the colour of the northern army) shot at soldiers or cavalry officers dressed in grey (the colour of the southern army). Of course, horses and men on either side would both go down in that hail of bullets. But horses, Claire learned, were not just the victims of stray bullets. The horses were targets.

Claire listened with horror. It seemed that one of the horses' jobs was to haul cannons to the battle site. Once there, the horses would be untethered from the big guns, but one man would hold them close by in case the cannons had to be moved quickly. The loss of a cannon to the enemy was a great loss and one to be avoided. If there were no woods or tall rocks to shelter behind, the horses were easy targets for sharpshooters on the other side. A sniper with a long rifle could hit a target half a mile away, and a horse was an easier target than a man. What better way to acquire your enemy's cannon than to eliminate the horses required to move them?

When Jacob began to describe—passing on his cousin's account—the sound bullets made when they entered horse-flesh, Claire wanted to plug her ears. Jacob likened it to the sound a pebble makes when dropped into mud. And when a bullet enters a horse's neck, Jacob said, he will try to shake it off, as he would a bothersome fly. Monsieur Weldon simply said, "I know, son," when Jacob said that horses would rise and fall, rise and fall, sometimes after receiving five bullets. Monsieur Weldon explained to Jacob that nothing in a horse's life could possibly prepare him for such a death. Not when rifle and rifleman were hundreds of yards away, often beyond even the horse's senses of smell and sight and hearing. No horse on earth could imagine a predator that killed so easily and without ever showing his face.

Claire wondered how Jacob could speak of such things without emotion. His account seemed cold, as if he were bemoaning the loss of an expensive saddle or fine leather boots. Best not get attached to a horse, he seemed to be saying. In war, a horse was here today, gone tomorrow.

Years later, Claire would look back on that day spent in the dark box and remember it as one of the saddest of her life. The hell she seemed headed for sounded as bad as the one Père Boivin used to warn about in church back home. She wondered what she had gotten herself into. But there was no going back now.

Tomorrow, they would be at Missisquoi Bay and begin that long crossing of Lake Champlain. The ice she had raced on with Beau Albert would be their highway to the horse-eating monster whose face Claire had clearly seen in the darkness of that box.

<hr />

Around L'Ange-Gardien, life went on. The disappearance of Claire Vigere was simply one more loss, and though runaways were unusual in that region, losses were not. Families lost fathers and sons, mothers and daughters. They buried their dead or succumbed to poverty and moved on. There were crop losses, losses of faith; children got lost in the woods and were never seen again. Prized horses died in their traces and farm animals were butchered for their meat.

Yet there were births, too, and rejoicing when mother and child came out of it alive and well. There were baptisms and confirmations and weddings and gatherings to mark birthdays and feast days. Ambrose used to say that the English had yet to learn how to laugh. A roomful of French people, he would say, "can sail into the night on a fiddle and a crock of wine and greet the dawn with delight. The English, on the other hand, tend to be sweet and sour—sweet on going to bed early and sour in the morn." Then he would point out that his blood was half-Irish, and the Irish, he said, were like the French. They liked music and drink and nights that stretched into morning.

Much of that joy had been drained from the Vigere family. Still, they had no choice but to soldier on. Horses had to be fed, wood split and fires tended to, meals prepared and eaten. But everyone in the family walked with a heavier tread now, and none more so than Ambrose.

One morning he was behind the barn investigating a ruckus—Babette had chased a rabbit into its hole and was letting everyone know—and Ambrose caught the outline of something under the snow, below the overhang of the roof. When the old man gently dusted aside the snow, he spotted those telltale black curls of Claire's on the snow, and he knew in that instant where she had gone and what her plan was. He bent low and put one of the curls in his pocket before going back inside the cabin.

Then he got out his pipe and sat by the fire, while one hand lingered in his pocket and stroked the lock of hair. It would be ten days or more before Jean Vigere returned from Calumet, and Ambrose was now certain his son would come back alone. Best, Ambrose thought, to say nothing. Bad enough for the family to imagine Claire fending for herself somewhere in the Canadas. He would not burden his family with all that could befall her in a land at war with itself.

CHAPTER 7

The Crossing

Claire awoke with a start. For several seconds, she had no idea where she was, and then it hit her: the darkness of the box, the smell of the horse blankets and her own unwashed body, the sound of the wagon's runners gliding over ice. She felt a powerful ache and longing for home. She even missed her brothers, especially the wide-eyed innocent Jérôme, for whom she had a soft spot. But she was a long way from shedding a tear.

It took a lot to make Claire cry. Not that she was hard of heart—far from it. She was simply made of sturdy stuff. Still, she was hungry, cold and lonely. And while she knew her family would be worried sick about her disappearance, she also knew they had each other to lean on. At her first opportunity, she would send them a letter to ease some of their concerns. So it was not the seven Vigeres back home who now occupied her mind. It was the two horses, Beau Albert and Tibeau.

Both horses, she knew, would be on high alert, their little ears swivelling this way and that, their eyes wide. In a herd this size, each horse would soon lose sight of the other. They would be like two oak leaves that had tumbled into the rushing current of a swollen river.

Claire struggled to hear the sounds of horses calling to each other, the crack of hooves on thick, hard ice, some evidence of the herd. But there was none. Just the easy clip of Monsieur Weldon's grey and the muffled sound of the wagon passing over snow or the *shissssssssssssssh* sound as it skimmed over ice.

Then, suddenly, it sounded as though the herd was running just ahead of the wagon, and Claire had to resist the urge to lift the lid and try for a peek at her beloved horses. For a long time, that was her company: the sound of horses on the fly, that rugged thunder she knew so well. Then the sound would fade and disappear. And it struck her how hard it must be for men on horseback to contain that river of horses. The stallions and senior mares, for example, would put on a burst—go wide or forward—to test the mettle of these men, try to break free of their circle and turn for home. The urge to gallop, she imagined, would move through the herd like ripples in a pond when she tossed in a rock.

That's why Monsieur Weldon brought up the rear, Claire thought to herself. He didn't want his grey and his wagon caught up in the unfolding frenzy. The pace of the herd would slacken, then quicken, then throttle down. Walk to trot to canter to gallop and everything in between. At times during the trek the herd would be no more than a speck on the horizon for Monsieur Weldon. Then, gradually, he and the grey would catch up. It was a game of tag, and they played it all day long.

Claire knew that Missisquoi Bay was five miles wide, but she also knew that as you headed south on Lake Champlain the lake widened to almost ten miles before it narrowed again.

A long, thin island called Grand Isle would keep them company on the right flank as they headed south, but when they passed by the island and the lake truly widened, the men and horses would think they were at sea. The far shores to the east and west would seem perilously far away.

The middle of the lake was the place to be when you were herding a few hundred horses. No farms out there, for farms meant other horses to distract the herd. No forests either, where the bolder horses might have run and hidden. For men herding horses, the middle of a frozen lake was as good as it got.

Sometimes, after the herd had settled into a more leisurely pace, one of the men would drop back and chat with Monsieur Weldon. One—in her mind Claire called him Froggy for his habit of clearing his throat every time he spoke—seemed quite unnerved at being on the ice.

"Huhhh," Froggy began, "you know, Captain, one of the boys was sayin' that he was on a trip like this once and men and horses went right through the damn ice! That so, Captain?"

"Yes," Weldon replied. "It can happen. The currents play tricks. But it's been a cracking cold winter. The ice must be a foot thick at least."

"Huhhh-huhhh," Froggy replied, causing Claire to believe the man truly was fearful, for the throat-clearing was getting louder and longer. "You see, Captain, I cain't swim. Never learned."

"I wouldn't worry," the man in the wagon replied. "If you went through the ice out here so far from shore, swimming wouldn't help." Tip Weldon did not elaborate, but he didn't have to. Froggy must have taken in this information and dwelt on it for he fell silent. Eventually he rode on, taking his fears with him.

"Do you mind if I set with you a spell, Captain?"

"Nope."

"I'm obliged," said this new man. His was a voice Claire had not heard before. Blind to the world, Claire was relying on tones of voice to get a sense of the speaker. And what she caught, right off the mark, was a thinly veiled hostility between these two. Monsieur Weldon's "nope" had a little edge to it, and the other man's excessive politeness had a swagger buried inside. Being in hiding in her cupboard, Claire thought, was like being all ears and only ears; you never listen so well as when you listen in the dark.

"How many of these horses been broke, Captain?"

"Don't know, Mr. Huntley. I reckon half. You have quite a bit of work ahead of you. And I don't need to remind you that even the ones that are broke need to be ridden—so I get a sense of what they know and how to assign them."

Huntley must have just nodded. Then he added, "Never broke Canadian horses before. Some of 'em look on the puny side."

"I think you will be surprised," Weldon said. "You may find yourself kissing the ground more times than you think. Some of those little Canadians may look round but they're lightning quick. And very, very smart."

"Don't want to brag, Captain, but I don't go to the ground easily. Been breakin' horses a long time and I don't mind a challenge."

"We'll see," Weldon offered, and Claire was sure he was smiling just a little as he said it. *Perhaps he is thinking,* thought Claire, *what I am thinking: Beau Albert, or Tibeau, one after the other, bucking this man over the moon and teaching him some humility.*

As the two men continued to talk, Claire began to get her bearings. They were, it seemed, headed due south for a place called Williamstown, just across the Vermont border on the Massachusetts side. The horses would be corralled there, and some would be assigned right on the spot to various cavalry troops. The heavier horses would pull gun carriages and wagons; the fleeter horses would serve as couriers; the ordinary mounts would go to troopers in the cavalry; the fittest and most handsome horses would go to colonels and generals. This man, Huntley, was the one who would ride each saddle horse to get a sense of that horse's capabilities, manners, temperament and athleticism.

Claire had the feeling that Huntley was as rude with horses as he was polite with humans. She imagined him with a toothpick in his mouth, or maybe a hand-rolled cigarette. Maybe he had his hat tilted back on his head, the head, too, tilted back so he could look down his nose at every horse and human who crossed his path.

Claire remembered a picture book that Ambrose had shown her when she was a child. There was a drawing of a "bronc-buster" (she would never forget the phrase because her grandfather had spent a long time explaining it to her) walking wide-legged across a corral while dusting his leather chaps with his hat. (Ambrose somehow knew that "chaps" was pronounced *"shaps."*) In the background was the horse the cowboy had just ridden into submission, lathered in sweat, head dropped in exhaustion. A spirited horse had lost his first battle with a rider, and the rider wore the face of the victor.

As a child, Claire would stare at that drawing. The artist had taken sides, given the horse-breaker—not the horse—the limelight. Claire thought otherwise. All her sympathy lay with the horse.

When Claire was a child, Ambrose would tell her stories of cowboys and Indians on the Plains, or, closer to home, of what the Iroquois had done to the Jesuit missionaries. Killed them, slowly, with scalping knives and tomahawks and necklaces of fire. The stories portrayed the black-robed priests as martyrs and the Iroquois as savages, but Claire would have none of it. She always sided with the Indians. Indians, Ambrose used to say, believed in talk and touch. He had read the accounts of George Catlin, an American artist who had spent time in the 1830s with the Comanche, the so-called "horse people" of the American South. Claire would listen in rapture as he spoke of their way with wild horses. Their method was to approach a captured horse extremely slowly, talking all the while—uttering deep grunts *("hoh-hoh-hoh")* or calming sounds *("shuh-shuh-shuh")*. When the horse seemed ready for it, the Indian would touch the horse's nose and head, and then his whole body. He would breathe into the horse's nostrils, aware that horses smell first, trust second. Over the course of days, man and horse would engage in what Ambrose called "a conversation."

Sometimes, Plains Indians would break horses in the shallow water of rivers and lakes. The hard work of moving through water would tire the horse, and, as Ambrose put it, winking as he said so, "it made for a softer landing."

But he had sympathy for the bronc-buster, too. He might even have had some sympathy for Monsieur Huntley, or at least for his skill and courage. These men specialized in the dangerous job of breaking horses, and for many, many years the rate of pay was the same—five dollars a horse. The quicker the job was done, the better the pay. Some horse-breakers—the young and foolish ones, anyway—would somehow get a saddle on a wild horse, hop on and hope for the best. A few horses were so gentle that they put up no fuss. Even spirited horses could be ridden into submission, each buck tamer than the one before. But some horses were too haunted by memories and bucked as if their very lives depended on it.

"You see," Ambrose told Claire, "some of those wild horses had narrowly escaped encounters with cougars—who would leap on the horse's back from a high rock or tree and rake the horse's flanks with his claws as he tried to hang on." Horses who survived such an ordeal would buck with a fury whenever anything—saddle or rider or blanket—was put on their backs. The memory of that big cat was too strong. Seeing scars on a horse's back, the bronc-busters—the smart ones, anyway—generally passed on that horse.

"The English," said Ambrose, "have an expression 'to pass the buck.' It means to give someone else the responsibility. We have bronc-busters to thank for that one."

Wary of bucks, broken ribs and shattered bones, horse-breakers tilted the odds in their favour. They would tie one of the horse's hind legs to a rope collar around the horse's neck; that took away the horse's ability to buck. Saddling and riding came quickly then, for the horse saw the futility of his situation.

"It wasn't about getting the horse to co-operate," Ambrose explained to Claire. "It was all about control, and it was all about time. On a cattle drive, one cowboy might need five horses. Morning horse, day horse, night horse, a few spares. I imagine cowboys don't have time to go slow breaking horses."

"It's not fair to horses," the young Claire replied. She thought of the gentle Canadian horses in their barn and she got angry just imagining them being roped and ridden hard by men with spurs.

There was one horse-breaker Ambrose admired greatly. His name was John Solomon Rarey, and he had won a name for himself training rude and wild horses all over the world in the 1850s. He had even written two books on training horses. One was called *The Modern Art of Taming Wild Horses* and the other was a mouthful called *The Farmer's Friend: Containing Rarey's Horse Secret, With Other Valuable Receipts and Information*. Ambrose owned both books.

John Rarey had grown up in Ohio and he broke horses the old way. The bronco-busting way. But eventually he did what Ambrose did: he asked around. He talked to cowboys, circus trainers, other horsemen, and read all he could. There had to be a better way, he figured, than fighting with horses and breaking bones.

And there was a better way. If Rarey had a secret, it was an old secret. He learned not to fight with a spooked horse, but to tire him. Let him spend his anger, his frustration and his fear in pure labour. Put him in front of a cart and make him trot forty or fifty miles. Use hobbles and gag bits only if need be, and remove them at the slightest hint of co-operation from the horse. Above all, use your hands and voice with the horse. Talk and touch, talk and touch.

"Just like the Indians!" Claire said to Ambrose, as if a light had gone on in her brain.

And Ambrose slapped both knees as reply. Yes yes yes.

<hr />

When she next awoke, Claire knew it was night. No slit of light, no sounds of the herd or of men talking. Just the whistle of the night wind on the lake as it tested the opening of her cramped little home and found its way in.

I'm as stiff as old Babette, she thought as she roused herself. Claire slowly lifted the lid of the box, looking left and right and then behind as best she could. The only light came from a sliver of a moon and a million stars, and it was a few moments before the girl realized she was staring into a face. A horse's face. It was Tip Weldon's grey, and he whinnied softly to her as if they were old friends.

She stroked his head and softly said his name: Mac. Claire had heard Monsieur Weldon address him, and now the big horse bowed to her touch. She had also heard the Captain sing Mac's praises, and she knew in her bones he was a good horse, an honest citizen.

Claire smiled. It was her first exchange with another creature in days. How many days? Three, she thought, maybe more. She climbed down gingerly from the wagon and stretched, put her arms out wide and raised them high over her head.

"Merde," she said under her breath. It was the one curse that Ambrose ever allowed himself. The word meant what came out of a horse's back end, and Claire had decided that she had now also earned the right to use the word. She was cold, stiff, hungry (the venison and bread were long gone) and desperately thirsty. She had just leaned down to scoop up some snow to eat when she noticed the grey's water bucket, and she plunged her hands into the ice-cold water and scooped the bracing liquid into her mouth as fast as she could. The water was so cold it set her teeth on edge but she had never tasted water as sweet as this. Besides, Mac didn't seem to mind sharing.

Then she relieved herself, crouching low and using precisely the same spot that the grey had used. Claire had always been open and honest, but she was learning to deceive and cover her tracks. Now there was the matter of food. She had none and would have to steal it.

Feeling a little like the Indians in Ambrose's stories, she crept back up into the wagon to get some perspective. She could make out a second wagon, a long, wide hay wagon now unburdened of almost all its hay. She could see where the men had dropped bales onto the ice, the bales a fairly precise sixty feet apart to form a large rectangle. The horses, in groups of nine and ten, had encircled each food supply. The horses must have been exhausted after running for days and they would have needed at least some hay just to stay warm. The horses were mostly quiet as they ate, just the odd squeal from a mare as they all sought a place around their dinner tables. Here and there Claire could see fires, with men gathered round them for warmth. Her first thought was, *How did they manage it without burning a hole through the ice and dousing the flames?* Her second thought was, *Should I join them?*

In her pocket was the note she would thrust into the hands of the first person to challenge her. The note was written, as neatly as she could manage, on lined paper. It read:

I am a runaway boy.
War orphan. Deaf. Name is Clint Flynn.
Good worker. Good with horses.

It was her calling card, and much thought had gone into choosing those seventeen words. Even the boy's name had been carefully picked; she had an English cousin in Calumet named Clint, and the name seemed a proper cousin to her own. Close enough but different all the same.

Why not, she thought, *go to that fire?* She was weary of the cold, sick of hiding in that dark box, and her belly was as empty as the Vigere fruit cellar at the end of August. But the thought of hoping for kindness and good sense from men the likes of Huntley and Froggy gave her no confidence. She had read in books about actors who played the part of other people, memorized lines, dressed in costume. But she had never acted before, and the role she was about to play seemed too big and complicated for a novice.

Claire was a girl trying to pass as a boy. She was a hearing person trying to pass as deaf. A Canadian trying to pass as an American. And she had no idea how her audience would accept her. The only man she was inclined to trust was Monsieur Weldon, and she had no idea where he was on this frozen expanse or whether her instincts about him were reliable.

Claire hung her head and felt, for the first time since fleeing home, a deep sense of despair. But as she looked down, she spotted a leather satchel on the seat of the wagon. *Please,* she said to herself, *let there be bread. Du pain du pain du pain,* she said over and over, wondering if the French word might do a better job of delivering what she prayed for. *Bread.*

"*Mon Dieu,*" she gasped when she flipped open the bag and saw what was inside. A loaf of bread, several thick slices of ham wrapped in paper and a goatskin bag. Her own goatskin had been dry for days, the milk long gone. Claire hoped Monsieur Weldon would forgive her as she tucked into that banquet. Never had food tasted so fine. As for the contents of the goatskin, the liquid warmed her, whatever it was. How, she wondered, could a cold drink deliver such heat to her throat and body? When she had had her fill of bread and ham, she tossed back several long slugs of the warm drink and then a few more. Claire got dizzy then, and she felt a rising panic as she folded her body back into that dark cupboard. Then came sleep, sleep like she had never known before.

Claire awoke with a pounding headache and the sound of Froggy clearing his throat and claiming his innocence.

"Captain, I ain't no thief, and I truly am sorry to hear someone was into your satchel. Truly. Huh-huh-huh-huh ..."

"Damn it!" shouted Monsieur Weldon. "I want the man who did this!" And then he must have reached back and slammed the top of the wagon's cupboard with the palm of his hand. Claire thought she would die, so delicate were her ears, so loud was the explosion in the box that now felt like a coffin. Everything hurt: her eyes, her tongue, her teeth and especially her head. Ambrose used to complain in the morning after weddings and wakes. "*La maudite* booze," he called it. "The damn booze." He had then what he called "*une gueule de bois*—a wooden jaw.*" Claire understood for the first time in her life what the phrase meant. She was hungover.

"I feel sorry for people who don't drink," she remembered Ambrose telling Vinet Leblanc one day. "When they wake up in the morning, that's as good as they're going to feel all day." Claire took from her grandfather's joke a little hope: that as the day progressed she would feel less awful.

At least the wagon wasn't moving. Any sort of motion and all that ham and bread would have exited her body in a hurry. Both body and soul suffered that day. The body from the rum, or whatever it was, the soul from all the guilt she felt as, in turn, each man in the company was called before Monsieur Weldon and grilled. He never flatly accused anyone. He simply asked each one, "What do you know about this?"

Though she battled that wooden jaw, she had enough curiosity about the little drama unfolding just a few feet away to dwell some more on Monsieur Weldon. Claire imagined that someone so adept at reading horses was also a keen judge of human character. Any tightness in the shoulders, any hesitation or dropping of the eyes: the Captain would have been on to that man like a hornet to a sugar pie.

Finally, Huntley was called to the wagon. But he was as calm and overly courteous, as proud as ever. He wasn't the thief, and Monsieur Weldon knew it.

"Just one more thing, Captain?" Huntley asked.

Monsieur Weldon said nothing, for he was a man of few words and wasn't about to waste one on this fellow. He must have used his eyes, or maybe an upward nod of the head to indicate, *What*?

"My horse stepped on his rein this morning. Snapped it. I sewed the two leather pieces together but it's not the best. Mind if I borrow one of your sets till we get to Williamstown?"

"In the back," said Tip Weldon, and at hearing this, Claire's heart began to race. She had thought she would be able to choose the moment when she would reveal herself. The long, thin box just inches from Monsieur Weldon's back had begun to feel a little like a sorry home, yet somehow hers. Now Huntley, of all people, was about to discover the stowaway child from north of the border. Maybe the note wouldn't work; maybe she would be sent back in disgrace. Beau Albert and Tibeau would press on without her and she would never see them again.

Her father had once told her that an animal, a young deer, say, being stalked by wolves will sometimes freeze rather than run. As if stillness could make the poor creature invisible. That's how Claire felt as she heard Huntley get off his horse. She could hear the crunch of his feet on the snow as he got closer; she could feel the wagon tilt and groan as he stepped up on the side. Then his hand was on the lid and the lid was being lifted. All of this happened slowly for Claire, like those times when she fell off horses back home and hit the ground. Later, she would replay the moments leading up to the fall and be struck by how quickly it had all happened in real time, and how slowly it had seemed to unfold in her head.

Then the lid was up and Claire was staring into the face of Huntley, though his eyes were averted.

"Matter which reins I take?" he was asking Monsieur Weldon. Huntley had a dirty red kerchief tied around his neck and Claire's eyes were as drawn to that as to the brown tobacco stains around his moustache and beard where the whiskers met his hard little mouth.

"There's a black set," replied Monsieur Weldon. "Leave it. You can take any other."

But before Huntley could lower his eyes and meet Claire's, two shots rang out and all business ceased. The lid came crashing down and Claire winced at the sound. A rider approached the wagon at a full gallop and came to a halt. "Captain," the man shouted, all out of breath, "those two black horses you like so well. Just made a run for it. They're headin' north up the lake!"

"Shit!" The voice was Huntley's.

"Captain," the man continued, "they're smart, those little buggers. We almost had 'em turned, and they split up! One went east, the other west, and after they'd outraced us, they joined up again and veered north. I never seen such a thing!"

The calmest head belonged to Monsieur Weldon, though clearly he was not pleased and he most certainly wanted those two horses back. Claire was willing to bet her last bit of bread that those two horses were Beau Albert and Tibeau.

"Huntley," he said in a soft voice, "take Jeremiah and ride north, but well to the east so those horses can't see you. Ride hard for half a day, rest the horses and then turn due west and south. Byard, you go with Zachary and do the same on the other side. Hard north but well to the west, rest your mounts, then come back east and south. Those horses are tired and they're still hungry. They won't gallop long. And bring bull-whips with you. Use them for herding, mind. Don't use them on those horses or I'll use the bullwhips on you. Understand?"

The men must all have nodded in assent, for nothing was said. Claire sat with her hands clasped over her belly, too worried to touch the bread, too wary of the goatskin to quench her thirst. The thoughts of the runaway girl were now all with her runaway horses.

CHAPTER 8

Two Horses Heading Home

A crow flying over Lake Champlain that grey morning in January of 1864 would have easily spotted the two black horses silhouetted against the white snow and the glare ice. Their manes were flying, their tails swaying rhythmically behind them, and they were moving at a quick and easy trot. They were heading north, as if following an old and familiar trail.

Tip Weldon's plan was a good one, and it should have worked. Huntley and Jeremiah were riding fresh horses on the east side of the lake; Byard and Zachary were doing the same on the west side. All were cantering, eating up those frozen miles. Sometimes they would ease back to a trot or walk, but soon they were speeding again, the men up out of the saddles to save their horses' backs. These horses were in excellent condition and had supped on grain to fuel this pursuit. They were the reserve horses on this horse drive, so they were well rested, well watered. And saddlebags, blankets, rifles and all the other items that would have otherwise loaded down a rider had been left behind with Tip Weldon and the camp that had suddenly formed mid-lake. There was little risk that the herd would bolt; they had their hay now, and, besides, they were weary of the long march.

Beau Albert and Tibeau, meanwhile, were tired, not just from the long trek but from lack of sleep. There had been no rest, not a minute, in that shifting mass of nervous, frightened, angry horses. A horse in that herd closed his eyes at his peril.

The two black Canadians, the formidable father and his elegant son, had managed to eat only a little hay. As for grain, that was a luxury last enjoyed at the Vigere Farm—the destination both horses had in mind. Nor had they drunk any water. Like the rest of the herd, they had been making do with snow.

Most horses in these circumstances would have tried to conserve themselves. Once the enemy was apparently behind them, they would have seen no urgency and they would have walked for home. Horses seem to have a compass for home—and no one really knows how that is. Dogs have it, too, and indeed many animals have an uncanny sense of home.

Claire knew the story of Vinet Leblanc's old cat—a fat tabby named L'Orange. The cat had slipped into a picnic basket one summer when relatives from Halifax were visiting and was only discovered when the visitors arrived back home. But L'Orange eluded capture and fled, and the visitors sadly wrote Vinet that his beloved cat was gone. Six months later, the tabby showed up at Vinet's cabin door. The six-hundred-mile journey had been hard on him—he was bone thin and one ear seemed to have been left behind on the trail—but he was back.

No, there was no doubt that the two black horses could find their way home. Huntley knew that. He had chased and roped wild horses on the American prairie and he was well versed in how horses react when pursued. He was certain that

these two horses were walking north, and that once encountered they would be no match for four horsemen.

Huntley was too steamed to entertain other possibilities.
Privately, he questioned even pursuing "the damn things," as
he called them. Why hold up the whole drive for two runty
horses? The young one was not bad looking but he was barely
sixteen hands; the older one was too round for his liking, too
thick at the neck, and not much past fifteen hands. The
Captain was normally a good judge of horseflesh, Huntley
thought, but some horse-trader had sure pulled the wool over
his eyes with these two. Huntley was of a mind to shoot them
if they gave him any trouble and then make up some story to
the Captain about how "the poor things" fell and broke their
legs on that slippery ice. Jeremiah, Byard and Zachary would
go along; no one cared to mess with Huntley.

Huntley was on the short side himself, but he was thick and
powerful. His hands were as huge as hams, and though his
green eyes were thought handsome, they did not look warmly
on the world. What a cold stare he could muster. It seemed
significant that Huntley was always called by his last name.
Surely he had a first name, though he never offered it and he
gave no one the slightest inclination to ask it. Being with
Huntley was like riding through a patch of prickly ash; you
just wanted out of there.

After riding north for four hours, the riders from east and
west met in the middle of the lake, certain they would have an
hour or so of rest before the two black horses appeared on the
horizon. It did not work out that way.

What Huntley and the others saw, clear as day, were two
sets of tracks heading north up the middle of Lake Champlain.
Beau Albert and Tibeau had beaten them.

"SHIT!" was Huntley's only response. Even the other men blinked, so loudly had he said the word.

—⁂—

That crow flying overhead, had he stuck around, would have seen two black horses trotting side by side. The older horse on the right, the younger one on the left.

Beau Albert was making the decisions—how fast to go, which direction, when (if at all) to pause. Tibeau's job, apparently, was to keep the journey light. Now and again he would reach over and try to nip his sire, who flattened his ears in response. Tibeau had youth and beauty and he had yet to lose his sense of play. The old man had his pride and a deep well of strength to draw on. They made quite a pair.

Their ancestors had prepared them for a dash home like this. For almost two hundred years, *habitant* horses had been a breed apart. The Americans had their horses, some fine ones, too, but those horses stayed on the American side of the border. The *habitant* loved his tough little horse and had no interest in other breeds. That horse, this land, seemed made for each other. It was as if the land itself—the boulders of granite, the tall white pines, the biting wind off the St. Lawrence River—had sculpted these horses.

Eventually, each side of the border discovered the other's horses. Some of the *habitants,* anxious to win ice races, bred their Canadians to Thoroughbreds and other breeds. On the American side, the carriage trade, the racetrack and breeding stables had all discovered the Canadian horse.

Ambrose said he had no interest in trying out other breeds. He let it be known that he liked his Canadian horses pure, and Albert and Tibeau were among the finest and purest he had ever seen. Ambrose would think nothing of hitching Beau Albert to a *berline* and taking him all the way to Calumet, maybe pausing once or twice to relieve himself in the woods. On lesser journeys, he would tie Tibeau to the back of the *berline* for what he called "*un peu d'exercice*. A little exercise."

These black horses could trot all night and all day, and it was a quick pace, too. Like farmers all over Canada East, Ambrose used the same horses to pull logs from the forest and to take him on his long journeys. The one labour laid on muscle, the other built up their wind.

And when times were tough, in winter especially, when hay ran low, farmers would release their horses into the forests, where they happily foraged and even seemed to thrive. One year, Ambrose had only frozen fish to offer his horses when the hay and grain ran out. The horses nibbled on that—nothing surprised them.

So, despite their deprived circumstances on their dash for home, Beau Albert and Tibeau were not at all overwhelmed. They, and their ancestors, had seen it all before.

***

Down the lake, Tip Weldon was anxiously eyeing that northern horizon. It was almost dark, and still no sign of Huntley and the runaway horses. A part of him was angry at this sudden turn of events, and he could imagine the military brass in Boston fuming at the delay. On the other hand, he was reminded once more of the quality of these two horses and his wisdom in buying them. You had to admire their spirit, their boldness, their stamina.

He thought of all those evenings with Ambrose, plying him with rum (Jupiter, that man could tolerate his drink) and trying to coax his price down. But the more Ambrose spoke of the horses and their lineage, the more stories he told to illustrate how clever and athletic they were and how much his granddaughter prized them, the more he stood firm and even showed signs of abandoning the sale altogether.

When night fell, Captain Weldon left the wagon and joined the crew around the fire. Spirits were good among the men, he thought. They were like the horses, glad of the rest. Goatskins of rum were being passed around, and while the Captain cautioned the men against drinking too much in case the horses began to move, he was not about to cut too deeply into their fun.

By midnight on this moonless night, everyone around the fire, the Captain among them, had settled into his blankets. Rum and a long day had done them in. Only two sentries on horseback were posted on the herd's eastern and western flanks, and, judging by the way the men's chins had sunk into their chests, they, too, were fast asleep.

⸺⸳⸻

Emboldened by the dark, Claire left her cupboard behind and walked about freely. There was plenty of food lying around: she helped herself to a beef stew in a cauldron by the fire, tucked into a loaf of bread, enjoyed the remains of someone's tea and had some hard biscuits that someone had carelessly left by the fire. These were moments of pure pleasure for Claire. She felt completely relaxed, warming herself by the fire as if she were invisible.

So that's how they make fires on the lake, thought Claire, as she eyed the contraption. She had seen these fires from a distance and couldn't imagine how a hot fire wouldn't simply melt the ice into water and douse the flames. The solution was ingenious and simple: Monsieur Weldon must have been carrying in the back of his wagon several thin but strong sheets of iron, maybe four feet square and a quarter-inch thick. The men would set these on flat rocks so the metal sheets were a few inches off the ice.

There must have been wood as well in the back of that wagon, and Claire could see that it was mostly birch they were burning. They would have bought it on the Canadian side. Watching the white and peppered bark curl as it burned and crackled and snapped, taking in the smell of the woodsmoke, she felt the tug of home. It was like getting a letter from a loved one travelling in a distant land. Claire reminded herself of her promise to write home. She would do it at the first opportunity, but—and she laughed at the thought—mail service in the middle of this lake was likely poor.

Claire stayed there a long time into the night, even feeding the fire as if it were hers. She smiled at the thought of the men rising in the morning and taking stock of things. *Some angel,* they would say, *has tended the fire all night long, for look, it still burns bright. And some devil,* they would then complain, *has been into our stew, bread and biscuit*s. The mystery of the camp thief would deepen, until all the men were looking at each other in a new way.

The other thing that gave Claire a feeling of contentment was the fact that Huntley and the others had not returned. This was a good sign. Claire retired to her box and dozed off just before dawn, and her last thought as she closed her eyes was of Albert and Tibeau galloping over the frozen horizon with Huntley and the others falling far behind.

"SHIT! SHIT!"

Two cuss words, thought Jeremiah. Huntley was really mad now.

The four riders had followed the tracks north, Huntley's fury rising with every stride. Each passing hour drew them farther away from the warm fire back at the camp, the goatskins of rum they knew were being passed around, the beef stew that Froggy—the cook on the expedition—had promised would be a fine feed. As light faded, Huntley and the rest knew they faced either an exhausting night of riding or a frigid one huddled around a fire on Grand Isle. And every stride north would have to be retraced when they headed back south.

The double cuss that Jeremiah remarked on occurred late in the day, when the cold had settled into their fingers and toes and the men with beards and moustaches had to speak through icicles. The tracks had suddenly veered west towards Grand Isle, Huntley noted. The damn horses were heading into the bush!

Were they doing this because they somehow sensed they were being followed? Huntley knew about the hearing of horses, how they would foretell thunder hours before it arrived. Could they hear the hoofbeats on the ice of the horses chasing them? Or were they just going into the forest to look for food? Were they both foraging *and* trying to throw off their pursuers?

Huntley was astonished by how fast the two escaped horses were going, but he was not filled with admiration. It was resentment that cooked in his brain. His fingers clenched that bullwhip and he felt a great longing to use it. Jeremiah, Byard and Zachary gave him an even wider berth than usual.

Near dark, Huntley resigned himself to a night in the woods of Grand Isle. The men tethered their horses, built a huge fire and huddled around it. The other riders took their cue from Huntley. No one said a word, and all three found themselves sneaking glances at Huntley as he stared into the fire. They needn't have bothered with their sly looks, for Huntley seemed almost unaware of their existence. He just stared into the fire while seeming to take little comfort from it. Jeremiah grew alarmed at Huntley's face, the squint of his eyes, the clenching of his teeth.

Jeremiah was from Salem, Massachusetts, where his father, a preacher, would often quote the Bible. "He that is slow to anger," his father would say, and if he thought you didn't know, he would quickly chirp "Book of Proverbs" and start again. "He that is slow to anger is better than the mighty; and he that ruleth his spirit than he that taketh a city."

Jeremiah took a deep breath. The proverb would have been lost on Huntley, for he was quick to anger and had no interest in ruling his spirit. *God have mercy,* Jeremiah said to himself, *on those two horses.*

Huntley and the others could not have known this, but the horses they were searching for were only a half mile away. Both Tibeau and Beau Albert were at home in the forest, nibbling on cedar and pine and even small branches. The younger horse was content to let his sire be the lookout, but any sudden noise brought both horses' heads up high and their ears forward.

Most nights around the Vigere farm, one could hear howls from wolves. Every horse in the region had seen a wolf or had a brush with one. Europeans and Americans who came to the Canadas in winter and saw Canadian horses for the first time inevitably remarked on two things: their woolly coats and their alertness. Even in summer, the horse of iron seemed to sleep with one eye open. A horse never knew what was lurking in the high grass or in the snow-white forest. When allowed to forage in the forest for too long, some horses took on an almost wild demeanour. Close encounters with wolves and cougars made them jumpy, and even older, quieter horses weren't happy to have their feet picked up and cleaned after being too long in the bush. The foot was his prime defence against a wolf, and many wolves learned the hard way to respect those feet. To surrender his feet was to give over his chance to flee, and the Canadian horse too long in the bush had to be coaxed into letting any human lift his foot.

Albert and Tibeau, then, were alert on that island, but they preferred the forest to the wind-blown lake. Albert, especially, couldn't relax on the ice. Ice made him think about racing. The forest seemed calm, by comparison, and reminded him of home. And there was far less wind in the woods, plus a chance to nibble on something.

Father and son even settled into some mutual grooming. It had been a while. Each would rest his head on the other's back and work that area gently with his teeth. *You scratch my back, I'll scratch yours,* was the deal. For the first time in many days, the two black horses closed their eyes and each, in turn, let go one of those big sighs that horses deliver when it's nap time.

"Least the snow is holding off." They were the first civil words that Huntley had spoken since all had left the main camp.

Snow would cover the horses' tracks and, without tracks to follow, the four men faced the prospect of continuing north even as far as L'Ange-Gardien. None of them relished that possibility.

They broke camp at dawn, their horses still fresh but not as fresh as they had been. No one had anticipated that hunting down those renegade horses would take this long. Quickly enough, the horsemen found tracks leading off the lake and into the forest on the island. Huntley was absolutely certain that they would find the two horses in a clearing. Roping them, he thought, would be easy.

Inside of an hour, the four horsemen spotted the two horses. A frozen marsh at the southern end of the island gave way to hills farther north. The hills afforded Huntley what he wanted: the element of surprise. The two black horses couldn't use their delicate ears or their extraordinary eyesight to give them warning. Suddenly the men were up on that rise and coming down in a flat-out gallop, shrieking all the way.

The goal was to make the horses panic and freeze. With luck, the horses would spend a few precious seconds deciding what to do, which way to go. In that time, the men would get close enough to let fly the ropes.

The horses didn't respond as expected. When Tip Weldon later asked him for his version of events, Jeremiah said, "Captain, I couldn't believe it. It was like they'd put their heads together in the night and planned their strategy. It almost worked."

The horses, as it happened, split up. Beau Albert headed west and drew Huntley and Jeremiah. Tibeau ran east, with Byard and Zachary in hot pursuit. A lone horse in a forest has an advantage over a pursuing horse and rider. The pursuing horse has to carry the rider and manage the rider's sudden shifts of weight; a careless rider can be swept off the saddle by a low-hanging branch. But in the end it was a branch that was Albert's undoing, not his pursuer's.

Uncanny how fast a horse can gallop through dense forest, even in the night. Any rider who has trusted her horse's night vision as they galloped on the trail through pitch-black woods knows how exhilarating it is: the wind in her face, branches beating at her legs, her hands in her horse's mane as she *pump pump pumps*. She tucks in behind her horse's head and she *pray pray prays*.

Beau Albert was flying through that forest, relying on his balance and surefootedness to see him through. There was no trail, only moments of light and patches of space in the otherwise dense forest. He could sense his pursuers but they were starting to lag. Albert threw caution to the winds, and the men had almost lost sight of him when the ragged limb of an old cedar put a dramatic halt to his run. The limb, as heavy and sharp as a spear, was hidden behind the foliage. A smaller branch he would have bulled past, but this one grabbed him at the shoulder, knocked him off his feet and left him upside down, wedged between two fallen trees.

Beau Albert struggled mightily for a few seconds, then he knew. It was hopeless. He relaxed, blinked, shook his head and let loose a loud whinny. It was a call for help.

❧

Tibeau was having an easier time. The place where Huntley and the rest had come upon the horses was close to the edge of the forest, and in less than a minute Tibeau was on the lake and sprinting for his life.

He had his ears pinned back and he had found another gear. Byard and Zachary were falling behind, and though they spurred their horses on and shouted for more speed, their horses, too, had clued in. The black horse was a runner.

Then suddenly he stopped. Stopped as if someone had drawn an invisible rope across the lake. Tibeau pricked his ears and turned to face the island. The old man was calling him. Tibeau must have heard some urgency in the call and he struck off in a new direction. The mad dash north had suddenly become a race to the place where Beau Albert was belly up. As Ambrose might have put it, the proud, stout horse was "in a pickle."

"Well well well." They were Huntley's first words as he came upon the downed horse.

Jeremiah was pleased to hear them. A nice change, he thought, from "SHIT!" and "SHIT! SHIT!"

Albert had no reason to like these men who now loomed over him. They had taken him from his good and kind keepers, driven him across a frozen lake for days with little in the way of food and no water, and then chased him when he and his stablemate had had the good sense to strike for home. Now he was upside down, his feet in the air, his shoulder hurt, and he could feel the blood trickling down his neck.

But the black gelding stayed calm. Horses are optimists, most of them, most of the time. Albert simply assumed that these men, whoever they were, would help him out of this jam. A smart horse knows when he needs human help.

But Beau Albert had never met a human like Huntley. The man approached him, still saying, "Well, well, well," in a soft voice the horse must have taken for kindness. Then the fist came back and Huntley landed a blow right between the horse's eyes.

Albert wasn't much bothered by the blow. His head was hard, harder than Huntley knew. "SHIT! SHIT! SHIT!" screamed Huntley as he held his right fist in the palm of his left hand. Jeremiah smiled, a small smile just in case Huntley saw.

Tibeau chose that moment to arrive on the scene, only slightly lathered from his run. Huntley removed himself to let the others do the work. They roped and hobbled Tibeau just in case he had ideas, secured Albert with a rope, then used more ropes and horsepower to pull one log aside and free the downed horse from the wedge.

Albert had a gaping wound at his shoulder—Zachary used snow as a bandage—but both horses looked otherwise none the worse for their adventure. If anything, the horses looked pleased and even haughty as they followed the horsemen (with two ropes around their necks as a precaution against another escape). Jeremiah, Byard and Zachary were happy to be going south again, and, though no one was saying it aloud, they all thought Huntley pretty much deserved his sprained hand.

There was something menacing about Huntley, and the men feared and disliked him. What a pleasant change to laugh at him; they would enjoy telling this story behind his back. It was like watching a man you despise slip on a patch of grease while carrying eggs in a basket. The laughter stayed with you long after he had landed on his bum and the last egg had broken on his noggin.

CHAPTER 9

From Claire to Clint

By noon, Huntley's party had reached the camp, where Tip Weldon awaited them beside his wagon with arms crossed. He was quick to note the injuries—Beau Albert's shoulder and Huntley's sore paw.

"What happened to your hand?" asked the Captain, staring at Huntley.

"Messed it up in the capture," was all he said. The other men were content to let Huntley explain the business of the sprain. If pressed, in private, Jeremiah would tell the Captain what he had seen.

"And the horse's shoulder?"

"He was runnin' from us on the island, Captain," said Jeremiah, "when he ran straight into a mighty sharp branch. Looks worse than it is, I think. But I tell you, he's quick, and the younger one is *real* quick."

The Captain told the men to get some grub by the fire and to release the younger horse into the herd. He had Jeremiah hold Beau Albert while he sewed him and doctored him.

Claire almost gasped aloud when she heard the business about the wound. Through the slit in the cupboard top she could just make out Monsieur Weldon's hands as he closed the gash with needle and thread. "Good boy," he would say every minute or so. "Good boy." Like the trooper that he was, Albert stood quietly. He was a horse who liked to be fussed over, even if the fussing meant sewing his skin as you would a torn sail.

Claire thought of all the times she and Ambrose had tended to horses in just this fashion after mishaps in the pasture or the forest. "They love people," Ambrose would say of his Canadian horses. "It has to hurt to be sewed up like that, but they trust us not to harm or hurt them needlessly."

When he was finished sewing the wound, Monsieur Weldon reached into his satchel and applied an ointment. Among the few possessions Claire had brought with her—it lay beside her in the box—was a leather bag with neat strips of cloth, powders for poultices and various ointments. (And, for good luck, the maple locket.) Claire had pondered unveiling herself that night had Monsieur Weldon not tended to the horse. The thought of Albert injured and not doctored was almost beyond bearing.

Claire had had her fill of the box. She was sick of her rank clothes and body, she was tired of stealing food, and she was weary—most of all—of doing nothing. Throughout most of her thirteen years, she had worked. There had almost always been something in her hands: a pitchfork, a needle and thread, a wooden spoon, the reins of a horse. For four days, this coffin box had been home and she wanted out.

Listening to the chatter around her, she learned that they would head for Williamstown within the hour. There were big corrals in the town where the horses would be sorted according to the tasks fated to them. The men could rest in the town, find hotels where they could spend their wages on beer and rum. And, there, thought Claire, a deaf boy named Clint Flynn would make himself known.

———— ∞∞∞ ————

The rest of the day unfolded much like the others. The horses were frisky after a day and a half of rest and hay. Monsieur Weldon and the grey moved along at their usual pace, with the herd surging forward and easing back. The game of tag between wagon and herd picked up where it had left off.

"Pay attention to those two black horses," Monsieur Weldon had advised the men. He wanted no repeat of the previous escapade. But if Beau Albert and Tibeau were scheming, they gave no sign of it.

With an end in sight, the journey to the town passed quickly for Claire. It was dark by the time they arrived in Williamstown, but one of the men must have ridden on ahead to let the military know about the new batch of horses coming. The town was far bigger than L'Ange-Gardien and didn't seem to get sleepy after dark the way the village did. Wagons came and went. Men and women walked up and down raised wooden sidewalks. Music from pianos and loud laughter filtered out from hotels. After the quiet of the lake, the noise hit Claire like a slap.

Still, when the wagon pulled into a livery stable and Mac was unhitched, she knew it would be only moments before she said goodbye to her home of the past four days. She heard the heavy door of the stable close, waited for a minute to ensure no one was about, and then eased her stiff frame out of the box.

Claire packed up her sack of belongings and found a spot up in the loft amid the hay. She curled up like a mouse and had the best sleep of her life.

At dawn, she found a bar of soap and a pail and treated her face and body to a much needed wash. She looked down at her chest where little nubs were forming. Depending on how quickly they became breasts and how much time she spent in the army, she might one day have to wrap herself in cloth to mask their existence. Army grooms named Clint Flynn didn't have such things.

There was a mirror in a back room where the stable manager would shave himself, and Claire was shocked at the girl who stared back at her. Dark sacks around her eyes. The face thinner than she remembered. And her lovely hair, shorn badly. She had seen sheep after shearing look better than this.

Claire took the scissors from her bag and cut off even more hair while trying to tidy up the first job done behind the barn at home. She was not vain, or, at least, not as vain as some girls she knew back in L'Ange-Gardien. But if four days had been this hard on her, what would forty days do? Or four hundred? How many days would pass before she and the horses could go home? She could not contemplate going home without them, or some terrible event befalling them. That was not in the cards.

Home.

She dug into her sack and found the picture book Ambrose had given her. Which one should she send? This one, she decided. It was a painting of the magnificent Montmorency Falls, the water seemingly frozen in mid-spray, with dozens of men and women in sleighs and *berlines* admiring the falls from its base. It seemed logical to Claire to choose this one. The frozen ice of Lake Champlain, the frozen falls at Montmorency. *Years from now,* thought Claire, *my brothers and I will laugh at how my brain works.*

With her pen, she wrote a note home—in French, of course. In English, it would have read like this:

> *Dear Papa, Maman,*
>   *Père-père, Mamie,*
>   *Léo, André and Jérôme:*
>   *I will write you every week, I promise. I want you to know I am well. I am working in a stable. Don't worry. I will return, one of these days. I love you all (even my brothers).*
>   *Claire*

She hoped the letter struck the right note. The business about working in a stable was not true, but it would shortly be true if things went according to plan. And she hoped the little joke at the end would reassure them, for if she were unwell or cold and hungry, she might not have felt up to some silliness.

In fact, Claire felt like a colt on a spring morning. The sleep in the hayloft, where she had been able to stretch her arms and legs, had done her a world of good. She was up and about and breathing stable air—her favourite kind—and not the stuff in Monsieur Weldon's cramped box. She was clean, and that felt wonderful, too. And even writing the letter had brought its rewards: for the first time since leaving home, she felt more like a traveller abroad than a runaway. The letter, written on the back of Krieghoff's painting of the falls, had the feel of a postcard sent by a rich girl from some exotic locale.

Claire Vigere sends her best to her family back home. She wishes them to know that her trunks have all arrived safely, her well-appointed room overlooks the ocean, and the weather is divine. She wishes they were here ...

Claire's little reverie in the loft ended abruptly when a man came in and tossed a few cups of grain into Mac's stall, then just as quickly left. She had business to attend to. Get a meal into her belly. See where the horses were being kept. Mail the letter.

And Claire Vigere knew just the person to do all those jobs. A deaf boy named Clint Flynn. The boy went down to the mirror, adjusted his wool cap so it sat low on his head, took a deep breath and opened the stable door.

The town in that bright winter sun was even livelier in the morning than it had been the evening before. The boy could hear bells coming from every direction as horse-drawn sleighs moved up and down the wide main street, and he had to remind himself that he was deaf. There would be no bells now. No church bells, no sleigh bells, no sound of any kind. Only silence. If there was a shout, a gunshot, a bark—the deaf boy could not respond.

No one took much notice of the boy as he moved up the street. He soon found what he was looking for: a small hotel with a sign outside that read "Room & Board & Home-Cooked Meals." The boy had in his pocket an American one-dollar coin, lifted from a wrangler's satchel as its rum-soaked owner slept around the fire on that frozen lake. (It was one more sin that Claire would have to confess to Père Boivin when she got back home.)

The boy entered the hotel and found a seat at a table by the window. A woman with a cheery face soon appeared at his side. "What'll it be, young man?" she asked.

The boy looked at her pleadingly, pointed to his right ear and shook his head. "Ah, you can't hear," she replied. "Poor thing." She came back with a pencil and pad and offered it to him in hopes he could read and write.

"Big breakfast," the boy wrote on the pad, and showed her his American dollar.

"Comin' right up," she said, and she put a thumb in the air to make him see that she understood.

Either people around here were quick-witted, Claire concluded, or there were lots of deaf people about. She had expected more difficulty in explaining her (no, *his*) deafness and in making herself (*him*-self) understood. This was the conversation in the boy's head, and he bit his lip and said *"Merde!"* under his breath. *Deaf … boy,* he said silently, *deaf … boy, deaf … boy.*

On the wide streets outside, a wagon stopped. The boy in the restaurant found himself being stared at by a girl, maybe two years old, holding her mother's hand. The boy averted his eyes with one hand, then poked his head around. The little girl smiled. It was a game that Claire and her brothers used to play in the cabin, and apparently children in Massachusetts knew about it too. They played peekaboo for what seemed a long time, and the boy in the restaurant was almost sad when it ended. He waved to the child, who did not return the wave but followed the boy with her eyes as the wagon pulled away.

There then appeared at the table the biggest breakfast Claire had ever seen. She might have stretched it to feed everyone back home. There was a huge bowl of porridge with brown sugar and cream on the side, three eggs, three slices of bacon, a stack of toast with marmalade, a large glass of milk, four pancakes with maple syrup (not quite as good as

Magrette's but very good nonetheless) and a cup of coffee. The last was the only item she had no appetite for. The rest, in time, found its way into the boy's belly.

Clint kept his hat on as he ate. He felt more like a boy with the hat on and he hoped no one would remind him of his manners. No one in the place did. And when he was finished, the bright woman who had served him took his dollar coin and came back with seventy-five cents change. She also put the pad and pencil in his right hand and squeezed that hand with both of hers. The boy gave her a generous smile in return.

Before the boy left, he wrote on the pad: "Post office?"

The woman nodded, took him outside and pointed him to the general store across the street. The boy bowed slightly. The move, which came to him instinctively, would serve him well in the days ahead. A deaf boy's sign of thanks to the hearing world.

The boy now had the hang of pencil and pad. For simple requests, it seemed to be working. "Envelopes? Pen?" he wrote inside the general store, and a young clerk brought up several envelopes from a shelf below, along with a quill pen and a small bottle of black ink. On the counter, the boy folded the page in three, placed the letter inside and wrote on the outside: "Ferme Vigere, L'Ange-Gardien, Canada East." The clerk took note of the address and then laid on the appropriate ten-cent stamp. On the apple-green stamp was the face of a man in a white wig, George Washington, with the words "U.S. Post Office" overtop and below "Ten Cents," with two Xs in the bottom corners. X, Claire knew, for her mother had taught her, was Latin for ten. The boy in the store paused to admire the stamp before handing the letter back to the clerk. He then nodded as both thanks and goodbye.

Out on the street, the sun on his face, his belly still full from that marathon breakfast, the boy felt tall as he walked. He looked straight into the eyes of every passing Yankee. Aside from matters of fashion (no one wore bright cloth belts as they did at home), folks here looked not so different from folks in L'Ange-Gardien. But the town was far bigger than L'Ange-Gardien, and it sat in a deep valley with green mountains all around.

The boy was taking in this new landscape—gawking, more like it—and that was how he missed the approach of Tip Weldon on that wooden sidewalk. In fact, by the time Clint noticed Monsieur Weldon, the boy had the sense that the man had been staring at him. But for how long? One second? Three? Clint walked past and hoped his face conveyed none of the terror that Claire felt. He wanted desperately to turn around, but if Monsieur Weldon had recognized the boy as Vincent Beaupierre and turned at the same moment the boy did ... the game would have been over, and Claire or Clint or whoever he or she claimed to be would have been sent packing on a coach or train heading north. But the boy did not turn around. He had more sense than that. Instead, he waited a few moments before casually crossing the street and from the other side followed the tall man in the wide-brimmed hat. Sooner or later, Monsieur Weldon would lead the way to Beau Albert and Tibeau.

Monsieur Weldon—flanked by two men—was walking north. The boy trailing them had the sun to help with direction. Within ten minutes, the bustle of the town lay behind them, and the houses began to spread out. The houses became farmhouses and, on both sides of the road, the boy saw how the land had been carved into neat farms.

Just at the moment Monsieur Weldon turned down a lane, the boy heard the sound of horses. But not the sound he had hoped for: the sound of horses playing in a pasture, of horses romping. What the boy heard quite distinctly was the sound of a horse in distress.

Monsieur Weldon and his companions joined a number of other men who had taken up positions leaning on a five-foot cedar rail fence. The rails formed a small, round pen, maybe one hundred feet in diameter. What all the men were looking at was Huntley on board a young bay horse who was doing everything she could to toss that thing on her back.

The boy could hardly bear to look. He had the sense that this was the young horse's first time with a rider and saddle on her back. The wide eyes, the violent bucking, the pitiful cries and pig-like squealing—this was the filly's introduction to the world of men. It wasn't long before even little jabs from Huntley's spurs failed to get a response. The horse was lathered and spent. The rider got off, grinned as if well pleased with himself and called out, "Next!"

And so it went for most of the afternoon. The boy noticed many Canadian horses coming for their bouts with Huntley, but there were other breeds, too. Monsieur Weldon wasn't the only horse-buyer who had brought in horses for grading. All the heavier, stockier horses had already been taken away, soon to be married to gun carriages and supply wagons for whatever time was left to them.

The boy was soon sick of the spectacle and was about to leave the pen for the much larger paddock alongside—where all the other horses nervously awaited their fates—when a black horse caught his eye. It was, without a shadow of a doubt, Beau Albert. The boy's eyes never left him. His handler brought him in and must have been taken in by the black horse's low head and apparent calm. But the second the horse caught sight of Huntley, there was chaos in that round pen. The horse whom Huntley had dismissed as small and unworthy of a chase across the frozen lake was now up on his hind legs and looking very, very tall. The handler fled for cover, and even Huntley—who had a notion of standing his ground—dove between fence rails as the horse rushed at him with teeth bared.

Huntley had mostly recovered from the sprain to his hand, but Beau Albert remembered all too well that fist to his head and who had delivered it. And now it was the horse's turn to wear the smug look. The black horse trotted around the now vacant pen like a prince, his tail bent and high in the air, his reins trailing on the ground. *Fais attention,* the boy thought to himself, though really he was talking to the horse. *Better watch out, Albert.*

Within a minute, six men were inside the pen and tossing ropes over the black gelding's head. They had seen his kind before, and every man knew what to do. But it was twenty more minutes before he was subdued enough that a rider dared get close. Still, the stout black horse had the men cursing as he issued kicks and bites and spins that sent them sprawling.

Now Huntley approached, dead calm. His eyes never left the black horse's, and the horse returned the hard stare. Some horses you can stare down; Albert was not one of them.

"Hold him, boys," Huntley ordered the six men. Another ten minutes passed while Albert sidestepped some more, reared and backed. The men along the rails were now quietly placing bets on the likelihood of Huntley weathering this storm. While the drama unfolded, no one took notice of the young boy looking on. He was simply one more spectator watching the battle that always ensues when a man rides a defiant horse.

It wasn't that this horse was young or had seldom or never been ridden: far from it. He simply had reason to hate his rider. And it wounded Claire deeply to see a horse she knew so well and cared so deeply about being roped by men. To be treated by this rider as a nuisance, a hurdle to be overcome and the quicker the better.

And, for a few moments anyway, it looked as though the hurdle had been overcome. The horse seemed, quite suddenly, to have thought better of fighting this particular rider. Huntley had him trotting around that ring smartly now, like a preacher out for a Sunday afternoon jog.

"If that horse could salute," someone shouted from the side, "I do believe he would." More than half the men watching wore a look of disappointment. They had each bet a dollar that the fiery black horse would put Huntley in the dirt at least once, and it seemed they had bet badly. But then the black horse picked up a canter, followed by a full gallop, and Huntley's eyes grew wide. He hadn't requested this speed. Round and round they went, faster, then faster yet, and Huntley seemed to grow smaller as all his attempts at stalling the horse—hauling on both reins, hard to the left, hard to the right—had no effect. He was reduced to shouting "Whoa! Whoa!" but he never got out a third "Whoa!" The horse, all in one motion, put on the brakes, dug in with all four feet and lowered his head almost to the ground. Huntley flew into one of the side rails and a fountain of blood began pouring from his nose.

Many of the men, now standing with their feet on the lower rails, pounded one fist into the palm of the other hand. It was what men sometimes did when luck turned from bad to good, when one dollar looked to be lost and suddenly was transformed into two.

The boy looking on almost forgot himself. He was about to shout, in the voice of Claire Vigere, in her best French, "*Bravo, Albert!!!!*" when good sense saved him. But now what? The black horse retreated to the middle of the pen and stood with his head high waiting for another rider. He looked like a gladiator in a Roman amphitheatre who had vanquished one foe and awaited the next. The horse may have grounded the bad man, the man who stank of sweat and tobacco, but he or another man would surely come for him now. Horses knew this of men, that men did not take defeat lightly.

The next rider, the horse saw, was tiny compared to the one he had just tossed. The boy had leapt off the railing and was now approaching the horse, who eyed him suspiciously. But horses have the most extraordinary eyesight and the most remarkable memory. The boy's body language, the set of his shoulders, his eyes, all were almost instantly recognizable to the horse. Beau Albert knew it was Claire. He whinnied gently, and his head dropped low to greet her. He went to her like a dog would go to his master after too long an absence.

The men looking on, Tip Weldon among them, said nothing. They were too astonished. The black horse and the young boy had quite suddenly come to occupy centre stage, and no one from the audience was about to interfere or stop this intriguing play from proceeding to the next act.

Claire, in fact, had no plan or preconceived notion of what to do next. If this was a play, there was no script. She knew only that she had to go to the horse. Then, moving quickly, she undid the girth, slipped off the saddle and, using the horse's mane as grip, launched herself onto the horse's back. The horse stayed perfectly still while he did so.

"Will ya look at that!" one man said from the side, speaking in a low, astonished voice. He was speaking for all of them.

What they observed next was the boy seeing the makings of a gap in the railing where only a few men were. He made a motion to them to get off the fence, holding each arm up in the air and moving it to the side. Some of the men would later say it made them think of the story from the Old Testament, Moses parting the Red Sea. And if one or two of the men didn't right away catch the boy's drift, they soon did. Boy and horse began to gallop for the gap and the men hightailed it out of there.

Some of the men would talk about what happened next for the rest of their lives. A boy came out of nowhere, got up on just about the wildest and most cantankerous horse they had ever seen, a horse who had just put their best bronc rider "on his ass." Then the boy stripped off the saddle. Was it that the stirrups were the wrong length and the boy had no time or inclination for adjusting? Or, the men later wondered, did he do it for effect? Riding bareback just added one more touch to the story. For the story was that the boy, riding bareback, then took the horse "over the damn fence."

That's how they would tell it. They couldn't just say "over the fence." The word "damn" somehow seemed essential to the telling. For the damn fence was a five-foot fence, and the horse was not much more than fifteen hands high. And if the storyteller seemed amazed every time he told the story, so, too, were his listeners.

Claire and Beau Albert had jumped many fences together, though none as high as this. But Albert was so glad to see his old pal again, and so anxious to leave that awful pen and the men in it, that he would have attempted the moon had she asked him. Whatever plan Claire had for rescuing Albert, she was making it up as she went. As they soared over that fence, the rider gripping the horse's mane and tucked in behind his neck, time seemed to slow down. It felt to Claire as though they were up in the air a long, long time, time enough to ponder the next move. High over that fence, floating and floating, men and fence below and behind her, Claire felt an overwhelming desire to just keep galloping upon landing. Head north, hope for the best.

They were now flying down that road, going so fast there were tears in Claire's eyes, when the solution came to her. Escape was futile. They would hunt horse and rider down, all the way to L'Ange-Gardien, if need be. And even if they did get as far as home, Monsieur Weldon had bought the horse fair and square. Besides, Tibeau was back there, and she couldn't leave him behind. No, going back home was not an option. Claire would have taken Albert "from frying pan to fire," as Ambrose sometimes put it. Or, "*de mal en pis*—from bad to worse," as Magrette would have said.

So she stopped Albert, stopped him with just a hint from her seat and the lightest tug on his bridle. What Huntley couldn't do by hauling with all his considerable strength Claire had accomplished with *politesse*.

Then she asked Albert to pick up his canter again and they headed back towards the round pen. The place where they had stopped was still within sight of the pen and none of the men—not one—had left his place on the railing. Back, at the same speed, came horse and rider. And again, horse and rider took that fence, in the same spot, only this time from the outside. It spoke volumes of Albert's trust in Claire that he willingly re-entered the hell he had just escaped.

"Then the boy gets off the damn horse," some of the men would later say, "and he heads straight for the Captain and hands him a note. Turns out the lad is deaf as a post. Deaf as a post! But I tell ya, he rode that horse over that fence like my granpappy used to play the fiddle. Just as sweet as Jesus."

CHAPTER 10

Army Life

When she handed Monsieur Weldon the note, Claire looked down, hoping he would take it as a hint of shyness and not try to meet her eyes. They stood in the centre of the ring, and all the men looked on as the three faced each other: man, horse, boy.

Tip Weldon took but seconds to read the note that introduced the runaway, the war orphan, the deaf boy named Clint Flynn who had so dramatically presented his calling card: "Good worker. Good with horses."

"I'll say you're good with horses," Weldon said with a chuckle, though as far as he knew he was talking to himself or the clouds above. "Deaf or not, the army could use a groom like you."

Then Monsieur Weldon did what Claire had dreaded he would do. He slowly put out his hand, laid his forefinger on her chin and tilted it up so he could look directly into her eyes. He had met her once, though briefly, but that time seemed so long ago. Would he remember Vincent Beaupierre, or had he seen through that disguise? Would he send him/her packing back north? Or would the note and the cropped hair derail any such memory? It made no sense that a girl from a village in Quebec would suddenly show up hundreds of miles away in Massachusetts, did it?

Claire did not blink and tried with every ounce of her being to disguise her terror. She felt herself biting her lip and immediately stopped, and tried to frame a smile. Tip Weldon had bent down low to peer into her eyes and it seemed he was looking right into her soul, so long did he hold her gaze.

Long afterwards, Claire would come back to that moment and try to understand what Monsieur Weldon was thinking. What a poker face he had, impossible to read. Was he simply staring at her, as all the men stared at her—out of pure amazement? He looked to be taking her in, as if he had found a bright gem in the dirt of Williamstown and was now taking the time to admire it. Or had her whole adventure become instantly clear to him—Canadian girl loves horses, girl hides away in his wagon, cuts her hair, poses as deaf to hide her French accent ...

Monsieur Weldon had a gift with horses. He must have asked himself how a perfect stranger, a mere boy, could generate instant trust with a very angry, very nervous and very fearful horse. This boy had to *know* this horse. And "the boy" had to have looked familiar. If Monsieur Weldon could remember details about the two hundred horses he had bought on his trip north, surely he would also remember the young lad who had so impressed during those races on Missisquoi Bay.

But maybe, thought Claire, Monsieur Weldon was the kind of man who would have great respect for someone so young and yet so bold. Ambrose would have told him about Claire, and perhaps he had used her attachment to the two horses as a bargaining chip: "My granddaughter would never forgive me if I sold those horses …" Maybe the thought of a girl fleeing home for the sake of horses tugged at some romantic part of him. Maybe he had had that same feeling for horses when he was thirteen. Maybe the awful business of buying horses for war hadn't entirely eroded that connection with these noble creatures, and with good and fine horses especially. Like the one now pawing, with his left front hoof, the ground beside Claire.

And maybe, just maybe, thought Claire, Monsieur Weldon was a practical man, too. If those two horses were even half as good as he thought they were, then young "Clint" was the key to their good manners. And if the older black could put Huntley through the rails, the younger one would do likewise. Clint would be their guardian angel.

If Monsieur Weldon knew Claire's identity, he gave no hint of it. He put the note in his pocket and called over one of the men—a stubby fellow in a blue uniform with three stripes on his sleeve.

"Sergeant McDermott, this lad is looking for work as a groom. Sign him on, find him a uniform that fits and give him some food. He's deaf, you understand, so you'll have to communicate with him using pencil and paper. Another thing, there's a horse in the herd over in the other paddock, a buddy to this one," he said, pointing at Albert. "The other horse is younger, taller, all black, a stud with a white sock on the right hind. Separate these two horses. Put them in stalls in the barn. I've got special jobs for them."

Then, in a quieter voice so that no one else could hear, he added this: "And Daniel, take care of this boy. Huntley's nose is broken. His nose is also out of joint, and he'll eat this lad for breakfast given half a chance."

The Sergeant just nodded. Then he led the boy and the horse out the gate that was now being opened for them. When the boy ran to the railing to gather up his bag and all his earthly possessions, the men followed him with their eyes. But their stare lacked hostility or suspicion. It was a look of welcome and admiration, as if the boy had just walked across a pond. *How,* the men all wondered, *did he do that*?

Daniel McDermott seemed a trustworthy sort. Or, at least, he seemed so to Claire as they walked towards what looked to be a sea of white canvas tents set out in precise rows on a vast field. At one point he reached back to give Beau Albert a pat on the head, and the horse seemed grateful. Monsieur Weldon liked this man, and so did Beau Albert—that was as good a recommendation as a man could get.

At last they reached a tent with the number forty-two written on a small white board atop the tent's front pole. The Sergeant reached into a satchel just outside the tent and produced a small pad of paper.

"Stay here, OK?" he wrote.

The boy had no idea what "OK" meant but he knew enough to stay, and he nodded. The Sergeant then took away the black horse, who went agreeably enough, though every few feet he would turn back to eye the boy. For the first time in a long time, the boy smiled.

Outside the tent, one grey blanket had been rolled into a pillow, with the letters "U.S." printed in the middle. Someone had gone to the trouble of rolling the pillow in such a way that its owner, the American government, was clear to all. Yet another blanket lay rumpled alongside, a sloppy cousin to the neatly rolled one. It seemed too inviting a bed to resist, the sun too warm, his exhaustion too sweet. The boy let his head hit the pillow and he fell into a deep sleep.

———— ⚬⚬⚬⚬ ————

When her eyes opened, Claire was staring into the face of Huntley. His nose was smashed and crooked, with blood at the nostrils, but he wore a smile. He was so close she could smell him—the tobacco stains on his fingers, the bitter whiff of old whisky and unwashed skin. Ambrose, too, had a scent, but his—a blend of strong soap, pipe tobacco, black tea and rum—was almost pleasant and certainly familiar. What came off Huntley was offensive and sour, like a sack of potatoes or apples gone bad.

He had a knife in his left hand and he was juggling it in the air. Then he stopped and made a motion with his right hand, the finger coming across his own neck from left to right. Claire knew what that meant: "I'm going to cut your throat ..."

Then he was poking at her shoulder. Harder and harder ...

Suddenly Huntley was gone. It was Sergeant McDermott poking her shoulder and he had his hands in front of his chest. "Easy boy," he was saying, "easy. You were havin' a dream is all." The Sergeant hadn't forgotten the boy was deaf, but he said the words anyway. They were a companion to his touch on the boy's shoulders and the look of concern in his eyes.

Claire was breathing heavily and her eyes were like saucers. She kept looking around—inside the tent, down the spaces between tents, behind the Sergeant. No sign of Huntley. Claire was like a fit horse: she got excited pretty quickly yet found her calm just as easily. Sergeant McDermott smiled at her, and she returned the smile.

"That's better," he said. Then he wrote on the pad, "OK?"

Claire wrote underneath, "OK." The French language took so long to say what it wanted to say; American English seemed so much more efficient. Imagine, she thought. Two letters meant "All is well" or *"Tout va bien."* Two letters did the work of ten.

Then the man handed her a uniform and pointed to the inside of the tent. Claire had no idea how the Sergeant had managed to find a uniform to fit her. Clearly soldiers came in all sizes, including petite. Worried that someone would enter the tent as she undressed, Claire moved quickly. Off with her old pants and shirt, which sorely needed washing in any case. On with the sky-blue pants, the dark blue coat with the high collar, the black leather belt. She even counted the buttons on the coat—twelve. Infantry, she was later told, had only nine buttons. A black felt hat with a small peak topped off the ensemble, and though there was no mirror to look at, Claire looked down at her new clothes and thought she looked rather handsome. She had also been given a canvas knapsack (not nearly as nice as her leather bag), a tin canteen and a grey blanket like the one outside.

The Sergeant had anticipated the boy's desire for a look at his own reflection. From a nearby post he took down a shaving mirror and offered it to him. The boy, he noticed with pleasure, couldn't stop smiling. Then McDermott pointed to a small chevron on the boy's right sleeve. It was a wide and flattening V, like a goose in flight but seen from a great distance.

McDermott wrote on the pad, "Clint Flynn, yr a private in the Union army. And I'm yr sargint, yr boss, OK?" And he pointed to his own chevrons, three large ones stacked one atop the other.

"Yes sir," wrote Claire on the pad, thinking herself rather clever for that reply.

Then McDermott took the pad back and wrote, "Stay here. I'm goin to get somewon to show yu the ropes."

Ropes, thought Claire. Why would he want to show her ropes? *Mon Dieu,* she sighed. Was this another American expression she would have to learn? Like "OK"? She waited. In the army, she instinctively knew, that's what you did. You followed orders. You waited for someone to show you things, like ropes.

About ten minutes later, Sergeant McDermott reappeared with a boy about Claire's size, though taller and thinner. The boy wore the same uniform that Claire did and he walked with a slight limp. He had a ready smile and teeth as white as a cloud. And his eyes, big and brown as almonds, gave the impression that the boy looked on the world with something between pure wonder and pure surprise. But what was most extraordinary about him, what took Claire completely by surprise, was his colour.

The boy was black. No, she thought, his skin was more of a soft brown colour, the red-brown of the autumn sumach seeds that *Mamie* often used to dye clothes.

Claire had never seen a brown person before, and though her mother had told her that people came in all sorts of colours—shades of yellow, brown, black, red—this was her first encounter with the real thing. Her mouth was open, and the boy playfully held his right hand up and closed his fingers on his thumb, like a clam. Embarrassed, Claire understood immediately. She closed her mouth.

The boy then saluted her, or so Claire thought. He seemed disappointed when Claire did not return the salute. Actually, it wasn't a salute at all. The boy, it turned out, was deaf. Truly deaf. And he communicated in the language of the deaf, the one then used by almost all deaf people in the New World and in Europe. The black boy spoke sign language. He was saying, quite simply, "Hello." This boy clearly knew (likely from McDermott) of this new groom's deafness, and he had assumed the new recruit would share his knowledge of sign language.

Hoping to repair some damage, Claire grabbed her pad, pointed to her own chest and wrote her name, "Clint." The boy then took the pad, did likewise and wrote, "Moses."

The pad went back and forth as the two boys made each other's acquaintance. It was a slow process, but there was an intensity about it, too, that Claire liked. She found herself looking up from the pad to study the boy's eyes, his facial expressions, the movement of his eyebrows. It was like reading a horse. Every physical detail mattered when you "spoke" in silence.

Finally, Moses wrote, "I will teach you to sign."

"OK," wrote Claire.

Then Moses saluted again. This time he wrote, "Hello." Then he saluted again and pointed to the word. Claire nodded.

Then Moses put his right hand in the air—the creamy palm of that brown hand facing out—and he waved the hand back and forth. Now he wrote "Goodbye" on the pad. Then it was on to other words. Putting your hand to your mouth and sending it out, as if words rode on the hands: this was "Thanks." Two fingers, the index and the middle one, brought to a point just below the eyes: this was "See."

"OK," Claire wrote on the pad, smiling broadly so Moses could see her delight. Then she signed thanks. Hand to mouth and out again. Her first lesson had gone well and she was anxious to learn more. Moses made two more signs: two hands held out in front and moving sideways at the same time. Then one hand pointing at himself. "Follow me," he was saying. And off they went towards the paddocks. Claire went happily, for she was sure she was about to be shown some ropes. The girl from L'Ange-Gardien, the boy named Clint: both knew all about ropes.

Turned out there were ropes, all right, but being shown the ropes in the army was more about being introduced to a schedule. Everything in the army was done according to a schedule. You rose at the same hour, ate at the same hours every day, slept when the army said so. Everything—rations for men and horses, equipment, time—was measured. After a while, Claire found it a source of comfort. She hated being late and no one was late in the army—or if they were, they paid dearly for it.

In time, Claire would learn just how savage and cruel war could be. Whatever rules governed human decency, they would all be broken. But there was one rule that both sides in the war still obeyed in 1864, when the war was three years old. They took a holiday from killing during winter. This camp was a winter camp, and though many men slept in tents, some had also built small log cabins, with wooden chimneys lined with clay, or even wooden barrels pressed into duty. Claire would stare at these contraptions, dumbfounded at woodsmoke coming out of stacked barrels. But even the cabins had canvas roofs. If white was the colour of winter, it was also the colour of that camp at Williamstown.

In the days and weeks that followed, Clint and Moses fell into a routine built around horses. They rose at dawn to the sound of a bugle, though Claire had to remind herself at first that she wasn't supposed to hear that sound or any sound. She would wait for Sergeant McDermott to give her a poke in the shoulder.

The army called the dawn bugle "Reveille," and while the word was French it came out sounding something like *"Rev-ah-lee."* It was only when Claire happened to notice the word written on a poster outside an officer's tent that she realized the word's French origins. It was a mystery to her how a word from the Canadas could be turned so upside down in the States.

Her own world was also upside down, but she was warming to it. It was a world full of sounds she had to pretend not to hear. All her life Claire had been drawn to the sound of birds, and Ambrose had taught her to know them by their call as well as by their plumage. But turning to see a bird after hearing it would have given the game away. Men in training would sometimes shoot off their rifles, but the sound of guns firing was another sound she had to ignore. And it required discipline to keep her mouth shut and say nothing when she stubbed her toe or bumped her head. One *"Merde!"* and any hearing person within earshot would have wanted to know why a deaf boy was cussing—in French!

And yet saying nothing day after day after day was also a kind of blessing. All day long she worked with horses—feeding them, grooming them, cleaning their feet, exercising them—and she was starting to feel like a horse. Silent, watchful, happy in the company of other horses.

The heavy horses had all been sent off to the front to haul

guns and supplies. What remained were troopers' and officers' horses—Beau Albert among them—and the fast horses who would serve as couriers taking messages from one regiment to another or engaging in lightning raids into enemy territory. This was to be Tibeau's task.

Each horse was in training for his job. Sergeant McDermott would put Clint up on Albert (who had a new name now, Black Bull, the choice of the captain who would ride him) to get the horse used to the sounds of the army and war. Drums, gunshots, cannons, bugles, sudden shouts, bands in parades: the black horse was supposed to stay calm through all of this. McDermott was a good man with horses, and he would introduce each new sound gradually: first from a distance, then closer as the horse reacted less forcefully. Gunfire and the cries of men seemed not to bother Black Bull (which Claire thought the silliest name for a horse she had ever heard). It was marching bands that seemed to set him off, but after several weeks of exposure even they failed to unnerve him.

Tibeau, meanwhile, was getting full rations of grain and daily workouts. It seemed that the land at war with itself was also falling in love with horse racing. New tracks were being built everywhere, including a small one at the edge of Williamstown. McDermott's instruction to Clint was to take Tibeau (or Lightning as he was now called) to the track for workouts meant to increase his fitness.

Claire's anxiety seemed to fade away on that track. Winter had given way to spring, and spring was feeling more and more like summer. In the early morning, breezing down that track in an easy gallop on Tibeau (Lightning, she thought, was at least a better name than Black Bull), she felt alive and happy. Out on that track, her fears—about being caught and sent home, of the war, the fate awaiting her horses—disappeared. In that saddle, time seemed to stop. There was just the sound of Tibeau blowing through his nostrils, the wind in her face, as horse and rider rocked along and found each other's rhythm.

Afterwards, Claire would bring Tibeau down to the river—the Hoosic River, she heard the men call it—to let him cool off and graze in the lush grass on the banks. The town was what the Sergeant called "well watered," and when she lay on the riverbank Claire could hear water all around her, from the river itself and from the streams and brooks on the steep hillsides. She took comfort in those sounds. It was the music of home.

A small violet flower that Claire had no name for grew on the mossy banks of those streams. But the trees were familiar: hemlock, elm, maple, towering white pines. With her head on the grass, she would look up from her spot in the shade to the treetops, which still caught the rays of the afternoon sun. She wanted to nestle into the mountainside and she wished she could pull all that earth and rock over her and her horse, like a blanket.

Claire saw each horse every day, and, if she was sure no one was about, she would speak briefly to them in French. In their stalls in the barn, each horse would lift his head from his hay to hear those words. *"Salut, mon vieux. Salut."* After all their mischief—their attempted escape, Albert's bucking bronco routine in the round pen—the two horses had settled into a sweet calm.

Word of their escapades had spread, and soldiers would sometimes enter the barn in groups of two or three hoping for a glimpse of the two renegades. Claire could hear them talking. One storyteller with a loose grip on the facts (the tale kept growing taller) would entertain the others.

"That rascal there," a lanky corporal announced one morning to two fellow soldiers, "put our Huntley in thah dirt four times in thah time it takes to cook a egg!" But his listeners were hard pressed to believe the story because Albert would stick his head out the stall door hoping for a treat, and he would lick just about any hand put near him. For a monster, he had the manners of a pet rabbit.

Meanwhile, back at L'Ange-Gardien, the Vigere family had received that first letter from Claire. They each took turns holding it, turning it over to look at the familiar falls at Montmorency, the unfamiliar American stamp. Ambrose even peered inside the envelope, as if he hoped to find her there.

The letter was proof that Claire was alive but gave no hint of where she was. Somewhere south of the border, working in a stable. Claire had spared them the details: following Tibeau and Beau Albert into a civil war. Ambrose pretty well knew that wherever Tip Weldon was the horses were as well, and Claire would be close by. But where Monsieur Weldon had gone, Ambrose had no idea.

So he continued to play dumb. He spared the others and said nothing. The adults in the cabin were all playing the same game. All had an inkling, all said nothing. It was how some families coped with crisis. Comfort the others as best you can, hope and pray for the best, never mention the unmentionable.

As long as the letters came every week, there was the hope that Claire would come back alive.

Claire and Moses worked from dawn to dusk. Evenings were free, as were Sunday afternoons.

Some days Claire longed for some chatter (chatter in French would have been even nicer), but she was also discovering the joys of silence. No pressure to make conversation, no worries that silence from your companion signalled something wrong. If she and Moses wanted to talk as they walked, one would tap the other in the side, then they would seek out each other's eyes and "talk."

Day by day, Claire's vocabulary in sign language grew. She could make small sentences, starting with the words "I am" (she would point to herself) and following that with whatever she was feeling at the time. To say "happy" she put one hand to her chest and rubbed up and down. Putting both hands to her waist and then down meant "tired," and there were many days when she was that. To say "cold," she held her fists in front of her chest and shook them (only at night was there a hint of the cold). Putting one hand to her forehead and another to her belly meant sick. To say "horse" you made your fingers into ears and put them at the side of your head. To communicate something in the future tense, you held your hand in the air and sliced forward. Something in the past, you sliced backward.

There was a logic to this language and a quickness that Claire came to love. Again, she said to herself: *French takes forever, English is quicker, but sign takes no time at all.*

Sometimes, she and Moses would talk about individual men in the regiment, and this required spelling out the name of that man—one letter at a time. It seemed at first a hard task to memorize all twenty-six letters of the alphabet, but even here some signs seemed natural choices. The letter *W* was three fingers in the air, the little finger and thumb of that hand joined below. The letter *I* was that same small finger, the pinky finger, held up. *Z* you traced in the air with your index finger. *Y* was thumb and pinky up, other fingers down and out of the way. *L* was index finger up and thumb outstretched in the shape of a capital *L*. This all made perfect sense.

Still, she often had to remind Moses to slow down. When he got excited, his fingers were a blur. Claire would shake her head, hold her right hand flat in front of her and slowly lower it. *Slow down, Moses. Slow down.* And he would. Pad and pencil were always there if needed, but as the days passed and turned into weeks, Moses and Claire relied on them less and less.

Moses and Claire both loved their free Sundays. When the weather allowed it, they would walk into the forest at the edge of Williamstown. They would find a soft spot under a certain oak, lie on their backs and watch the clouds racing overhead. The game was to spot the animal shapes in the sky—the lion's head, the lean white dog, the huge dragon, the galloping horse, the fat frog.

When he got excited, Moses would make noises. Grunts, loud nonsensical calls. He would take in a breath and then expel it like a dog panting. At first Claire was troubled by it, but she grew to like it. The sounds he made were his music, the measure of his delight. Sometimes he would take a regimental drum with him into the forest and beat it with drumsticks. Moses told Claire he could feel the sound in his body and it gave him great pleasure. At first it was all racket, but then he would settle into delicate and beautiful rhythms. Claire wanted to tell him how beautiful it sounded, how much she wanted to dance to it. But she couldn't, of course. She would lay one hand on the drum to feel the sound, then give him a thumbs-up sign of approval. Claire was an audience of one, and it seemed that was all Moses needed. He would smile at her, then close his eyes, and play on.

Claire found her own delight in seeking her place in this foreign land, with her horses, with her silent companion. The war lay to the south, and they would soon head to the fighting. But for now she was absorbed in discovering a new language and a new world. The world of the deaf.

CHAPTER 11

The Story of Moses

Moses Odell was Claire Vigere's opposite. He was black, she was white. He was a boy, she was a girl. He was deaf, and she had perfect hearing. He communicated by a sophisticated language of sign and gesture, and in English; she had a voice and her mother tongue was French. He was a slave's son who had become his master's property the moment he took his first breath; she was born free (as free as an *habitant* could be) and had no real sense of what it meant to be a slave. "Slave" was not a word that any Vigere had ever taught her.

The education of Claire continued as the summer of 1864 dawned in Williamstown. There was a rumour making the rounds that the regiment would be moving south and into battle within a week. The plan to reach Boston had apparently been scrapped by the generals.

Though Claire and Moses would not be directly involved in fighting, they would be close to it, perhaps too close. One afternoon, when the two grooms were sitting on stumps and oiling some tack, Sergeant McDermott chose the moment to let the lads know what might lie ahead. He was sitting a little higher than they were, on the flat end of a wooden barrel.

Both man and barrel had the same look: sturdy and low and wide in the middle. Sergeant McDermott, who was a plain speaker, tried to warn them. "If I were a bettin' man," he wrote on the pad, "and I ain't, I'd bet you two wont see the elafant."

Moses looked at Clint, but Clint wore the same look of astonishment. Neither had heard that elephants were being used in this war. McDermott saw the confusion and tapped each boy on the shoulder, then shook his head. Now he wrote, "Its what we say when new recrutes get their first taste of batle. Dont know why. But thats what we say. You lads will be behint the lines, but lines can be brokin. OK?"

The two grooms nodded. But they both wore a look of such dread that the Sergeant felt compelled to tousle their hair and offer some sort of reassurance. McDermott wished right away he hadn't been so blunt. He had seen platoons overrun by the enemy and he knew that men with bayonets did not stop to ask polite questions about an enemy soldier's age. Anyone in uniform, anyone seen to be aiding the other side, was a target. Soldiers in grey would go after these boys in blue, no matter their age, no matter their lack of weaponry. A soldier in battle was like a savage dog: he turned and spun and bit whatever moved within his range. McDermott had seen many things and he had no words to describe them, just a darkness that sometimes got the better of him.

Still, he was kind in his bones. It was just that he had not been around young people much and he had forgotten how vulnerable they were. He seemed genuinely touched by the easy friendship that had developed between Moses and Clint. He assumed it was because they shared the burden of deafness.

Daniel McDermott was a reliable soldier, one of Captain Weldon's favourites, but he kept to himself most of the time. He had high standards in everything—he prided himself on the neatness of his uniform and the polish on his buttons, the meals he sometimes cooked for himself that were a cut above the rest, the methodical approach he took to horse care. He loved perfection. Men in the regiment respected him but were cowed by him, and so he had no one he could call a close friend. Still, the notion of friendship appealed to him and he liked to see it flourish. He would cozy up to it like a cat to a fireplace. McDermott would look on as Clint cut Moses's hair or Moses cut Clint's. The Sergeant thought they groomed each other in the manner of two horses chumming in a paddock.

Claire wanted her hair kept short and not too neat. A tousled appearance, she thought, would make her look more like a boy. And Moses was enough of a poor barber that tousled was what she got. She also insisted on bathing in private, claiming modesty. Neither Moses nor McDermott objected; everyone liked Clint and allowed him this eccentricity. The story of him taking that fiery black horse over the paddock fence had won him respect in the camp; he had earned the right to be different.

As for those budding breasts of Claire's, they were too small as yet to warrant wrapping, and the bulky blue coat masked them in any case. She worried about the hot summer days to come, when Moses might ask her to join him in a swim at some lake or pond. She had heard the men talking about "skinny-dipping"—swimming naked to ward off the heat. Claire would deal with that problem when the time came.

It was during a haircut (Moses was trimming Claire's) that Sergeant McDermott plunked down beside them on the barrel that still served as his campfire chair. "You ever hear bout

Annie Etheridge?" he wrote on the pad. "You know women fite on ower side?"

Claire felt a cold panic. Why was the Sergeant suddenly talking about women in war? She had been holding a mirror to watch Moses as he hacked at her black curls. Now she tilted the mirror so she could observe the Sergeant. Was he just making conversation? Was he curious to see how she would respond? Or maybe he was doing what she had suspected Monsieur Weldon of doing—knowing perfectly well that "Clint" was Claire and pretending not to know.

Claire returned her gaze to the mirror and her own reflection. What she saw was a weathered face. Long days outside under the spring and summer sun with only a soldier's peaked cap for protection had given more colour to her skin than she was used to. The high collar of the uniform added some toughness to her look, she thought. As for the hair, it was just about the worst haircut she had ever seen. It gave her the look of a *gamin*—a street boy. Or so she hoped.

Yet Claire was not entirely blind to her own beauty. The soft line of the chin, the delicate blue eyes, the milky skin of her throat. Her great fear was that others would likewise not be blind to female beauty, no matter how buried or disguised. And now the Sergeant—perhaps by coincidence, perhaps not—was writing madly on the pad about some heroine named Annie Etheridge.

It seems Annie had joined a regiment called the 3rd Michigan and signed on to wash clothes and blankets. When the regiment was called to the front, the other washerwomen went home. Not Annie. A small legend would grow around her name. The story had passed among the men of the Union army, from one regiment to another, like a good-luck charm.

It helped that she was young and pretty. "Rite smart lookin," McDermott wrote on the pad. Moses put down his scissors, Claire her mirror, and they followed the tale as McDermott chronicled it in his neat and tiny handwriting.

Annie marched with the men and slept in tents with the men all the way to the front lines. She was quiet and a good worker and they all respected her and saw to her safety. Anyone who swore in her presence, or showed any other sign of disrespect, would have been set upon by the others. It was like having someone's mother join the troop, and there was hardly a boy or man there who did not miss his mother. At the front line, little Annie served as a nurse, putting dressings on wounds. Finally, the army gave her a horse and a saddle, a distinctive black uniform and a sergeant's three stripes.

"Just like these," the Sergeant wrote, and pointed to his own sleeve.

Witnesses in battle described her as cool under fire, and as one who never worried over her own fate but always cheered those around her. She sounded, thought Claire, like Joan of Arc—that peasant girl of the fifteenth century who led the French of France against the English soldiers. Ambrose liked to tell that story to Claire while they mucked out the barn, but he would never finish it. He simply called her a young girl who was born to lead but who suffered what Ambrose called—Claire could hear in her head exactly how he said this—"*une fin triste*. An unhappy ending." Claire wondered if Annie would meet the same fate.

In one battle, McDermott wrote, the bluecoats were about to abandon a heavy gun when Annie came along and talked them out of running. They went back to firing their cannon, and one soldier later said that no officer could have persuaded them quite like—as McDermott put it—"that brave litle sargent in peticots."

"You said she was in uniform," Clint wrote on the pad, then looked at McDermott with a puzzled look on his face. A petticoat was a kind of skirt then worn by women and girls as an undergarment.

"Unaform," he wrote. Then he added, by way of explanation, "Peticots just a manner of speakin."

"What ever happened to Annie?" Moses wrote on the pad.

"Dont know," the Sergeant wrote. "I herd she got wounded last year at Chancellorsville, lost a hand, got sent ta home. Another story says she married an offacer and the two are still fightin in Virginia. Caint say.

"Ther was another famus nurse," wrote the Sergeant, who seemed in a talkative mood this night. Her name was Mary Ann Bickerdyke, though all the wounded men in her care called her "Mother" Bickerdyke. McDermott would write furiously on his pad, then show it to his audience and go back to writing. Moses and Claire would scan his text, then nod, and the Sergeant would quickly write some more. The teller, the told, each kept pressing the other to go faster. The story had a life of its own.

It seems that Mary Ann Bickerdyke was in church one Sunday morning during the early days of the war when the minister read of the grim circumstances at a military hospital near her home in Illinois. She was forty-four years old and a widow, and when the minister made a plea for someone to transport supplies to the hospital, she volunteered. Four years later, "Mother" Bickerdyke had become a legend amid the wounded soldiers in Georgia.

The Sergeant knew a line much quoted among the northern wounded. "She is a power of good," one patient had said of her. "We fared might poor till she came here." Those who had seen her in the flesh remarked on her strong chin, her piercing eyes, the granny glasses. "Mother" Bickerdyke was a bear for cleanliness and efficiency and it wasn't long before the surgeons and the generals were obeying her orders.

"One time," said Sergeant McDermott, "she cot a docter with his fingr in the cookey jar." The nurse had a pretty good notion that one of the surgeons was skimming off some of her supplies—food and medicine intended for the wounded. *Her* wounded. She marched into his tent and saw his table full of the jellies and preserves meant for her storeroom. "Mother" Bickerdyke swept everything off his table, mounted her horse (a gelding called Old Whitey), galloped off to the nearest general and had that surgeon dismissed.

She was a force, was "Mother" Bickerdyke. She knew a great deal about herbal medicine, what she called "botanic medicine." But her real strength lay in her fierce determination to do all she could for the wounded, whom she saw as her children. Claire heard her story and right away thought of Magrette. Sergeant McDermott ended his story by writing this on the pad: "She sounds like my own ma. Nobody messed with my ma."

Claire took solace in the Sergeant's tales. She seemed reassured now that he was simply telling stories, something to pass the time. He wasn't staring at her, wasn't assessing her response to the tale. She thought of Madame Lacoste, the elderly teacher at the school in L'Ange-Gardien. If she had evidence that a certain boy had taken a pencil home without her permission, she would ask the boy if he knew what happened to thieves in the next life. The boy right away knew that the teacher knew. Madame Lacoste was making a game of it, like a cat toying with a mouse.

Claire had seen cats in the barn at home teasing mice in corners and she hated how those fierce little predators prolonged the agony of their prey. The mice had to be eaten, for grain was too precious to share. And the cats were only doing their job. But couldn't they at least, thought Claire, do it without cruelty and games?

It was what she loved about horses. How direct they were. Claire remembered Ambrose's favourite expression to capture the honour of horses: "As honest as the day is long. More than I can say for some people."

⸙

There was much to like about Moses Odell. First and foremost for Claire was his respect for privacy. One day he signed to her, *Home?* (Moses put one hand at his mouth then raised it towards one ear). *Where?* (He stretched out both hands, then moved each one towards the middle in a scissors action.) *Where,* he was asking, *do you live?*

North, she replied by pointing in that direction.

Moses took her answer as an invitation to ask other questions. *Family?* he asked, and he made the sign for marriage—two hands clasped.

But Claire didn't want to get into details. She was afraid that if she named a town, say, in Vermont, word might spread in the camp. Someone from that town might be in the camp and he might want to know more. Her last name. What street she lived on. "And surely, Clint, you know the Crowe family, owned that big horse farm on the edge of town?" One lie would lead to another and the whole house of cards would eventually come tumbling down.

Too sad, she signed to Moses. She cupped both hands in front of her chest and brought them down.

Moses put his hand over his heart and rubbed that space to say he was sorry. That, and the look in his eyes, conveyed better than any words could the depth of his compassion. Claire was speaking a kind of truth when she described her story as too sad to talk about. She had left hearth and home, and though she had landed—for the moment, anyway—in a soft spot (with Albert and Tibeau, Moses and McDermott)— she dearly missed her family and regretted the pain she had caused them. It was sad, and the small tear that gathered at her right eye was the real thing.

But then the boy named Clint pulled himself together. He wanted to shift focus, to let Moses know he wasn't as sad as all that. He pointed at Moses. *Family?* he asked.

Moses spread his arms wide and grinned to signal that his family was large. He was the youngest, with three older brothers and three older sisters. All the children had worked with their mother and father on a cotton plantation east of Atlanta in the state of Georgia. The smile on his face faded as Moses finger-spelled these letters of the alphabet: S-L-A-V-E-S.

Then he stood and lifted one pant leg, the right one, to reveal a deep scar that ran across the back of his calf. The slash had healed over and was almost beautiful, the skin pink as lips against the surrounding brown. This was why Moses walked with a limp. He explained to Clint that the master of the plantation had sent a message to every family: he had cut into the tendon of the right leg of every family's youngest son. Not so deeply that the boy would never walk again, but deeply enough to cause a lifelong limp, and deeply enough to send a message. All over the South, slaves were running away to free states in the North or to Canada, with the aid of a long line of sympathizers. Some called it the "Underground Railroad"—a network of churches and families opposed to slavery and intent on helping slaves to their freedom.

But the plantation owners were fed up with runaways. They issued a warning. If Moses's father or anyone in his family tried fleeing, Moses—if caught—would be cut again. And this time both legs would be cut and he would never walk again.

Claire took in all this and was left with a deep admiration for Moses's father. He must have been a brave and wise man. He had taught Moses how to read and write, a crime that would have brought him a severe whipping had he been caught. And one night about a year ago he had gathered his family behind the shed they called home and announced they were fleeing North. He had heard of black regiments that were forming up there and he was desperate to join one.

It seemed the country was at a crossroads. If the North won the war, slavery would be abolished—as President Abraham Lincoln had said it would. Southern victory would put the Negro people back in the cotton fields.

Moses's father said they would risk the plantation owners' dogs, the men on horseback paid to round up fleeing slaves, the starvation they faced if they got no help or sympathy along the way. They ran that night.

But their freedom was short-lived. Camped in a corn field, they were set upon by the slave owners' dogs, and the seven family members scattered to the four winds. Moses escaped, but he had no idea how the others had fared or where they were. If he survived the war, he would go back to the farm in Georgia and try to track them down from there. In the meantime, he had no family.

You family, he signed to Clint. *And Sergeant.* Then Moses turned away, perhaps so no one could see his tears, and, without looking back, he gave the white boy a *C'mon* sign. He was running for the paddocks. Horses were family, too.

It was while running to join Moses that a foot came out of nowhere to trip her. Claire never saw it coming. She had barely stopped tumbling when someone else's face was in hers, inches away.

Huntley. It was no dream this time. Claire had not forgotten Huntley, not by a long shot. But he seemed almost to have disappeared from the camp, and she had hoped he had. Sometimes she would spot him in the distance, which was not hard, since he was one of the few men in camp not wearing the blue uniform. But he seemed always to be walking away, or leading a horse, or talking to the Captain. Claire hoped that work would consume him, that time would soften his anger and his desire for revenge.

Now he was back, the cold stare was back, the faint grin. Claire's eyes were drawn immediately to his nose, still bent and misshapen.

He said nothing, just leaned over her. And even after she heard Sergeant McDermott's voice—"Huntley, leave the boy alone!"—she stayed frozen in the grip of his green eyes. She could smell old rum and cigarettes and whatever he had had for breakfast; it made her long for the breath of horses and the sweet smell of wet hay and apples. Another few seconds must have passed before Huntley put something in her hand and walked away.

Claire stared at the paper in disbelief. It was one of the Krieghoff paintings from her book. Huntley must have come in the night, searched her bag, found the book and ripped out a page. Claire felt a surge of emotions. Fear, because Huntley had been so close to her as she lay sleeping. Outrage, because he had dared take a page from her precious book. Fear again, as she understood exactly what he had done and why.

His burglary went far beyond settling an old score; to pull it off he would have had to think and scheme and plan. Claire wondered if he had put his hands around her throat, like an executioner sliding a noose around a man's neck just to check for the fit. He hadn't come in the daytime, she thought, for that would have been too risky, too hurried. The night had offered him cover and given him more time. Maybe Huntley had casually gone through her possessions by the light of a full moon, debating which item to use to drive home his dart with the message attached. The note might have read: "I was here in the night and I will come again when it pleases me."

The painting torn from the book was one called *The Blacksmith's Shop,* and it showed horses being unharnessed from their *berlines* and led inside a small barn attached to a handsome little cabin with a porch at the front. Snow was falling, and you could tell by the set of the horses' heads that they'd been there before and looked forward to the shelter of the barn. But three areas of the painting had been set on fire. The holes were jagged in shape and edged with brown where the match had done its work. Claire knew the painting; she had studied it as closely as she had all the others. Missing now were the small boy with a bucket of grain on the far left of the painting, and two horses, one just entering the picture on the left, the other stopped in front of the cabin.

If the intent was to terrify Claire, it worked. If he could make the boy and two horses disappear from the painting, he could do the same to Clint, Black Bull and Lightning.

Moses and McDermott arrived alongside her and took in what had happened. Moses, for his part, seemed as alarmed as Claire, even more so. The Sergeant tried to reassure both Clint and Moses. McDermott wrote a note about posting a sentry by the tent to stop any more of what he called "thievery" and added that he would mention the incident to Captain Weldon.

Claire had seen what happened to thieves in the camp. One man was accused of stealing money from another soldier, his own friend, who had been injured during war games. The thief's head was shaved and a wooden sign was hung at his chest proclaiming him a thief and describing details of the crime. The punishment seemed aimed at humiliating the soldier by under-lining his disgrace. Several soldiers—their rifles carried strangely, with bayonets dragging behind them—marched the man out of camp to the sound of music from a pipe and drum.

Claire had also seen what happened to soldiers accused of drunkenness or other conduct the army didn't approve of. These men were tied to trees, sometimes with their hands bound over their heads and bayonets propped in their mouths.

Huntley deserved such a fate, for army rules were army rules and there was no denying the theft. But Claire, Moses, McDermott—they all knew that Huntley was too valuable a regiment resource to be let go. Besides, he was not actually a soldier; he was a civilian in the army's employ. Yet he was too nasty to be left unguarded. And how do you keep an eye on someone twenty-four hours a day?

Later that day, as the light was beginning to fade and after the campfire had been lit, McDermott settled down to supper with his grooms. It was the usual fare—salt pork ("sowbelly," the men called it), a small potato and a slice of turnip. When the meal was done, McDermott slipped eight-inch-long hunting knives to both Moses and Claire. He made a motion, as if he were sliding an invisible knife into his own boot. A sign to let them know where they should hide the weapon. Then he put his raised index finger to his lips. *Tell no one.* The two grooms nodded solemnly.

Moses knew a great deal more about human cruelty than Claire did, but whatever innocence she possessed was being eroded, bit by bit. Even Moses was taken aback by this new threat from within the camp. By taking the knives into their possession, Claire and Moses both knew that a corner had been turned, and each had to wonder where this path would lead.

⟨⟩⟨⟩

The following day was a Sunday, so there was time to walk into town and mail another letter home. It felt good to reconnect in some way with her folks, but the words for this letter came only slowly. Claire ripped out a Krieghoff painting called *Settler's House, Laval*. It looked like a scene from late winter, with most of the snow melted from the roof of the cabin and the *habitant* lightly dressed as he unloaded firewood from his *berline* and his young son accompanied the horse to the tiny barn.

Claire liked the fact that the horse was not being led on a rope but simply walking alongside the boy. The detail spoke of the friendship and trust between the two. The *habitant's* wife stood at the cabin door with her daughter, who looked about two years old, and the family dog, a perky black mongrel whose tail would surely wag if that painting could come to life. All had come outside to greet the man of the cabin on his return from the forest.

The painting was shaped like an egg on its side. Forest rose into the hills on the left, with mountains set behind. The cabin, thought Claire, looked snug and warm. She wanted what they had—the comfort of the familiar. She longed to hear French again, even the sound of her brothers squabbling. Finally, she wrote on the back of the painting a few words in French. Like the other letters, this one was put in an envelope and posted to the village of L'Ange-Gardien. In English, the letter would have read like this.

> *My dear family:*
> *The weather is good, and so are my spirits. I hope all is well at home. I am a little sad sometimes, but I get over it quickly. I have a good job, and I save my money. The horses here are fine, though not as beautiful as ours.*
> *My love to you all,*
> *Claire*

⌘

Early in May, the tents were taken down and the five hundred or so men and officers of the Massachusetts 1st Cavalry prepared to ride south. They were sick of the endless marching, the drills, the cleaning of their rifles. But if the troopers had any notion of riding glorious chargers into battle, their battle-hardened sergeants soon cured them of that idea.

Men in the cavalry at least rode to battle, so they were spared the ordeal of the infantry, who marched and marched and marched. But once at the battle site, the cavalry hopped off and fought alongside the men on foot. One cavalry trooper would hold the horses of three others, who would march against the enemy. Sometimes, the cavalry would form raiding parties. Sometimes, northern cavalry would take on southern cavalry. But most times troopers fought from the ground. If they had hoped that life in the cavalry would get them up from the mud and the dirt, they were mistaken.

And now the men were breaking camp. The noise was so overwhelming that Claire almost envied Moses the quiet in his head, though Moses, too, would have felt the rumble in his body. Officers were shouting orders, covered wagons groaned under the weight of many barrels and boxes of food and supplies, and what amounted to a sizable village slowly began to uproot itself.

Williamstown must have been sad to see them go. The soldiers had been good for business, especially the general stores that sold flour and bacon, coffee and sugar, and the hotels that sold beer and whisky. And yet, thought Claire, the land around the town would now be glad of the time to recover. The army's woodcutters had taken hundreds of trees for their campfires and cookfires, to build wagons and gun carriages. There were stumps as far as the eye could see.

"*Laide*" was the French word that came to her. Ugly. The army had stripped the surrounding land of its trees and the land now looked like her hair after Moses had been at it with the scissors. Like her once lovely hair, the land would recover, but the healing would take a decade or more.

It was while surveying that bruised landscape that Claire caught a glimpse of Monsieur Weldon driving his wagon—the long runners below now replaced by high wheels. He was going back north for more horses. Their eyes met briefly as he passed. She thought he nodded. He might even have smiled, though she couldn't be sure. Claire followed him with her eyes as Mac, the grey, and that wagon she had once called home clip-clopped down the road. She was about to turn away when he stopped.

Monsieur Weldon called to a soldier on the side of the road and got him to hold Mac while he walked slowly back towards her. His wide-brimmed hat was low over his eyes so she couldn't see his face. Perhaps he wasn't coming back to her at all but was on some other army business that had nothing to do with her. But no, he came straight to her.

Again, Claire felt panic. She drew this image in her mind: Monsieur Weldon reaching her finally and grabbing her. "C'mon, little girl. You've had your adventure and now I'm taking you home!" She imagined herself screaming, squirming like a snared rabbit, and all the men aghast: *Turns out our "Clint" was a damn girl, and not one bit of deaf!*

When he got to her, Monsieur Weldon looked her in the eye. Nothing was said for a while, as if each of them was thinking what to do next. Finally, he made a motion, as if he were writing on an invisible pad of paper. He knew the deaf groom always carried pen and paper, and these the groom now passed to him.

Monsieur Weldon hastily wrote a note, then folded it and handed it to the boy standing in front of him. He then saluted the boy, who was too astonished to salute back. Finally the Captain walked slowly down the road, nodded to the soldier and put the old grey into a loose and easy trot. They ascended the hill and were gone.

Claire opened the folded paper. "I know," Monsieur Weldon had written. "And your secret is safe with me. I have spoken with Huntley and I will have his head on a platter if he touches you or your horses. But be careful. He is bad business. I will see your family and find the words to say that you are well."

Claire sighed with relief and gratitude before refolding the note and placing it in her pocket.

Before the day was done, every man in the regiment was assigned a horse, and this, too, contributed to the noise and chaos. Everywhere Claire looked, men were saddling and bridling horses. Not every horse was pleased with his or her new master, for some troopers had only a vague sense of how to ride, and some lacked that skill altogether. The feeling went the other way, too; Claire could hear some of the better riders complaining about "my bag of bones" or "this little runt" as they climbed on board. But most of the horses were Canadian horses, and she knew that most of those men would be singing a different tune in days to come.

McDermott was nudging Moses and Claire down to the smallest paddock, where officers were to meet their horses. She was especially curious to see who had been assigned Beau Albert and Tibeau.

They arrived just in time to see Beau Albert being saddled up by a young soldier. The horse was wide-eyed and he seemed very glad to see Claire on the scene. Officers didn't tack up horses; that was what enlisted men and grooms were for. When the soldier saw Clint, he gladly passed on the job.

Claire wished she could speak to Beau Albert—that horse loved the sound of French as much as she did—but stroking his neck worked the same sort of magic. She had put saddles on horses a thousand times, though no saddle as fine as this one. It was black with a deep seat and the letters *HD* stencilled on both flaps. As she tightened the matching girth and set the equally elegant bridle into place, Claire had this thought: *Beau Albert has never looked so handsome*. He was ready for his officer.

The man who would ride Black Bull had come forward. He was blond and squarely built, and Claire found her focus split between his green-blue eyes and the shine off his high black riding boots. As impressive as the saddle was, its owner was more so. He began circling the horse, and Claire couldn't read from his manner whether he was admiring the horse or eyeing him with suspicion. Sergeant McDermott then approached the officer and saluted, quite snappily, and held it longer than usual. Whoever this officer was, he was an officer McDermott admired. Then the Sergeant relaxed as they walked a little to the side and exchanged some words—though Claire couldn't hear with all the horse and human chatter around her—and she could see the officer nodding. Then the Sergeant was pointing at her and beckoning her over.

"Zo, he chumps, ziss horse?" the officer said, and Sergeant McDermott hastily produced his pencil and pad to write the words down. Whatever the Sergeant had said to the officer, it was clear that the officer was looking to this young groom as an authority on the black horse.

But the accent, thought Claire. That wasn't an American accent. It was like no English she had ever heard.

Then McDermott scribbled something else on the pad and showed it to her. "Germin offacer. Good rider," the note said, and he had underlined "good" three times. Claire had no idea what a German was doing fighting in the American Civil War, but just then she was more worried about the partnership between this man and the horse she loved.

She took the pad and pencil from the Sergeant and wrote, "Good horse," and she underlined the word "good" three times. "Jumps anything. Hard worker. Smart. Smart. Do not hit. Do not hit."

Then slowly Claire handed the note to the officer. She had been in the army long enough to know that giving orders to an officer was not a good idea. Yet she loved Albert and she knew that spurring this horse or hitting him with a whip would be disastrous for both horse and rider.

Claire waited while the officer read the note as casually as if he were reading mail from an elderly aunt. "Good," the man said. Or had he? It sounded like *"Goot."* Then the man launched himself casually into the saddle while the groom held the bridle and the left stirrup. He rode the black horse in a wide circle, and Claire could tell immediately that he was a rider of great skill. His hands were light and low, his back straight, and he followed the motion of the horse perfectly. Then came a quick stop, up into a canter and elegantly over a fence nearby. The rider looked pleased; the horse looked pleased. Claire issued a huge sigh, for it seemed that Albert had found a rider worthy of him. The rider was Captain Hubert Dilger.

Now Claire began to search frantically for Tibeau, for she would not rest until she had seen his rider. Sergeant McDermott had anticipated Clint's anguish and was leading him to another

paddock, where higher ranking officers were being paired
with their horses.

Claire quickly spotted Tibeau. He was at the centre of a great
column of dust as two soldiers tried valiantly to stop him from
swinging his backside in ever grander circles. The would-be
rider, an officer notable for his small stature and youthful
looks, stood off to one side. He seemed not at all bothered by
Tibeau's shenanigans and patiently waited for the dust to settle.

When Claire arrived on the scene, the horse greeted her but
he also bobbed his head repeatedly. She took this to mean,
Where have you been? Then she stroked his neck and circled
him as she always did to calm him. The girl circled him left,
then right, backed him and led him forward, stroking him all
the while. Then suddenly the young officer was at her side—
he smelled fresh, thought Claire, like Magrette's laundered
sheets on the clothesline back home—and he leapt up into the
saddle without bothering with a stirrup. Yet he landed so
lightly that Claire took him for a jockey.

Tibeau was still fussing with his head, but Claire knew that
his little dance would soon settle. The officer sat on him as if
there were a cushion of air between the man's bottom and the
saddle. And it wasn't a wooden army saddle, either. This one
was brown leather, fine and handsomely cut, the saddle
compact like its owner. What Claire saw in the rider's hands
was strength and lightness of touch.

Again she breathed a sigh. Tibeau, too, had landed in the
hands of a fine rider. Still, she did want to pass on one word
of warning. Claire hurriedly wrote a note and passed it to the
Sergeant, who knew without being told what to do with it.

Sergeant McDermott called the officer by name and stood
ready with his salute. "Major Huey, sir?" The officer nodded

and the Sergeant continued. "This groom, sir, he knows your horse pretty good. Horse's name is Lightning. Turned four. Good horse, by all accounts, but the groom asked me to give you this note."

"Good horse," the note read. "Smart, very fast, brave. But," and this word was underlined, "is very afraid of chipmunks."

The officer, Major Pennock Huey, laughed out loud at the note. "Tell your groom I know this horse's story, and his groom's too, for that matter, and I'm pleased to be acquainted with both Mr. Clint and Mr. Lightning." Then he spun the horse in a flashy circle and took off in a cloud of dust, but not before shouting, "Thanks for the warning, Sergeant. Tell the private it's southern chipmunks we'll have to worry about!"

CHAPTER 12

The Long Road South

The Sergeant, flanked by the two grooms, made his way to the covered wagon that was to be their transportation as they headed south to the battlefields—would it be Virginia, Tennessee, Georgia? Claire loved the sounds of those places. They were names she had heard often in the camp as she listened to the men talking, listened without appearing to listen.

The men spoke in hushed voices of great battles—Gettysburg, Fredericksburg, Bull Run—and of generals with glorious names like Robert E. Lee and "Stonewall" Jackson, Ulysses S. Grant and William Tecumseh Sherman. Some men spoke as if they knew what was what in this war between South and North. But only a few of these men had actually been in battle. Letters from home, camp rumours, conversations with men who had recovered from battle wounds and were now being sent back to the lines, stories read in newspapers: these were the sources for their knowledge of war.

Sometimes the men would approach Sergeant McDermott and ask him plainly, "What's it like?"

"Like nothin' you ever seen," he'd say. "Don't ask, cause you cain't prepare for it and you cain't forget it neither. Maybe it'll be over, soldier, 'fore we get there. What do you say we all march a little slower?" and he'd poke the man in the ribs.

Or he'd tell them a funny story, anything to take their minds off things. One young soldier seemed worried about everything, perhaps because he was so young. Claire thought he was sixteen at best. Red-haired and delicate-looking, he was barely older than the regiment's drummer, who was, Claire was certain, younger than she was. And the Sergeant seemed determined to make this freckled boy laugh. So he told him the following story.

An old farmer in Vermont had a particular way of shearing his sheep, which were constantly leaping fences and getting mixed up with other flocks. The old man's method was to shear them but leave some fleece at the belly, so that when it came time to return lost sheep, his were instantly recognizable. Well, it seems the old man had sheep in his head—maybe he was counting them—when he nodded off at church during his nephew's wedding. The ceremony was nearing the end, and the minister was at that part where he asks if anyone has cause to object to this man taking this woman as his wife. "Let him speak now," the minister said loudly to his congregation, "or forever hold his peace." It was at that moment that someone gave the old man a shake of the shoulder. The old fellow, who had been drifting in and out of sleep, gave a start and said aloud to the church, "If she's got a tuft on her belly, she's mine!"

The young man bent low with laughter, and even the Sergeant seemed to enjoy the joke, as if he, too, were hearing it for the first time. Claire understood that the greatest kindness to someone going into battle is not to dwell on death but on life. She also liked that story, and had to turn away lest someone see her wide grin. One day, with luck and God willing, she would tell her family back home that story.

The caravan continued steadily south and west. Packed with rifles and ammunition, the Sergeant's wagon offered a bone-rattling ride. Claire thought back to Monsieur Weldon's wagon as they had crossed the ice and snow of Lake Champlain. She fondly remembered the wagon's smooth and quiet glide. The old crate guided by Sergeant McDermott leapt this way and that, and there was nothing to hold on to when it plunged and dipped. Nothing but the Sergeant's knees and elbows.

Moses and Claire would drive their boots into the angled board at their feet, but it did them little good. They marvelled at the way the Sergeant rolled with the wagon, like a sailor long at sea who bobs with his ship as it pitches and rolls in the wind and the waves. By the second day, Moses, in fact, was beginning to feel ill from all the motion. He tried to make the sign for "sick" (hand to forehead) but his hand kept slipping as the wagon tossed him around and it was a few seconds before Claire understood. Then she pointed to herself to let him know that she, too, was feeling seasick from that awful wagon.

When the huge caravan stopped at noon for a meal, the two grooms each begged McDermott to be given a horse, any horse, even a mule. Some of the spare horses, several dozen of them, were attached by lead ropes to a long picket—a tethering rope strung between trees. The Sergeant went to the line, bowed low to the two grooms and tossed out one hand in a flourish. *Take your pick,* they understood him to say.

Beaming, Moses and Claire walked up and down the line looking the horses over. Moses couldn't decide, kept shrugging his shoulders, looking to his fellow groom for guidance. Claire had chosen a compact chestnut Canadian mare and had her saddled up and ready to go in a few minutes. Claire liked the mare's angles, her back (not too long, not too short), but mostly she liked her eye—soft and trusting and kind. She was circling the mare, seeing what the horse knew, and Moses was eyeing a tall grey. The gelding looked on the bony side but Claire saw a sparkle in his eye.

Moses pointed at the grey and looked expectantly at Claire. She gave him the thumbs-up. By the time Claire and Moses had both horses saddled and tied to the back of the wagon, the Sergeant had the meal on.

He had driven two sharpened Y-shaped branches into the dirt and strung a long iron rod between them. From the rod hung two pots—the bigger one for stew, the smaller one for coffee. Claire had always admired Magrette back home for her ability to make a meal quickly. Suddenly the food was there, on the table, hot and good. The men had come in from the fields or the forest and had barely washed their hands when their plates were being filled. The Sergeant had the same genius for speed, though not quite Magrette's touch. Still, he was a fair cook, for a man.

Over the meal, Clint had questions for the Sergeant. Who were the men riding Black Bull and Lightning? What were they like? The Sergeant made a sign to say, *Look, can I just finish my stew?* Claire took no offence. She nodded, and smiled at the Sergeant. *Sure, I can wait,* the smile said.

Finally, he was done. Seated as usual on his favourite barrel, Dan McDermott used the back of his hand to wipe his mouth and then let out a series of burps. He seemed to be saying "Yowwwwww" as he burped, and what followed was not an "Excuse me!" but a pause as he geared up for another one. Claire thought it was, on the one hand, the height of rudeness and, on the other hand, the sign of a man comfortable in his own skin. Asked to choose between a good man and good manners, she knew which was more important.

Finally, the Sergeant got out his pencil and pad and started to write. Moses and Claire rose and stood behind him. They had all gotten used to this kind of storytelling, watching each word form on the pad, the story being built one letter at a time. The Sergeant had developed a kind of shorthand, linking phrases and images, not unlike sign language. He had no desire to write long, had no time for it. But he thought for a few minutes before he put pen to paper. This is what he wrote:

"Germin offacer on Black Bull. Captain Hubert Dilger. Called 'Leathrbreeches.' Doeskin pants?" And McDermott turned around to see if Claire had noticed the Captain's unusual trousers. She nodded vigorously.

"Body of a classik rider. Mind of a cowboy. Scouts like a Indian. Cool under fire. Fot Stonewall Jackson at Chancellorsville. Fot at Gettysburg. His men luv him. And he luvs Black Bull."

"Kind?" Claire wrote underneath.

"Fair," the Sergeant wrote. "And God bless him."

Claire pondered this for a few seconds, and then wrote, "Other officer?"

"Major Pennock Huey," the Sergeant wrote. And again, he took time to gather his thoughts. Either the Sergeant, thought Claire, didn't know him that well or he had mixed feelings about him. Finally, he started to write.

"West Point." And he looked to see the response—a look of confusion. "Milatary acadamee," he wrote. "Jockey, for a bit.

Smart, maybe to smart." Then the Sergeant thought better, and scratched out the last three words. Finally, he added, "Best coureeyer we got."

Then Claire wrote, "He likes Lightning?"

"They're still gettin akwainted," the Sergeant wrote, then put the pad in his pocket and ordered the two grooms to bed down for the night. He made a prayer sign with his hands and laid his cheek against them.

Soon, thought Claire, *we'll all be signing.*

The days got hotter and progressively longer as the caravan kept on its southwest course and was joined by other caravans, other cavalries, other regiments. They were a river of men and horses and white covered wagons, and they were pouring into the South. Claire very much liked her chestnut mare, whom she called in her head Minonette. The name seemed to suit the horse, who was just as agreeable as Minon back home but a shade smaller. Moses, too, liked the grey, whom he called Jacob, after his father. The grey was extremely sensitive along his sides and would rush forward at the slightest touch of a heel or calf—not at all like those sleepy mules Moses used to ride in Georgia. Jacob, a part-Canadian horse, was teaching Moses to ride quietly. When Moses forgot, Jacob got fast and Moses hit the dirt. But he always rose smiling. Claire would catch the grey, hold him, and on they all went.

Claire was glad to be off the Sergeant's wagon and in the saddle. She was even glad of an entire day in the saddle. The mountains had given way to rolling hills and grassland and she was content to take it all in. She had a traveller's optimism: every day was a new day, every weather was welcome.

But whoever had designed the heavy wool uniforms had not factored in the heat of summer. Now it was June and by noon the sun was a burning eye. The wool made Claire drip from every pore, and her skin became a magnet for all the dust that the endless caravan of horses and wagons kicked up. At night, she would try to run a comb through her hair and it would not budge. The comb would just stay there, rooted, like a stick in mud.

At night, if there was a stream or some source of water nearby, Claire would walk to the shore with her bar of army soap and scrub from her face and hands the dirt of Connecticut or New Jersey or Pennsylvania—whatever state they were crossing. If she felt especially dirty, or especially brave, she would take off all her clothes and do what the men did. She would skinny-dip, alone in the dark. If there was a better feeling in the world, she did not know what it was.

One night in Pennsylvania, when most of the men had been allowed into a nearby town for as much drink as their officers would permit them, Claire took Minonette down to the river. The Susquehanna, the men had called it. The falling sun cast a gorgeous pink over everything—the clear and boundless sky, the trees that lined the shores as if competing for a view of that wide and splendid river, the rocks peeking up from the water line. Sure that no one was about, Claire hung all her clothes on a low branch, then removed the tack from Minonette, leaving just her halter on. As Sergeant McDermott had taught Claire, the mare's rope was looped once around her neck, then gathered in a neat coil at her chest. It was called "the cavalry knot" and it meant that the lead rope was always there, ready for any use but tidy and out of the way. The knot was a neat trick she would take home with her. Finally, girl and horse strode out into the water for a swim in the beauty of the dusk.

It was hard to tell who enjoyed the cool water more. Both horse and rider appeared to be smiling. On Minonette's back, Claire would go out as far as she dared, then circle back towards the shore. She could feel beneath her the power of the swimming horse, her legs tickled by water as the mare cut through the current. Claire decided she would let the chestnut mare determine when they would go in. But every time she turned the mare for shore, offering the mare the hint that maybe it was time to go, the horse would circle back to deeper water. Sometimes Claire would ease down the horse's side, using the lead rope as grab-hold, then climb back on before slipping down the other side. A little ballet it was, of girl and horse and water. The river was so quiet that anyone on shore could have heard them. The horse churning the water, the girl singing to herself in French. It was Ambrose's song, the old one with the driving beat about always using the back door. *La porte en arrière.*

Night had almost fallen when they got back to the place where Claire had left her clothes and the tack. But the clothes were not as she had arranged them. Even the tack had been disturbed. The saddle and bridle now sat, neatly, not where she had put them, but on a flat limestone rock. The clothes, too, had been messed with. Boots, pants, shirt and cap—in that order—had been strung out on the sand over a span of some twenty feet. The cap, the last bit of clothing, now lay under a huge drooping willow.

Slowly, Claire reached into the boot for the knife. It was still there, and she mouthed the words *"Dieu, merci."* She tied Minonette to a tree, slowly put on the pants while scanning the shore and all the trees, then slipped into her shirt, boots and coat. Now she started walking towards that willow. The knife in her right hand, she took one step, then stopped and listened. Nothing but the low gurgle of the Susquehanna. Finally, she got to her cap and picked it up, taking her eyes only briefly off the willow in front of her. Only when she grabbed the cap did she notice what was underneath, written in the sand.

The letter *H. H* for Huntley.

Claire backed away towards the river. She half expected the man to come running out from behind the willow and she still held out the knife in front of her as she retreated. In less than a minute, she had the mare saddled and bridled and she rode with a fury back to camp.

Thank God, she said to herself when she found the Sergeant and Moses around the fire. She thought about telling them, but decided against it. There was no point. But as she stared into the flames of the campfire, she began to wonder about how much Huntley had seen, and heard. When had he arrived on the scene? Was there light enough that he had seen the outline of her small breasts, the curve at her hip? Had he heard her singing, in French? She cursed her own carelessness. What did he now know? And what, for God's sake, did he want? If he wanted to hurt her, or worse, why not just do it? Maybe, she thought, he liked to inflict a little torment.

"The world is a wonderful place," Ambrose used to tell her on those long buggy rides through the countryside, "and there is good in almost everyone. But you should know, *ma petite,* that some folk do the devil's work."

That night, she could not sleep. She could hear the Sergeant snoring, and Moses talking in his sleep, but she was used to the racket. That wasn't what kept her awake. Her head on a rolled blanket, her right hand clutching the bit of blue blanket, she stared into the dark. She thought of the man, the man she despised and feared, watching her from shore as she swam naked with her horse. He had ruined the moment, taken it from her. One more theft. Huntley had already invaded her tent and ripped a page from a book she saw as sacred. He had harmed Albert, another sin. Now he had invaded her privacy. Maybe he had seen her body, knew her secret.

Huntley was like a stain that had formed at the curve of her throat. It was on the skin, in the skin, and no amount of scrubbing would remove it.

In the middle of the page, a small decorative ornament separates the two sections.

As Claire and the caravan pressed on to Virginia and closer to the front lines, Tip Weldon was well into another horse-buying mission in Canada East. He was unsure whether Ambrose had horses to sell, but that was not why he had sent word asking for a meeting at an auberge in Farnham. The Captain was making good on a promise.

Monsieur Weldon was waiting for Ambrose at a corner table, and there were already two glasses of rum on the red tablecloth when the old man arrived. It struck the Captain that Ambrose had aged, even in the time since he had seen him last. They shook hands warmly, each raised his glass, and they looked each other in the eye.

Ambrose had an inkling of what Monsieur Weldon was going to say, and the Captain had a hunch that Ambrose had a grasp of things as well. For the longest time, neither said a word. They were like arm-wrestlers, each one waiting for the other to make the first move.

Finally, the Captain blinked. "Ambrose," he began, "what I am going to say to you is in strictest confidence. Are we agreed?"

Ambrose assured Tip Weldon that he would say nothing. Then the old man said, "You have news of Claire." It wasn't a question. It was a statement. And the Captain nodded.

"So her name is Claire, is it? I do know she's an extraordinary girl, but I'm sure you know that, too. You remember the last time I was here. Your horse had won that race on the bay, with a young boy driving—a boy with a lot of horse smarts—behind that black speed demon. Beau Albert. You called him Beau Albert."

"*C'est ça,*" said Ambrose, knowing Monsieur Weldon would understand, for the Captain had picked up some French on his many trips north.

"Well, some weeks later, in a small town in Massachusetts, my best horse breaker just about gets killed trying to ride that demon of yours. And into the paddock steps a young boy who reminds me an awful lot of your boy, the racer on the bay. This boy rides that horse, bareback, over the fence—a five-foot fence!—then rides him back over the fence once more. Gets off the horse, gives me a note to say he's a deaf runaway, a war orphan, wants to join the army as a groom. Get the picture?"

"*Ben, oui,*" said Ambrose, half sighing and half smiling. "Is she well?" he asked. "Is she happy? Is she with Tibeau and Albert?"

"Yes, to all those questions," the Captain replied. "And no one but me knows her secret. At least, I don't think anyone else knows. She's paired up with a fine young Negro groom, a deaf lad about her age, and I have my best sergeant looking after the two of them. Ambrose, I'm not going to lie to you. She's with the 1st Massachusetts Cavalry, and by now they'll be pretty close to the fighting. But my hope is that she'll be spared the worst of it." The Captain stopped with that; there was no need to muddy the waters with mention of Huntley.

There was a silence, then, as each man swallowed the rest of his rum and pondered what was on the table between them.

"You know, Ambrose," the Captain began again, "I had a mind not to speak to you at all. I worried that you might hold me responsible. I thought you might be angry. Demand to know why I didn't just grab her and bring her back on my wagon this trip. But she would have just run again. You know that."

Ambrose nodded. "Yes, I do know that."

"And if you were to complain to your government, the Union army might put me in hot water. Strange things are happening in my country. Good sense has fled. The prisons are full, and there are bands of renegades tearing up the countryside on both sides. People calling each other traitor and turning friends and neighbours over to vigilantes. I tell you, Claire is probably in a fairly safe place—inside a regiment. Anyway, I trust you, Ambrose. I knew you'd make no trouble for me. But I like you, too, and I had a hunch you knew where your granddaughter had gone and would want to know for sure."

"I appreciate your kindness," said Ambrose. "But I do have one question. How did she get all the way down there and manage to stay with our horses?"

"Ah," replied the Captain. "Took me a while to figure that out. But one day I was taking some blankets out of my wagon's cupboard and I found some bread crumbs and a wineskin I thought was lost. The little pirate was camped out in my cupboard the whole way south!"

Both men laughed at this, then the Captain told the rest and Ambrose took it all in. The Captain described the mysterious camp thief on the frozen Lake Champlain. The mad dash for freedom by Albert and Tibeau. A longer version of the vaulting of the fence. A sketch of the two officers now riding the two Canadian horses, since renamed Black Bull and Lightning.

"Black Bull?" Ambrose complained.

"Sorry, Ambrose," the Captain answered. "Wouldn't have been my first choice, either."

"*Pauvre* Albert," Ambrose sighed. "*Mon pauvre ami.*"

The Captain was fairly sure that Ambrose was saying, "Poor Albert. My poor pal." And he reassured the old man that both horses were well treated and in good hands.

Each man now settled into the other's good company. Ambrose told stories of his own life as a gatherer. He told the Captain, "If I meet a man I do not know—in the market, after Mass—I will chat him up. But what I'm really after is news of the man's horses. How many do you own? How were they trained? What bit do you use? What feed? What are your thoughts on breeding? What books have you read on the subject of horses?"

"I do the same," the Captain replied. Ambrose smiled to hear that.

Ambrose told Monsieur Weldon that he never tired of watching horses, greeting them, touching them. All his life he remained hungry to know more about the animal he considered the noblest and wisest of God's creatures.

"If I see a man whose horse is ill shod or ill fed," he told the Captain, "if his coat is dull or his eye a sad one, I know the man has nothing to tell me about horses. No, this is a man in need of help." If a man's horse was fearful and looked to have been whipped, Ambrose said he would swallow his own anger and appeal to the man's decency. Or, if that failed, his pocketbook. "Look after your horse," he would tell the man, "and he'll look after you. Who wants to do business with a horse dealer and end up with a horse worse than the one you've got?"

Ambrose and Monsieur Weldon—each of them horse dealers—gave each other a knowing look. There was no awkwardness between the two men, none.

Tip Weldon loved horses, undeniably, but his job was to send them into war. Ambrose Vigere likewise loved horses, but he had sold his two best horses into war. How could two men who loved horses betray them? The question never came up in discussion that night, but it was there all right. Maybe it was why Ambrose now told the Captain about his little campaign aimed at stopping cruelty to horses.

"On many occasions," he said, "I've put a little fear in a man who has been cruel to his horse. I might tell him the story of another man I know who was cruel to his horses. Whipped them for their fears. Starved them as punishment. Used awful bits in their mouths. But one day, the man was careless in the company of an old gelding he had bullied for years. The man was taking off some harness when the horse caught him with a hoof. The horse was loose, you see, and he didn't just strike the man once, but many, many times. That man never walked again. You can hardly blame the horse, now, can you? I don't need to tell you, Monsieur Weldon, that a horse remembers every kindness, every loss of temper, and the author of each."

"Do your sermons ever work?" Tip Weldon asked Ambrose.

"I can't say," Ambrose replied. "My last resort would be a letter to the man. 'Dear Sir,' it would begin, 'I know you have inflicted great harm on your horses. This practice must stop. If it does not, I will come and take your horses when you are sleeping or lead them away when you are at market. Know that I am watching you, and think better of your horses than I do of you, sir.' And I would sign the letter, 'A friend who knows.'"

Tip Weldon nodded and smiled at the boldness of Ambrose's little campaign.

"But here's the thing," Ambrose said. "I have sent many, many such letters. And evidently, people must talk about the letters, though no one knows that I'm the sender. Old Vinet Leblanc has told me he's heard of men in other villages who have ill treated their horses and lost every one when *'l'avocat des chevaux'*—you would say, 'the horse's lawyer'—came and took them one night. And that when the man bought new horses, and laid his whip on them, too, the same thing happened. Of course, nothing like that has ever taken place. I would no more steal a horse than beat one. But my letters must have had some influence, for they have launched a small legend around here, and I intend to write them, Monsieur Weldon, till my days are done."

Just then, Vinet Leblanc, of all people, entered the inn. *"En parlant du loup,"* Ambrose said when he saw him. "Speak of the devil." Vinet was an old friend who lived nearby in the village of Saint-Alexandre, and he had stopped in at the inn to warm himself before heading home after a day with friends. When he spotted Ambrose and Tip Weldon, he joined them for what he called *"une petite bière"*—a small glass of beer.

Bald as an egg, Vinet had a habit of running the palm of his hand over that dome when he was about to tell a story. And he was always on the brink of a story. When Ambrose and the Captain filled him in on the fate of Claire, he launched into his own story on the Vigere girl, *"la jeune fille Vigere."* He had seen her work her magic with excitable young horses and he had started, years ago, to call her "the horse's shadow."

"Why shadow?" Tip Weldon asked.

"You know the story of Bucephalus?" Vinet asked, certain his questioner did not. (He was wrong about that, but the Captain politely shook his head to invite the old man's story.)

"Ben ..." Vinet began. "Well ... a long long time ago, even before the time of Christ, there lived a king in a land called Macedonia. And this king had a mind to buy a black stallion, but this was a very hot horse. You know, Monsieur Weldon, that a hot horse has nothing to do with the weather—hot, when you're talking of horses, means excitable, nervous, spooky. This black horse's own grooms stayed clear of his teeth and hooves. But the owner saw real quality in this horse—in his eye, his body, the way he moved—and was asking a great deal for him.

"'Take him away,' the king ordered with a wave of his hand, for the horse was prancing and pawing the air. Then the king's son, the prince, who was watching all this, spoke for the first time. 'What a horse they are losing,' he said with sadness. The prince thought much of the horse and precious little of his handlers.

"The king challenged his son. 'Do you think you can do better?' The prince was so sure he could that he offered to pay the full price of the horse if he failed." Here Vinet paused, for horse dealers are always curious to know the asking and selling price of a horse.

"This was ancient times," said Vinet, and they didn't have Canadian dollars, but talents, and the asking price for this stallion was thirteen talents—or more than ten thousand dollars!"

Vinet had told this story many times, and normally there was a gasp from his listeners, who could barely conceive of such a sum, and Vinet would let them settle before he returned to his story. Ambrose and the Captain were harder to impress; they just nodded.

"Imagine if the prince, who was only a boy of twelve, had failed to calm the horse," said Vinet. "Imagine his loss of face—not to mention all that money. Up in the air," said Vinet, "like smoke." And he let his fingers dance and flutter over his head to illustrate the point.

"The young prince, whose name was Alexander, approached the horse with confidence, took him by the bridle and turned him towards the sun. And just like that"—here old Vinet snapped his fingers—"the horse calmed. Can you guess why?" Vinet asked Monsieur Weldon.

In all his years of telling the story, no one had ever guessed the answer. Tip Weldon knew, and so did Ambrose, for he had heard the story many times, but common courtesy kept both men quiet.

"I'll tell you why," Vinet jumped in. "Prince Alexander had noticed something that no one else had. This horse, though superb in every way, was still young and silly—he feared his own shadow! And as far as the horse was concerned, this young man had rid him of his tormentor. So, the boy stroked the horse, spoke softly to him, mounted him, and they took off in a gallop. They came back at the same speed they had left and everyone looking on was amazed, for the horse was absolutely his. That horse would become a famous warhorse called Bucephalus, and that boy would one day be called Alexander the Great, and he would conquer much of the known world—not including New France." Ambrose smiled at Vinet's irreverent remark.

"Alexander and Bucephalus were partners for thirty years," Vinet continued, "and when the horse died in battle the King was overwhelmed with grief, and he named a city after his horse. All this because a young boy was paying attention when a young horse showed fear.

"Little Claire Vigere," said Vinet, ending his tale, "has the young prince's eye. Around horses she notices even small things, and she reacts. The horse thinks he has found someone who understands him, speaks his language, and he is always grateful. Many horses live all their lives and never meet anyone like that. One day I watched Claire moving among a herd of horses, and it seemed to me that they had accepted her as one of them. She looked neither horse nor human, but something in between, more like a horse's shadow. But not one," he added, "to spook a horse!"

His beer done, and his story likewise, Vinet Leblanc now rose and warmly shook the hands of Ambrose and Tip Weldon before taking his leave.

The two men went on sipping their rum. They would now and again touch each other on the shoulder as they talked on and on—of war and peace, the folly of man, the wisdom of children. They drank to each other's good health and that of the runaway deaf boy called Clint. And they drank, of course, to horses.

"Long may they run," said the *habitant*.

"Long may they run," said the Yank.

They perhaps should have stopped with that toast. Maybe Monsieur Weldon should have retired to his room in the auberge and Ambrose Vigere should have climbed into his *berline* and asked Minon to take him home, for she knew the way as well as he did. But they didn't stop there.

There was genuine friendship between the two men, and the rum was giving it more warmth than it really possessed. Ambrose was feeling a torrent of emotions—relief, anxiety, a sense of loss almost as deep as when Claire had run away. His only granddaughter was, on the one hand, well and safe for the moment, but she was also riding into the jaws of war. And, somehow, Monsieur Weldon offered a connection to Claire. He had touched her when he bade her adieu back there in Williamstown, he had talked to her, he had seen her just weeks ago. No, they would have one more drink. Well, two. They would drink in the manner of his Irish relations—with an ale in one hand and a "wee chaser" of Irish whisky in the other.

Ambrose was reaching into his pocket for a dollar and Monsieur Weldon was at the same time waving his hands—for that's what men do when they drink. They fight good-naturedly over who will buy the next round. Monsieur Weldon then reached into his pocket and showed Ambrose the letter Claire had used to introduce herself as a war orphan and deaf groom. "Good with horses ..." Ambrose took hold of the note, admired the penmanship, the intelligence behind the words.

Ambrose, too, had something to show Tip Weldon. Ambrose's hand reached into his right pocket and closed on the Krieghoff *carte-de-visite* letters that Claire had mailed home. He had put them in his pocket, intending to show them to Monsieur Weldon if, as Ambrose hoped, the Captain had word of Claire.

After they sorted out the matter of payment (Monsieur Weldon insisted on buying), Ambrose put the two tiny paintings on the table. Monsieur Weldon stared at the art with great interest, then flipped each page over to see Claire's handwriting before coming back to the art. "They're called *cartes-de-visite*," said Ambrose. "By a fellow who lives here in Canada East, a man named Krieghoff."

It was then that a tall, grey-haired man with a slightly wild look, as if high winds had been at him, pushed back his chair from a table nearby and approached them.

"Did someone mention my name?" he asked. And then he presented himself. "Cornelius Krieghoff," he said while bowing deeply to them both. "At your service."

Well, this was a night of surprises! Ambrose and Tip (he was "Tip" now, no longer "Monsieur Weldon") at first eyed him with suspicion. They were all loose with drink, and perhaps this man before them was "telling a tale in hopes of an ale." Every auberge had them, men with a great thirst and no money, but charming enough and bold enough to enter the circle of men who did have money and didn't mind paying for a little entertainment.

But it seemed he was who he said he was. He was able to describe to Ambrose all the other paintings in the book, as well as the book's unusual golden lock with its centre cut out in the shape of a four-leaf clover. The man then pulled from his pocket a calling card. "Cornelius Krieghoff, Artist," it proclaimed.

Of course they bought him a drink and introduced themselves. It was like reading a book in a library and having the author of that book chance by, sit down in front of you and chat you up. They were honoured to buy him a drink. Monsieur Krieghoff was as close to a celebrity as the cities of Montreal or Quebec had to offer in the 1860s. He had lived in both places, as well as in the United States and Europe. His first language was Dutch, for he was born in Holland, but he also spoke German. He had married a Québécoise, so his command of French, Ambrose noted, was very good. This right away endeared him to the old man.

It turned out that Cornelius Krieghoff had even served in the U.S. Army: in the Indian wars of Florida in 1837 he had built artillery fortifications. This gave him an instant connection with the Captain, who praised Krieghoff's command of English. And he had an interest in horses, Canadian horses especially, and had given them pride of place in hundreds of his paintings. Suddenly, this stranger was no stranger at all.

"Gentlemen," said Krieghoff, raising his glass, "let's drink to army life," and he nodded to the Captain. Then he said, "And let's hope for a fine harvest in the fall," before bowing to Ambrose. "And to the artists among us," he ended the toast. They all drank to that.

Cornelius Krieghoff was a learned man, a fine musician and a painter of considerable reputation. He knew all about the *habitants,* how they lived and worked and played, and had made a living telling their story in oils and watercolours. But his finances were almost as unpredictable as those of the farmers.

The man whom Ambrose and Tip met in the auberge that night was a curious and contradictory sort. He was refined, no doubt about that. Here was a man at home in fancy parlours, sipping brandy with judges and bishops, men and women of high rank. People liked him instantly, for he had wit and charm and he seemed genuinely interested in the lives of others.

Yet there was something seedy about him, too. He was a tall man, almost as tall as Monsieur Weldon, with a pink blush to his face (likely from too much whisky) and wild, unruly hair. Ambrose had never met an artist before and he simply assumed that artists weren't like common folk. Krieghoff had mutton chops—long, curly sideburns that ran down the side of his face and gathered under his chin. He was cheery, yet there was fatigue in his eyes and worry in his thin lips. The starched collar, the cravat he wore at his neck, his overcoat: all were frayed and rumpled. Had it not been so late in the evening, Ambrose would have guessed he had just gotten out of bed, and had worn his clothes all night.

As the evening wore on, Ambrose switched to tea. "If I don't," he warned the others, "even Minon won't be able to get me home." Tip Weldon likewise turned to water. The owner of the inn had told Monsieur Weldon that the water came from a nearby spring. "It's very sweet," said the Captain. "Besides, my head will thank me in the morning."

Only Cornelius Krieghoff pressed on with the whisky, by turns listening to Ambrose and Tip and then offering tales of his own. By now, there was no one left in the inn's dining room. The owner had gone to bed and left on their table the whisky bottle and the few inches of honey-coloured liquid that remained.

Talk turned, finally, to how they had all come to be at the inn that evening. It seemed that Monsieur Krieghoff had been asked to paint the portrait of a bishop who had retired to a village nearby. Then Ambrose Vigere and Tip Weldon told the story of Claire. How Ambrose had bought the *carte-de-visite* book for her, how she had run away in pursuit of two beloved family horses. Drink had killed discretion by this point, and so the two men also told Krieghoff of Claire's secret. A thirteen-year-old French girl was living as a deaf boy, a private enlisted in the Union army.

Krieghoff was astonished at the tale. He had seen and done much in his forty-nine years, and travelled widely, but he had never heard the likes of this.

"Do you have an image of her?" the painter asked.

"*Ben oui*," Ambrose replied. "I carry it with me always. A few years ago, a man came to the farm. He said he would do a family portrait, a 'photograph' he called it. 'I'm looking for clients,' he said, 'and I can use this to demonstrate my art.' We could not afford to pay him, of course, but he left a copy of the photograph with us."

At this point, old Ambrose began to undo the buttons of his shirt, which slightly alarmed the other two. They wondered where it was kept, this family photograph. The answer soon revealed itself: around his neck. In those days, Roman Catholics wore a medallion at their necks, usually the face of a saint no bigger than a dime and attached to a thin chain. But around Ambrose's neck was the family photograph, tucked into a heavy cardboard sleeve much like Krieghoff's *carte-de-visite* paintings.

"I put this on the day Claire ran away," he explained, and he got misty-eyed as he spoke. "And whenever I travelled—to Montreal or Calumet or villages in between—I'd stop people on the street and ask if they'd seen this girl. I thought that wearing the photograph would spare it from being crushed in my pocket. And it was a way ..."

Here the old man paused, and the other two wondered if he could continue. He bit his lip and fought back tears. Tip Weldon touched his arm. Krieghoff wore a look of great sadness. They would all be crying soon unless someone rallied them.

"I'm sorry," Ambrose said, coming to their emotional rescue. "It's been very, very hard on all of us. But having the picture of Claire close to me somehow helps." He then slowly handed the photograph to Monsieur Krieghoff.

Krieghoff cupped the print delicately in his hands, as if it were crystal that might shatter if dropped. The black-and-white photograph showed the Vigere family gathered around the cabin's fireplace. Ambrose and Magrette, patriarch and matriarch, were seated and dressed in their Sunday best. Behind them, standing, were Jean on one side and Claudine on the other, with the boys—Léo, André, Jérôme—ranged between them. Everyone looked uncomfortable and stiff, which was not surprising since photography was still a new invention in those days and you had to hold your pose for a long time, not moving an inch until the photographer was done.

The only one who looked at ease was the twelve-year-old girl reclining on the wooden floor in front of her family. Someone, perhaps the photographer, or perhaps Ambrose, had decided to set the girl apart from the boys. Claire looked proud, even defiant. Her hair was long, her curls framed her face, her pose was entirely relaxed.

Tip Weldon, for one, was astonished. The sun-splashed private he had left at Williamstown was now revealed as some other creature. She was the centre of the photograph, and if the photographer knew it so did Tip Weldon—and so did Cornelius Krieghoff.

"Diana, returned from the hunt," the painter said. Ambrose looked at him as if he were mumbling in another language, though the Captain clearly understood the reference.

"Diana was the goddess of the hunt in Greek mythology," Tip Weldon explained to Ambrose.

"I must paint this girl, those eyes," said Krieghoff. "Yes, I'll paint a triptych. A three-panel painting," he said, anticipating confusion from the other men. "There will be three paintings, tall and thin, side by side: the girl as she was here, in her village. Then, in her uniform, the boy soldier. Then, as a young woman. Yes, I can see it so clearly, so clearly ..."

"Your subject, I'm afraid," said Tip Weldon, "is at this moment riding to war in Virginia. How do you aim to find her?"

"Do you believe in fate, Captain Weldon?" the painter asked.

"Maybe," came the reply.

"Well I do," said Krieghoff. "If I was fated to encounter you and Ambrose, then I am fated as well to meet Claire Vigere. And I know that one day I will. I will paint her," he said. "I will."

Ambrose slept most of the way home, but it was a troubled sleep full of dark dreams. Minon parked the *berline* in front of the cabin and had to whinny several times to wake her master up. *"Merde,"* he muttered to himself as he eased his old bones down off the sled before taking off Minon's harness and leading her into the barn.

Ambrose didn't want his granddaughter riding into battle in Virginia, and he was not at all comfortable with the notion of her as a painter's inspiration. Goddess of the hunt? *"Merde,"* he said again as he walked towards the cabin. Inside, he needed no light. It was one of the beauties of old age and spending a lifetime in the same place: he could navigate his way in the dark and find his own bed.

But would Claire find her way? He was not sure any more. It seemed she drew attention, all kinds of attention. Ambrose had liked Monsieur Krieghoff, but the sight of Claire had lit some fire in the painter. And Ambrose wasn't sure he liked its heat or its glow.

CHAPTER 13

Seeing the Elephant

As the 1st Massachusetts Cavalry made its way south and west, it grew larger by the day. Infantry from other regiments (including all-black regiments), horses pulling gun carriages small and large, other cavalry units from other northern states, more supply wagons and more supply wagons: all joined the march. From Williamstown, Claire's unit had moved along at a good clip, but now they were part of a bulky war machine. It took them longer to get rolling in the morning. That sea of tents had to be packed, all those men had to be fed, all those horses tacked up.

There was more work for Claire and Moses now. The routine work got more intense—doctoring sore and injured horses, filing hooves, repairing broken tack, laying down hay and grain and buckets of water for horses on pickets. And the Sergeant gave the two grooms chores around the mess tents: peeling potatoes, cleaning pots and the worst, emptying the chamber pots from the officers' tents.

Her exhaustion at the end of every day was beyond anything Claire had ever experienced, even during haying at home. Still, she slept badly. Huntley was always on her mind.

She had taken to sleeping with her Krieghoff book clutched in her hand, with her knife slipped between the pages. If he wanted the book, he would have to wrench it from her, and maybe pay a price.

Finally, Claire decided to speak to Sergeant McDermott. Telling him about what had happened back on the Susquehanna River risked Huntley spilling the beans. But Claire had had a lot of time to think about all this as she rode Minonette down those dusty roads, and it had struck her that there were worse things than spilt beans. Like spilt blood. Huntley, Monsieur Weldon had warned her, was "bad business." And whatever warning Monsieur Weldon had given Huntley, it had failed to stop him. Huntley was stalking her, and he seemed to be enjoying the hunt.

The Sergeant was so angry when she wrote on the pad about the incident at the river that she feared he would explode. He said nothing, just gritted his teeth and growled. Claire thought of Babette back home. When she was younger, that otherwise sweet pup would growl at anyone who went near her food. Ambrose would bring her down a notch by ignoring the threat, taking her food in his hands and defying her to respond. It worked. But the Sergeant's growling wasn't so easily stopped. He was still *grrrrrrrrrr*-ing as he stomped off, and the *grrrrrrrrrr*-ing seemed to get louder even as he disappeared over the rise.

"Where's that goddamned Huntley?" she heard him yelling to no one in particular.

The Sergeant was gone a long time. The campfire was almost out and the bugler had hours ago called for an end to the day.

When he returned, McDermott had cuts on the knuckles of his right hand but seemed otherwise fine. He looked at his young groom, grim at first, but then he smiled. He made a motion with his right fist against his nose, did it again quickly three or four times, then tipped his head hard to the left and closed his eyes. Finally, he wrote the letter *H* in the air and waved bye-bye. If Claire read him right, he was saying: *I smashed his nose, and knocked him out. He won't bother you again.*

Claire bowed thanks to the Sergeant and hoped he was right. In any case, she slept well for the first time in many nights.

The next day it rained. At first, the men were glad of the showers, for they kept off the mosquitoes that had been tormenting them and put a stop, for a while anyway, to the dust. But the cool rain kept on, became a cold rain, and the dust turned to ankle-deep mud. The men called it "gumbo," and they complained of it with every step they took.

Claire felt sorry for the men as they plodded on. And she felt sorry for the horses, especially the heavy horses hauling artillery, as they strained and slipped on the steeper hills and suffered the bullwhips. She even felt sorry for herself as the rain found every part of her, but she soon stopped thinking about her discomfort. She and the men of the 1st Massachusetts were beginning to see the things that war did, things beyond her imagining. Claire had yet to "see the elephant," but she now saw where the elephant had gone on his rampages.

Late that morning, the column came up over a rise and Claire gazed at a Virginia landscape that looked to her like the face of the harvest moon, but with none of the moon's beauty.

There was no living thing on that plain. The colour brown, and only brown, ruled here; green had been banished. There were no trees or bushes or fence lines or even a trace of them. Not a blade of grass, not a weed, not even a stump. Riding alongside Sergeant McDermott's wagon, Claire hunched her shoulders and gave him a look of amazement: *How did this happen?* He simply pointed down the hill at the heavy artillery carriages.

The land had been blasted. Churned up by many months' worth of cannon fire, the earth had turned to mud, then been baked by the sun. Now the rain just sat on that hardpan. The water found the caves the Confederates had dug as shelter against the cannons, with huge timbers framing the openings and several feet of hardpan on top. Now small lakes were forming in and all around the caves.

This was the first of many strange sights Claire saw that day. She was so unnerved by what she saw that she wrote down some of her impressions on her pad that night. Some day her family would want to know what she had seen, and she wanted it to be right. She didn't want to have these sights in her memory, but neither did she want to forget them. She made a list, a short, terrible list, with only a few words to capture each memory.

"1. Lines of men on ground," she wrote. "Men who saw the elephant and lost their shoes." Northern soldiers were burying the southern dead, but not before taking their boots and, sometimes, even their socks. Claire was shocked by the numbers of the dead, but it was their bare feet she kept staring at. A final insult to the fallen.

"2. Trains upside down, everything here upside down." Each side would tear up the other's rail lines, and a steam locomotive coming around a bend would have nowhere to go but down the hillside. Now dozens of men with ropes and horses were scurrying around the huge, black, upturned thing, like ants trying to move the body of a dead black beetle.

"3. Prisoners herded like cattle." Sergeant McDermott had explained in a note that for several years, the North and South had traded prisoners of war. Now the North, sensing victory, was trying to choke off the enemy's supply of soldiers. Union cavalry were marching their prisoners, many hundreds of them, off to some prison. "War is hell," the Sergeant had written. "War prison is werse." Claire had never seen men look so hopeless as they shuffled on. She would never forget their eyes, their hard stares, how young so many of them were. No more than boys her age.

"4. Guns and dead horses, dead horses and guns." Each side would focus its cannon fire on the other side's big guns. One side would overrun a line somewhere and take their artillery; farther up the line the reverse would occur. Horses bore the brunt of it all. Some fallen horses, Claire noted, seemed not to have a mark on them. The force of the explosion was enough to knock them down and out, and they never rose again.

"5. Chimney left, house gone. Where?" Sometimes a family had the misfortune to be caught in the middle between two armies. Like this house, which had been blown apart. Only the chimney, and a teakettle at the base of it, remained as evidence that, just days ago, a family had called this home.

"6. Slaves no more, but this is home?" They passed what people in Virginia and elsewhere were calling "freedmen's villages." They were, in fact, shantytowns. Claire saw people living in houses no better than chicken houses. As the northern army marched south, the slaves were freed, but they had no home now—just shelters they threw together using mismatched boards and roofs of tin held down by rocks.

Moses was greatly saddened to see black people, his people, living like that. The former slaves would come out of their shacks to wave at the passing army. Their children, especially, offered a warm welcome to Moses. One young boy saluted him while wearing a wide grin, but Moses was too miserable to reply. Somewhere Claire could hear a man's voice. He was singing a song. *"Hard times,"* the chorus went, *"hard times come again no more ..."*

Moses, riding alongside Claire, tapped her on the shoulder and signed his sadness: his fingers curved at his eyes and then dropping down to his mouth. Then he made the sign for weeping: fingers rolling down his cheek as if they were tears.

Claire nodded, then made a sign to sum up all they had seen this day. She took the thumb and middle finger of one hand and pinched the side of her wrist—the sign for "earth." Then she made the sign for "broken": her two hands grasped an imaginary object, maybe an arrow or a ruler, then she made a motion as if to break that object in two. *The earth,* she was saying to Moses, *is broken.*

<hr>

Beau Albert and his son, Tibeau, were also catching a glimpse of the elephant.

Riding a horse he knew only as Black Bull, Captain Hubert Dilger was doing what he did best. Taking risks. Going off by himself on daring scouting missions. Flirting with death and, so far, getting away with it.

One night around the campfire, Claire listened as Sergeant McDermott talked to several other men about the man they all called "Leatherbreeches." It seemed that at the Battle of Chancellorsville in the spring of 1863, where "Stonewall" Jackson and his Confederates crushed Union regiments, the German officer had distinguished himself. This was the fate of the brave and the reckless. Many such men died. The ones who survived got talked about by men like McDermott around campfires. The men would smoke their pipes or roll their cigarettes and stare into the fire, wondering what time was left to them.

Maybe, thought Claire as she heard the story, soldiers needed to hear about how brave their fellow soldiers were. But she had also heard the whispers. How some men, over-come by fear, ran from the fighting. Like some horses, they went mad in the smoke and the noise and the chaos. Deserters were hunted down like rats, and a man who fled his regiment had as much to fear from his own soldiers as from the enemy.

Leatherbreeches did not run. He was as bold as they came. At Chancellorsville, the artillery captain had ridden his horse a good mile into enemy lines. No one had authorized his little expedition. And when he returned and reported to senior offi-cers, no one trusted his German accent or believed him when he told them an awful truth: the Rebels were coming through the woods, woods that the northern generals had thought too dense to allow the passage of men.

The generals were wrong. Leatherbreeches was right. The woods and brambles were so thick that they ripped off many a Rebel uniform, but soon the men were free of the woods. Yelling that terrifying Rebel yell and firing away.

And while many bluecoats ran from the men in grey, the German captain held them as best he could all by himself. Swarmed by the enemy on the road, he took charge of a big gun and fired what was called "cannister." It was no more than a tin can full of lead slugs, but it sprayed widely and took down everything within about two hundred and fifty yards. Firing cannister was like firing a sawed-off shotgun—wildly inaccurate but deadly at short range.

"He'd fire a round," McDermott was saying, "then he'd retreat fifty yards and fire another round. Thing is, he was ridin' the damned heavy horse haulin' the gun. Finally, when the Rebels had 'bout surrounded him, he takes his sword, cuts loose the harness and rides that big horse bareback on up the road to his own line." Leatherbreeches's own horse had been lost in the battle. And that was how the German was portrayed in these campfire chats. Cantering a plough horse, feet as big as pie plates, the cut leather traces flying behind him. A man escaping in slow motion.

Claire delighted in the story, for the young love to be frightened. But they like happy endings too, and Claire worried—now more than ever—about what lay ahead for Beau Albert and Tibeau. Would the bullets find them? Or would they have the same luck as Leatherbreeches and the plough horse?

In the morning, as the huge caravan assembled to continue on its way south, Leatherbreeches happened alongside the Sergeant's wagon.

"Mornin', sir," the Sergeant said. "That horse workin' out okay for ya?"

"Ziss is a *goot* horse. *Goot, goot, goot.*" He patted Beau Albert on his neck, and the horse lowered his head as if pleased by both the compliment and the pat. Claire listened with pleasure and pride. It seemed that some of the other officers had earlier mocked Leatherbreeches. They claimed to be sorry that he had been assigned "that stubby little fellow." But day by day, Albert—who seemed not to mind the awful name they called him—had proven his worth. "The little horse with the big leap," as some men called him, would jump fences the other horses declined. He was still going strong at the end of the day, when the others had their tongues hanging out. And he had developed a real affection for Leatherbreeches.

"I do not trade him for ze vorld," Captain Dilger said as he rode off in a handsome gallop.

Please, thought Claire, *look after him.* And she said a prayer for horse and rider as they disappeared over the next rise. It was not the first prayer she had said since leaving the village. It would not be the last.

As for Tibeau, he, too, was making a name for himself in the 1st Massachusetts. It was not easy keeping a regiment informed of what the head was doing when the tail was lagging so far behind. And now they were a regiment within other regiments, with infantry here and there and artillery everywhere. Officers like Major Pennock Huey were forever racing up and down the line passing urgent messages from one general to another.

In the early days of the regiment's march south, when they'd had more time on their hands, Major Huey would playfully race—and always beat—other couriers and their horses in the regiment. You could pick out the Major easily enough: the left side of his hat was pinned up and decorated with a long black feather. When Tibeau sprinted, the feather trembled in all that wind. Claire thought that horse and rider made for a dashing pair.

"I do believe," the Major would tell all who would listen, "that this stud has got some Thoroughbred blood in him." Claire, had she allowed herself a voice, would have denied any such thing. *Tibeau,* she would have said, *is a Canadian through and through.*

But Ambrose had kept his cards close to his vest. He had not told Claire everything. He had not told her, for example, that Minon's sire carried both Canadian horse blood and Thoroughbred horse blood. There *was* a touch, maybe more than a touch, of Thoroughbred blood in young Tibeau. Ambrose loved the little horse of iron, but he loved to win races, too. He was only doing what other breeders in Canada East were doing in those days: tossing some hot blood into the mix to gain a little advantage.

Tibeau had the strength and stamina of Beau Albert and his ancestors, what horse breeders call "bottom." But he also had that touch of pepper in his trot and canter, thanks to the Thoroughbred blood coursing in his veins. Tibeau wasn't like Albert, who would sit back when asked and wait for the moment to take the lead in a race. Tibeau was a front-runner. He would grab the lead and challenge anyone who got close to him.

Claire would watch them pass, the Major sitting Tibeau like the jockey he had once been. There was just a hint of air between the rider's seat and that fine leather saddle, with the handsome saddle pad of blue edged in yellow. The horse, too, seemed to float on the air as they cruised past. "There goes Lightning!" men would shout. And the Major would take off his hat to recognize their cheers and shout, *"Yeehaw!"*

Claire said a prayer for the Major and Tibeau as well. "May there be no chipmunks in Virginia," she whispered one night by a southern swamp where the frog choir sang only bass notes. "May the Major ride like the wind. May my black horse only see the elephant from a long, long way away."

At night they would sleep side by side, Moses by Claire. The Sergeant would be snoring nearby, along with several privates elsewhere in the tent. Fighting was not far off now, with cannon fire rumbling in the night. Claire could feel the earth trembling beneath her, and she was sure that Moses could too.

She tapped him on the shoulder. The light of a full moon entered the tent and she could see by his eyes he was awake.

Feel it? she signed. The middle finger of one hand moved up her chest.

Moses nodded. He made the shape of a handgun with one hand, then spread his hands apart. *Big guns,* he was saying.

Are you afraid? Claire then asked him. She held her hands out in front of her, as if to protect herself from some frightening thing.

Again Moses nodded his reply. The whole conversation took only a few seconds, for Claire's sign language was becoming more natural to her. It was not as rapid-fire as that of Moses, and she still had to make him slow down sometimes when he got excited. Often they didn't use their hands, just read each other's eyes. A furrow at the brow. A widening of the eyes. A squinting. A wink. One eyebrow up, the other down. All with their eyes, they could communicate worry, surprise, concentration, mischief, doubt. "The eye is the window of the soul," Claudine used to tell her daughter, and Claire never tired of looking through that window into the soul of Moses Odell. He was her ally, her companion, her friend.

She had never met anyone with such a sorrowful past who yet remained so bright and cheery. Bright to the bone. She could tease him about his riding and he never took offence. He could mock her for her modesty (Moses would make a show of wrapping himself in some invisible cloak whenever Claire went by herself to a river or stream to wash herself). But each seemed to know when to stop the ribbing, how far was too far.

Each claimed the other's favourite foods were inedible. Moses liked something called "hominy grits," a southern breakfast made of hulled and boiled corn. Claire would make her hand flat, like a knife, and tap her neck: the sign for *dirty* or *nasty*. Moses also liked fried green tomatoes, which Claire did not like but could tolerate. What Moses did, too, with great flare was cook fried chicken, letting it sit in buttermilk beforehand and cooking it in flour in a hot black frying pan.

Claire, for her part, would make—as best she could over an open fire—*tourtière* and *tarte au sucre*. She ate boiled oatmeal every morning if it was available, but Moses—who put away the pork and the sugar pie like a hungry horse—hated the oatmeal. Even layering on brown sugar and cream failed to change his mind. He would roll his eyes at the sight of her porridge, as she did when shown his grits.

All this food came courtesy of a band of thugs called "bummers." They were no more than bandits, and they would fan out—in front of the army, behind, alongside—and take what they wanted from the farmers who had the misfortune to lie in their way. The bummers were cutthroats riding the coattails of war.

Sergeant McDermott simply shook his head when he saw them coming, always whooping, always in a gallop. Their saddlebags often jingled with stolen silver cutlery; they sometimes wore leather boots that seemed too new, too shiny, too fine. The Sergeant would look at their torn and dirty trousers, then at their boots. He knew how they came by those boots.

"Juiced-up, light-fingered highway robbers is all they are," McDermott told any who would listen. "Takin' advantage of the war is what they're doin'." And then he spat on the ground.

The bummers shot any farmer who stood up to them, walked into his house and stole money, fancy dresses, gold watches. The bummer took what he could carry or haul. Over his horse's mud-splashed neck might be a clean patchwork quilt, another looted item to be traded for a bottle of whisky or a silver dollar. To the men and women and children of the South, they sometimes did far worse than steal, but stealing was their stock-in-trade.

The bummers filled the regiments' supply wagons with flour and corn, with chickens and sweet potatoes, fresh beef and southern ham. They were like a swarm of locusts, and there was no law to stop them. And when they had finished filling their wagons, filled them until the wagons groaned, the bummers would enter the farmhouse and smash the dishes, set the house and barns on fire and steal the horses.

When she first heard this, Claire took herself away from the tents and wept. She thought of her own family, how hard the Vigeres worked for the little they had, and the thought of bands of men coming along and taking it and then torching the homestead and stealing every horse ... cherished broodmares, beloved colts, fine stallions in their prime. Claire tried to imagine Minon, Beau Albert, Tibeau and every horse in Ambrose's herd taken by rude and howling thieves, *Mamie*'s dishes smashed on the floor of the cabin. The thought was too much to bear.

Claire went on making *tourtière* and *tarte au sucre* whenever the ingredients became available, but her eyes welled up with every bite, and she always put most of it away. Next day the regiment would inevitably pass a shantytown, and she and Moses would offer slices to the children. For the rest of her life, Claire thought of the bummers every time she thought of *tarte au sucre* or *tourtière*.

The bummers were a wild bunch. Some were deserters from both Confederate and Union armies; some were just taking a short holiday from the horrors of war; some were thieves along for the ride. Northern generals might have tried reining them in, but that would have been too much trouble. Besides, the bummers served the generals' purpose. The bandits were killing two birds with one stone: filling the army's supply wagons and laying waste to the South. "We'll make Virginia howl," one Union general had warned. "We'll make Virginia starve," he might have added. It was all part of the plan. The blue-coated generals thought that total war—waged against both soldiers *and* civilians—would break the will of the South.

The freed slaves who lived in their shantytowns or who followed the northern armies hoping for handouts of food got some of the excess. Moses hated the bummers, for they were as likely to hang a black man as help him out. But at least there was food for his folk. There was food and more than enough food—as long as you saluted the Stars and Stripes of the Union side. Those who honoured the Confederate flag, with its blue X on a red background, got nothing, or worse. Dixie, as the South called itself, was howling like a kicked dog, and the bummers were doing much of the kicking.

These were the last days of June 1864, and the men and boys (and Claire Vigere) of the 1st Massachusetts had finally arrived at their destination. The Tennessee River. Across that deep and wide river lay the elephant.

That night, around every campfire of every regiment up and
down the river, it was the same. Men were writing letters
home, letters of farewell. They told their wives and children
how much they loved them, gave some last bit of advice on the
running of the farm, told the eldest son that if anything
happened he was in charge.

Claire had never seen so many men so quiet, so lost in their
own thoughts. Some men could neither read nor write, and
they would ask others—such as Sergeant McDermott—to
write these letters for them.

Somewhere in the dark, a man was playing a harmonica.
Elsewhere, men were singing. One sang "Just Before the Battle,
Mother." It was one of the most popular songs of the war, and
every soldier knew the lyrics. Two lines stayed with Claire, for
the words seemed to capture what was happening around her.
They went like this:

> Comrades brave are 'round me lying, fill'd with tho'ts
>   of home and God;
> For well they know that on the morrow, some will sleep
>   beneath the sod.

Some men sang to their sweethearts, "The Yellow Rose of
Texas." They sang of their homesickness, with songs like
"Weeping Sad and Lonely." The tunes were as mournful as the
men who sang them. Even the horses, picketed by the thousands up and down the Tennessee River, had fallen into the
mood of the camp. They grazed silently.

Claire went down to the river, a lazy river about eight
hundred feet wide, and wrote her own letter home by the light

of the moon. She had ripped from the Krieghoff book one of her favourite paintings. It was called *Cheating the Toll Man*, and it showed three men on a *berline* being pulled by a dark bay Canadian horse. They were cheerfully racing past the toll collector, thumbing their noses at him, and the third man had an open bottle of wine in his hand. Krieghoff had painted the scene just the year before, in 1863. You were supposed to pay a toll to help maintain the roads, but poor farmers going to and from market resented this tax and sometimes broke the rules. Claire herself had been in Ambrose's wagon as he and Beau Albert had sped past such a tollgate. He, of all people, would appreciate this painting.

That night, Claire wrote this note home. In English, it would have read like this.

Dear family:
  I miss you all very much and think of you every day.
On the other hand, I have learned much and made new
friends—people named Moses and McDermott. I am
busy with horses (and always will be). It's hot here, too
hot for me. But when I complain to the horses, they
always listen. I love you all.
  Claire

There was no mention of the war, or the elephant or the bummers, for Claire was determined that her news would always be good news. She had caused her family enough worry.

Then she joined the long line of men dropping off letters at a tent set aside for that purpose. A boy with the beginnings of a moustache and haunting brown eyes held open a heavy canvas bag as each man dropped his letter inside. It reminded Claire of people at church back home, dropping coins into Père Boivin's collection plate.

Later, she motioned to Moses to follow her. She made three signs in quick succession. *See* (two fingers held in front of her to make a V shape). Then *horses* (fingers made to look like ears atop her head). And, finally, *goodbye* (a farewell wave).

Claire still worried about Huntley, though she had seen no sign of him since Sergeant McDermott had paid him a visit. Her worry was that Huntley still spied on her, that as she sat around her fire he was in the dark watching her. She had communicated to Moses what Huntley had done, and Moses was determined to do what he could to protect his friend. As Moses and Claire walked towards the horses on the picket line they looked warily to the left and right. Both had slipped their knives out of their boots and into their hands with the blade hidden up their sleeves. If Huntley appeared, they would be ready.

They were a while finding the two horses they wanted to see. Their own horses, Minonette and Jacob, were to stay with them behind the lines, but they, too, might eventually be called upon. No one knew what tomorrow would bring. Claire and Moses walked up and down the long picket, looking for Tibeau and Beau Albert. If they saw a soldier, Claire would just hand him her pad, on which she had written, "Major Huey's horse?" and "Captain Dilger's horse?" Every soldier they met just pointed on down the line.

Finally, they came to Beau Albert. He whinnied loudly when he spotted Claire and gratefully took the lumps of sugar she had saved for him. When she had her back turned to Moses, she whispered her old greeting. *"Salut, mon vieux.*

Salut." Then she stroked his powerful neck. She scratched Albert just behind the ears in that place he loved, and the horse opened his mouth and stretched out his jaw in pleasure.

Then she took the knife from her sleeve and cut off a lock of Beau Albert's mane and placed it in the leather satchel at her belt. There were tears as she did this, for she did not know if she would see him again. Claire hated to leave him. She walked away from him backward, and horse and girl stared at each other for the longest time. His ears were cocked at her and she thought she saw worry in his eyes. Then she blew him a kiss and turned away.

Down the line, they found Tibeau. He, too, was pleased to see Claire. He had been causing a commotion on that picket, nipping at his neighbours and pawing the ground. It was several minutes before Claire managed to calm him. She even got a little stern with him, tapped him on the chest with the back of her hand and whispered into his ear, "*Fais pas ça! Don't do that!*" And, when he had settled, "*C'est ça, c'est ça. That's it.*" Tibeau got the same treatment as Albert—a few lumps of sugar, a lock of mane taken. For luck, and just in case.

Then Claire rubbed him all over with her hands. She massaged his nose, especially the edges of his nostrils, then found the ears and rubbed them, too. Down the neck to the breast, down the forearm to the knee, all the way down to the hoof. You can never, Ambrose often told her, rub a horse too much. Claire rubbed Tibeau's withers, the top of his back, his sides, the croup and the stifle, the hocks and the legs right down to the hooves. Then she went back to his eyes, those lovely brown eyes, and kissed them as he closed them.

It was as hard to walk away from those horses that night as it had been to climb into Tip Weldon's wagon and leave home.

As she and Moses walked back down the line in the growing
dark, she could hear Tibeau calling to her. She had to pretend
not to hear him, for Claire Vigere didn't exist down there by
the Tennessee River. There was only Clint Flynn and Moses
Odell, deaf boys hired on by the bluecoats as grooms.
Tomorrow the bluecoats would all cross that great wide river,
and come what may.

That night, as she tried to sleep, Claire could hear men talking
outside a tent nearby. They were talking about "forest," about
"gettin' that damned forest." It took her a while before she
realized they were talking about a man called Forrest. General
Nathan Bedford Forrest. He was the enemy the bluecoats
feared and wanted badly. The men talking outside the tent
that night spoke of him with both admiration and hatred.

The name Forrest ranked up there with Jackson and Grant
and Lee. Soldiers who claimed to have seen these famous men
were often accused of lying and would have to back their
claim with particulars of time and place. And almost as
famous as the generals themselves were the horses they rode.

Jackson rode Old Sorrel, though some called her Little Sorrel:
the mare was so tiny that the general's feet almost touched the
ground. William B. Bate rode a famously brave horse called
Black Hawk. Nathan Forrest himself rode King Philip. Jeb Stuart
rode a horse called Virginia, whose fame dated from the time
the horse leapt a huge ditch to save the general from capture.
Robert E. Lee rode a storied grey called Traveller, so famous that
even the sight of that horse cheered the men in grey.

On the northern side, everyone knew Rienzi, later known
as Winchester, the fast black horse ridden by General

Sheridan. Grant rode Cincinatti. Joseph Hooker rode the seventeen-hand-high Lookout. Philip Kearny rode a white mare called Moscow, and though he loved her, he finally agreed with his comrades that the horse made for too inviting a target on the battlefield and he switched to a bay horse called Decatur. George G. Meade rode Baldy.

It was considered an honour to have caught a glimpse of such men (or their horses), to have heard these men speak, or to have shaken their hands. Robert E. Lee, the great general of the South, was once asked to name the best soldier under his command. He named a man who had served him for a grand total of one month: Nathan Bedford Forrest.

Because the bummers included in their numbers both Union and Confederate soldiers, each side heard and spread stories of the other side's generals. And so it was that the men outside Claire's tent that night on the shores of the Tennessee River knew so much about the man who may have been the most brilliant cavalryman of the Civil War.

The men by that tent knew, for example, that just weeks beforehand, at Brice's Crossroads in northwestern Mississippi, Forrest had pulled off one of the great upsets of the war. When Forrest challenged the bluecoat general at the crossroads and surrounded the enemy on three sides, he was bluffing. The other general didn't know that Forrest was vastly outnumbered.

"That damned Forrest," one of the men said, then spat into the fire. "I wish he were with us, and not agin us."

With less than three thousand cavalry, Forrest had defeated a Union cavalry of eight thousand men and horses. Forrest did what he always did: he had his men ride hard and fast to either side of the enemy and then cut in from behind. He would divide and conquer. His men would ride to a battle zone, dismount and fight like infantry, then ride on again. Forrest would chase down a retreating army and demand from its general absolute and immediate surrender. Or, he'd say, "I'll put every man to the sword."

Forrest was a tall, black-haired man with hard grey eyes and a small, thin beard called a goatee. The beard formed a small, perfect triangle—the end pointing down—around his mouth and chin. Born in Tennessee, he had climbed out of poverty and made a fortune as a plantation owner and slave trader. When he joined the Confederate cavalry in 1861, he did so as a private. He would leave as a general, one still unable to read or write.

His motto was a simple one: "Get there first with the most men." The men around that campfire by the Tennessee River said he was fearless. One fellow had a long list of impressive numbers on Forrest and there was a hushed silence as he rattled them off. The soldier claimed to know the number of horses shot out from underneath Forrest: twenty-nine. The number of times Forrest had come under fire: one hundred and seventy-nine. And the number of prisoners Forrest had taken: thirty-one thousand.

But it was the prisoners he *didn't* take that made some northern generals so determined to capture Forrest. There were, among the regiments that had joined up with the 1st Massachusetts, several manned only by black soldiers. They were freed slaves, and they would march the next day into battle behind flags that read "Remember Fort Pillow."

Claire listened, fearful yet completely caught up in the tale. Could there ever have been, she asked herself, a place with the most unlikely name of Fort Pillow? But it seems there was. Forrest's cavalry had overrun black regiments at Fort Pillow just months beforehand, in April of 1864. After a day-long battle, the Union commander had refused to surrender, and Forrest had made good on his threat to "put every man to the sword." At some point he had called off the massacre, but only eighty of two hundred and sixty-two black soldiers survived. Word of what had happened at Fort Pillow spread, and now the black soldiers marching with the 1st Massachusetts wanted Forrest as badly as Sherman and Grant did.

"He ain't lost a battle yet," one man said to another, "and I reckon he's a hard man to beat." Claire heard the men speak of battles where Forrest had shone. Shiloh. Murfreesboro. Chickamauga. One soldier said he had read in a newspaper that General Sherman had called General Nathan Bedford Forrest "the very devil. There will never be peace in Tennessee till Forrest is dead." The North was still smarting over Forrest's daring raid on a Union supply depot in Tennessee in which six million dollars' worth of supplies had been taken.

Claire did not sleep that night. It was bad enough that she was about to face the elephant. But riding the elephant would be the devil himself.

CHAPTER 14

Crossing the River

Long before dawn, Claire felt the Sergeant shake her shoulder; she and Moses were put to work tacking up the officers' horses. Claire was busy laying on saddle pads, hoisting saddles into place, doing up girths, adjusting bridles. But her mind was elsewhere, with her precious black horses. Somewhere down the picket line were Beau Albert and Tibeau; there would be no second farewell.

Worry had robbed her of sleep during the night, stolen her appetite in the morning, and now worry ruled her day. The whole point of running away had been to be with her horses, but as far as Claire was concerned, they were a thousand miles away. There was nothing she could do to protect them, and the thought made her sick at heart.

The regiment, meanwhile, was preparing for battle. The first task was to send hundreds of men on horseback into the river, which ran to the south. They would swim with the current, let the Tennessee take them for a mile or so and then climb the river's west bank. Another group would ride north, alongside the river, and they, too, would find a point a mile upriver before crossing and climbing the opposite bank. Then both troops would ride back in the direction from which they had come. It was a classic pincer movement by Union generals tired of being outflanked by Forrest. This time they would outflank the outflanker.

Next, the northern army would put many more hundreds of men into the trees all along the east side of the river. They were snipers, crack shots with the eyes of hawks. "Sharpshooters," as they were called, were much feared in the Civil War. You could be enjoying a cup of coffee well behind the fighting and a good man with a rifle half a mile away could end your days.

The problem with the battle plan, as the Sergeant saw it—and he complained to himself as he tacked up his horse—was that the only easy way across the river was over one covered bridge. McDermott's nightmare, the scenario he feared most, was that if Forrest were to put the run on the bluecoats, they would all bottleneck at that bridge. Or they would have to enter the river and swim back across, and the snipers in grey would pick them off "like partridge in a Sunday hunt," as the Sergeant put it. If that came to pass, it was hoped that Union sharpshooters would keep Confederate snipers at bay and cover any retreat.

Before he mounted his horse, the Sergeant wrote down some last-minute instructions for Moses and Claire. He numbered them.

1. Stay down for chrisakes.
2. Stay put.
3. If the Rebs com, get on yr horses and ride hard to the east. OK?

Then he looked the two of them in the eye for what seemed a long time. Claire thought she could see a wetness in his eyes, but then he quickly lowered them, gave each of them a mighty hug (Claire gasped at the strength of it and Moses made a *ffffffffffffffff* sound, as if air had been forced from his belly). McDermott did not look back as he rode smartly towards the covered bridge.

The 1st Massachusetts and their companion regiments were an impressive sight as they filed towards that bridge. All those bayonets of the marching men glinting in the early sun. The horses snorting, keenly aware of the tension all around them. The thunder as the guns and carriages rumbled across. The *brrrrrrrruump brrrrrrrruump brrrrrrrruump* of the drummer boys' beat as they marched west. If Forrest and his men were watching, they made no attempt to halt the army's progress. Claire wondered if the Sergeant wasn't right: the bridge seemed tiny and narrow for such a great mass of men and horses and artillery.

Moses had his horse, Jacob, saddled and tied to a tree nearby. Claire, likewise, had Minonette ready to fly if need be. There was nothing to be done now but wait and pray.

⸻

Claire was with Moses and they were tucked in behind a log, as they had been for hours. Now and again, like shy wild turkeys, one would brave a peek at the other side of the river. Smoke, thick and grey and black, was drifting across the water, riding the west wind. Off in the distance you could hear cannon fire and a wild sound that, had she not known better, Claire would have taken for an impossible mix of sounds— migrating geese, barking dogs, blacksmiths' hammers. Enough geese to blacken a sky, dogs in packs beyond counting, every blacksmith in the world hammering at once in the same place. What Claire was hearing was the sound of two armies clashing, and it was hard to know whether that awful sound was moving away or coming closer. Then came a voice from behind her, and she knew right away whose it was.

"Hey little darlin'. Ain't ya glad to see me?"

Claire gave Moses a tap on the shoulder, then pointed behind her. Huntley stood about twenty feet away, his handgun casually drawn and pointing down just a little. She had never caught more than a glimpse of him, and now Claire had to take him all in. She was drawn first to those green eyes of his. They were striking, but cold as the sea.

"Don't pretend ya cain't hear. I know damn well ya ain't deaf, and I know as well you ain't no boy neither. Now turn around, real slow."

Huntley still wore the red kerchief around his neck. He still had yellow-brown tobacco stains at his moustache and beard, stains Claire had noticed when Huntley had lifted the lid of the wagon and almost discovered her. Huntley's nose, thanks in part to Albert's buck and the Sergeant's fists, was flat and thick and bent. It was a boxer's nose, and none too pretty. He wore a wide-brimmed hat, a loose jacket down to his hips and pants that rode high up above ankle level. Her brothers would have called them "high-water pants," and they would have laughed to themselves about them in private. But there was nothing funny about Huntley.

"Tell your Negro pal," said Huntley, "to take his knife from his boot and put it on the ground. You do the same." Claire turned to Moses and made the sign for *knife*—her index finger making a slicing motion—and then pointed to the

soft black earth. Claire laid her knife down gently but Moses
drove his blade into the dirt in a show of temper.

"My oh my, ain't he a wildcat?" said Huntley.

"Don't you hurt him!" Claire said. She was already aware
of Moses staring at her, open-mouthed. He would have seen
Huntley moving his lips and had already put two and two
together. Unless Clint was suddenly able to read lips, Moses
would be thinking to himself, his "deaf" friend could hear.
And just now his friend had moved his lips, so Clint could
speak, too! *Please forgive me,* she signed to him, begging with
her eyes that he understand something beyond understanding.
Claire would explain it all to him later. If there was a later.

"Tie up your pal," Huntley said to her, and he threw her a
rope. "Around that tree, nice and tight."

Claire led Moses to the chestnut tree Huntley had pointed
out and tied him to it, the rope around his shins, his waist and
his neck. Her heart was pounding and there was a lot going
on in her head. She could sense how betrayed Moses felt, and
her own sadness and fear were welling up within her. Claire
tied him up, but she had the presence of mind to leave the
ropes looser than she had been told.

"Turn around, little darlin', if you please," said Huntley, all
charm, as if he were asking her politely to whistle his favourite
tune. Claire had her back to the river and Huntley was a little
to her right, so she could see both Huntley and Moses.

"You feel warm, darlin'?" asked Huntley. "Bet you'd feel
better if you unbuttoned that heavy coat of yours. Take off
that hat while you're at it." He still had the gun levelled at
her. There was a faint smile on his lips. "Too bad you don't
have a horse you could ride bareback into that river. Them
other boys over on the other side would like a peek at your

fine flesh too." The smile grew wider now, revealing yellow and crooked teeth.

Claire tossed her hat and was starting on the top buttons of her coat. Huntley had never ever left her thoughts, and through all those sleepless nights she had tried to imagine how she might defend herself against him. She had hoped the knife might help; if she could get in the first blow, it might give her time to run. Find a fast horse, leave her stalker far behind. But no, she couldn't abandon Moses.

She had one other option. She had thought of it one night when she was staring into the dark. *If "deafness" has helped me get this far, maybe "blindness" will save me.* But not her blindness, Huntley's. Ever since that sleepless night, Claire had kept a fistful of sand in both front pockets of her blue coat. Huntley, when he finally chose his moment, would be full of his own power. He would not anticipate her throwing sand in his face. The element of surprise would be on her side.

The moment she had heard Huntley's voice as she lay behind that log, Claire acted on her instinct to grab a handful of that good black earth from the banks of the Tennessee. He would have seen only her clenched right fist and taken it as a sign of her fear. Now, as she started to undo the buttons of her coat, using only her left hand, she advanced on Huntley. This seemed to please him. He liked to intimidate and he was used to being obeyed—by men, by horses, by girls and women. When she was five feet from Huntley, Claire caught sight of Moses. He had freed his hands from the ropes. His eyes were desperately seeking hers and he was giving her—as frantically as he could—a sign. Left hand back at his shoulder, elbow out; right hand moving up and down rapidly between that hand and that elbow: *Drop down! Drop down!*

Claire trusted Moses, trusted him with her life. All in one motion, she tossed the fine black earth at Huntley's eyes then dropped onto her belly, as if cuffed from behind. Huntley was, for the moment, blinded and astonished and angered. Claire reached into her left pocket and tossed more sand up in his face, then dipped into the other pocket and hit him with a third volley. Huntley threw up his hands, squinted his eyes shut and shook his head violently. He spat out dirt and began to speak.

"What the hell ya doin' ya little—?"

They were his last words. A bullet caught him in the chest and drove him backward and down on his back. Moses would later explain that he had seen movement in the trees across the river, saw the sun glint on a rifle barrel and figured a sharpshooter was making ready.

Now snipers on both sides of the river were looking for tell-tale smoke on the other side and aiming at its maker. The war, whose awful bark had seemed so far away, was suddenly here.

Claire now moved like a frightened deer. She grabbed the knives on the ground, cut Moses loose and took the pistol from the right hand of Huntley. Then she removed his holster, slid it onto her own belt and laid in the gun. She was shocked by the weight of it and hoped she would never have to use it. Claire stared down at Huntley: the man would go to his grave wearing a look of bewilderment.

Moses started madly to sign, wanting answers. Claire just kissed him on his right cheek, then on the left, in the French manner, and started to sign a quick explanation. *I'm not a boy* ... (her palm over her eyes, like an Indian scout). *I'm not deaf* ... (her hand pointed to the mouth and the ear). She was about to go further but the sharpshooters' bullets were taking down oak leaves all around them.

Moses and Claire grabbed Jacob and Minonette and tied them to trees deeper in the woods and beyond the sightline of the snipers. Then they crawled back to the log and waited to see who would come across that covered bridge. Would it be the 1st Massachusetts, moving proud and slow, flush with victory? Would it be their tattered remnants, fleeing from Nathan Bedford Forrest? Or would it be Forrest himself, his eyes fixed on the Union supply wagons on this side of the river and any bluecoat in his path?

Now there came the crack of rifles, not the occasional work of snipers, but the greater sound of guns firing in succession and unison. Smoke as thick as fog settled over the Tennessee River, making it impossible to see. "Blow, you wind, blow!" screamed Claire. They were the first loud words she had spoken since leaving the village that lay almost a thousand miles behind her.

Moses couldn't stop staring. The boy beside him—but no, he wasn't a boy, he was a girl—he, that is, she, had her mouth wide open and she was saying something. Even in the silence that Moses lived in every moment of his life, he could feel the energy she was devoting to her cry.

Claire, strange to say, found his look faintly amusing. She tapped Moses on the shoulder, long the gesture they had used to keep the other loose and not too serious, no matter what. Her signs came in a flurry. *Blow!*—her hand moved out from her mouth, as if riding a jet of air. *Wind!*—both hands before her, fingers spread wide, swaying quickly back and forth in unison, while her cheeks puffed up and she expelled air.

Had he been there, Ambrose would have said that Moses and Claire were punch-drunk. It is what tension sometimes turns to: silliness. And so Claire kept on screaming, "Blow, wind, blow!" And Moses joined her, watching her mouth and making the same shapes with his. From his mouth came a kind of joyful groan, timed to coincide with Claire's crazed pleading for a wind to blow away the smoke.

The snipers in the trees must have been stunned into silence. On both sides, they listened and could not believe their ears. A girl was calling for wind. And that other sound—what was that? Some animal, an ally of hers? The two of them were singing a crazed hymn to the west wind.

Years later, when Claire told the whole story—running away from home, hiding in the wagon, masquerading as a deaf boy, the war itself—no one had trouble with any of her tale. *This* was the one part no one would believe. That when she lay behind the log with Moses, the two of them, each in a different way, calling on the gods for help, the gods replied.

The trees overhead began to stir, the leaves to tremble. It was not just a gust of wind, it was more like what remained of a good honest blow from some western state. As if a wind from Wyoming, say, were passing by and heard Claire's call. The wind had about as much energy as a tired old horse being asked for a trot by a boy lacking skill or manners. The trot the horse gives him is slow and resentful, but the horse is generous in his way and it's a trot nonetheless. That was what the wind was like that warm day, the last day in June of 1864, on the banks of the Tennessee. It was just enough to clear some smoke and give two young grooms what they were calling for: a view of the covered bridge.

The wind did its work and the grey-black smoke drifted across the river like angry clouds warning of storms to come. Claire and Moses watched from behind that log for what seemed like many hours, and their hunger and thirst began to build as the light of day began to fade.

Moses tapped Claire, then made a motion with his hands at his mouth, the four fingers tapping repeatedly against the thumb like a talkative clam. *Let's eat,* he was saying. He had in mind to crawl on his belly back towards one of the supply wagons and get some food and water.

It was then that the covered bridge offered its first returns. Claire heard the sound of a horse galloping, that familiar beat—two-and-one, two-and-one, two-and-one—the hooves echoing in the chamber. He was a handsome grey gelding, an officer's horse. No sign of the rider. He was back there, thought Claire, either fighting on the ground with sword and pistol, or fallen. There was blood on the saddle, but the horse seemed otherwise unharmed. He emerged from the east side of the bridge and went straight to the picket line, what passed for home to a horse in war.

Then more horses came, some nowhere as neat and tidy as the grey. Some came in a flurry, crazed from whatever they had experienced back there where the smoke and the noise were thickest. Some bore awful wounds where lead and steel had done their work; some were lame and crippled; some were not long for this world. They came in waves, mules and heavy horses dragging their leather traces, troopers' mounts with their reins loose about them. It was a cruel parade, nothing like the one that had left in the morning with such promise of glory.

Now there came men on horseback, some tilted forward or backward in the saddle. The wounded, the half-dead, the men without sense of where they were, of why or when. They rode with whatever energy they possessed, which was precious little. They rode from memory, the setting sun at their backs.

Some riders would get as far as the east side of the bridge and then pitch forward and out of the saddle. Surgeons and their helpers were hauling such men into huge canvas tents, crude hospitals where the wounded and the dead and the dying lay on blood-soaked cots.

Finally, men on foot began to come back. Some men had converted their rifles into stretcher poles and laid sacks between them to carry the wounded. Some men limped forward, one arm slung over the shoulder of a fellow soldier. Some, apparently unhurt, walked with head bent low and one hand grasping the belt of the soldier beside them. They had seen the elephant and they would never see again. Many wore white bandages wrapped around their heads, hands, arms, legs, but the red beneath inevitably showed through. Some men walked as if in no hurry at all. The battle had taken the hurry right out of them and replaced it with something else. Claire looked at those soldiers and saw men who did not much care whether they breathed or not.

And still, riderless horses came pounding across that bridge. They, too, seemed to have lost all sense and would sometimes mow down men in their way. The noise of panicked horses was added to all the other noises: the shouting of officers trying to regroup their men, the sharpshooters on both sides of the river resuming their murderous work, the unholy racket inside the covered bridge as the 1st Massachusetts and its sister regiments hobbled home.

Claire kept looking for familiar faces as darkness fell and the bridge spewed out its last contents. Where was Sergeant McDermott? What about Captain Dilger on Beau Albert? And Major Huey on Tibeau? Claire could not pick them out. Maybe she had missed them? Maybe they fought on somewhere beyond the hills, a pocket of resistance to the west? Maybe they were gone?

Traffic was thinning out, just stragglers now. Claire had not given up hope entirely, but the situation looked grim. Only a faint light remained, and there was little to fear from the sharpshooters. She motioned to Moses and they both walked towards their tent, picked up their satchels full of veterinary supplies and continued towards the picket lines. Their own bellies would wait while they attended to the poor horses.

There were buckets of water to be filled; there was just enough light that Claire could go down to the river without using a torch, which would have offered an inviting target to the snipers. Some horses, at least, could still be saved. Their wounds would need cleansing and stitching; they would need a kind word and a bit of hay if some was left. Claire could talk to the horses now and she took comfort in that. But only a little. She was a runaway, and a runaway can often only count on a few people. The Sergeant had been one. Moses, of course. But Albert and Tibeau had been central characters in this little play of hers, and now they were gone. Claire could not bear the thought of them fallen in the mud of a battlefield.

She imagined them like this: riderless, running off into the hills and finding shelter in the woods far from the roar of the guns. The two horses were a pair again, they were free and away from the madness. Maybe a kind soul would find them up there, maybe a girl her age who would appreciate them, cherish them, discover the places they liked to have scratched.

This is what Claire dreamed of as she made repeated trips to the river for buckets of water. It was a hollow fantasy, and she knew it, but she embraced it like a child with a make-believe friend.

Just then, a whole new wave of bluecoats began tearing across the river. This one seemed a more orderly bunch, though it had its share of wounded and sad-eyed men riding wagons. Claire could hear Captain Dilger, in that distinctive German accent of his, shouting orders from somewhere on the hill on the other side of the river. Her heart leapt at that sound, for if the Captain had made it back, maybe Albert had as well.

Then came infantry, not marching and not running, but hurrying across with their dignity intact. Artillery pieces followed, dozens strong. Claire thought she saw a strange sight—the Sergeant riding one of the heavy horses hauling cannon. It made no sense. But as the carriage emerged from the covered bridge, she was sure it was him. His right hand was heavily bandaged, and even in the darkness she could see the stain of blood. One of the last men to head into the covered bridge was Major Huey, and this time there was no doubt in Claire's mind. Tibeau was calling out to Albert, no doubt angry and worried at being left behind, and she caught the flash of his white hind sock.

"*Dieu, merci,*" Claire spoke into the waters of the river. She ran up the bank as fast as her legs would take her.

Claire was a while sorting out how the men and horses she cared for had fared in the battle. There was a longer version of the battle to be told, but that would have to wait for another time. The casualty list went like this.

Sergeant McDermott. Alive, but his right hand had been hacked by a sword and the surgeons had told him they would have to sever it or he would almost certainly die. But the

Sergeant had seen too many soldiers lose limbs to surgeons, get their stubs tied up neatly in thread and be buried a few days later. "I'm keepin' ma damn hand," he said, and stormed out of the surgeons' tent. He was white with shock, but grim with determination, too. The Sergeant was a tough man and he treated the pain of his hand almost casually. It was then that he saw Clint and embraced him.

The Sergeant made a motion with his hand, as if to write something down. *Get your pad,* he was saying to Clint. He was going to issue instructions to the boy, for the Sergeant had an idea that he hoped might save his own hand. It would take longer to write with his left hand, but he would manage all right.

"No need for a pad," Claire told him.

McDermott looked at Claire as though he had seen a ghost.

"It's a long story, Sarge," she said, using the name the soldiers often used with him. "And some day I'll tell you everything. I am not Clint. My real name is Claire Vigere and I'm a runaway girl from north of the border. I followed Black Bull and Lightning all the way down here."

"Well I'll be pitchforked," he said. Then he managed a smile. "Had *me* fooled." He said her name aloud, rolling it around on his tongue, like some new flavour of candy he would have to get used to. "Claire, what was it, *Vee-chair?*"

"Vigere," Claire corrected him. "What about your hand, Sarge? How can I help?"

"Okay," he replied, all business now. "Go down to the river, get a bucket of water. Boil it on the fire real good and put about five handfuls of salt in the water. My grandma used to treat bad cuts this way. You dunk your wound in salt water, hot as ya can stand it, for as long as ya can stand it. And you pray, also for as long as ya can stand it."

Claire did as she was told. Later, it hurt her to watch McDermott drop that bloodied hand into the kettle. He had put a small oak branch in his mouth and bit down on it. He was too proud to scream but you could see the pain written on his face.

As for Captain Dilger, he had taken a bullet in the left arm. But the round lead slug had mercifully passed through without doing too much damage. The bones had been spared. In time, the surgeons said, he would likely be fine.

Major Huey had no wounds, none that anyone could see on his body. Yet no one could get a word out of him. He just stared into the fire and hummed a tune. This was what battle did to some men. It broke them in some terrible way, and many never managed the task of rebuilding. The Major still wore his hat, the one pinned up at the side with the black feather. It was a warrior's hat but the warrior was no more. For Major Huey, the Civil War was over.

Beau Albert was fine. When Claire gave the Captain the same short version of the Clint/Claire story as the Sergeant got (she would tell it several times that night, and eventually it made the rounds of what remained of the camp), he seemed not shocked at all. "Amerika," he told her, "is zo full of surprise." And when Claire asked Captain Dilger how Albert had been in battle, he got so excited he began speaking in rapid-fire German. One word he kept repeating was *"spitze"* (it would have sounded to Claire like *spit-zah,* and it means *excellent*). Whatever he was saying, it was praise. Of that, at least, Claire was sure. That, and the fact that Albert had no wounds save for a small cut on his forehead.

Tibeau had likewise emerged from the day of fighting with

no apparent wounds, though he was as wide-eyed as Claire had ever seen him. She stroked his chest and gave him lumps of sugar. "I guess you saw some chipmunks, didn't you?" she asked him. By his look and high carriage, she supposed that he had seen a great many of them throughout the day-long battle.

When she got back to the campfire, where the Sergeant was still soaking his hand, Claire noticed that McDermott and Captain Dilger were deep in conversation. The Captain's left arm was in a sling, the Sergeant's right hand was in water. Their heads were together, and anyone looking on might have guessed they were discussing their wounds. But when Claire arrived, they both looked at her. As if they had been talking about her.

"Clint," the Sergeant began. "I mean, Claire. Find Moses. We got jobs for you two."

Claire located Moses down along the picket line. A mule had been separated from the grey, the high, handsome horse who was the first to return from battle. The two friends were both kicking up a fuss, and as soon as Moses paired them on the picket line, order was restored. Now Claire led him back to the fire.

"Claire," the Sergeant began, "I'll explain to you and you can get the same message across to Moses later on. Okay? We're in a pickle here. The Captain is all that's left of our offi-cers. Rest are back there," and he pointed across the river. "Wounded, dead, captured. We don't know. Now, we're pretty sure we stung that Nathan Bedford Forrest pretty good today, but he may come again. Maybe across that bridge. We can hold him off for a while, but we don't want him gettin' into our supply wagons. We got a lot of ammunition in them wagons. We need someone to ride east about fifty miles to Lawrenceburg. Light riders to go that distance—as quick as Jack Be Nimble. You and Moses up for that?"

The Captain looked at her expectantly while she quickly signed the same message to Moses. Claire had no idea who Jack Be Nimble was, but she was up for the ride. Moses, too, nodded immediately.

"When do we leave?" Claire asked.

"Before ze dawn," Captain Dilger replied. "Unt you vill bose carry ze zame dizpatch, neh?"

Claire looked to the Sergeant for help in translation.

"Look," said McDermott, who had to gesture with his left hand, because the right hand was still immersed in the hot, salted water. "I ain't gonna lie to you. It's dangerous. The roads could be crawlin' with Rebs. But it's just as dangerous to stay here with us. Both you and Moses will carry the same letter from Captain Dilger to the commanding officer at Lawrenceburg. If somethin' happens to you ..." and he paused here and bit his lip, "maybe Moses gets through. Or if Moses don't make it, we hope you do. 'Course we think you're both gettin' through. We want you to ride Lightning, and we'll put Moses up on Black Bull. Ya both leave before dawn."

"Sarge," said Claire, "we'll fly down that road. But I have to tell you one thing."

"What's that?" McDermott asked, suddenly worried that the day had brought yet another thing. One more *damned* thing.

"Black Bull," she said with a smile, "is not Black Bull. He is ..." She wanted to say Beau Albert in the French way, so it sounded like *Bo Al-bear,* but she was worried that this little bit of French might be too much for the Sergeant. So she said, "His name is Good Albert," and she pronounced the hard *T* at the end, as the English did. "As for Lightning, his name is ..."

Oh dear, she thought, *same problem.* Tibeau was perhaps also too hard for the Sergeant. It would come out sounding hard and dull, like *Tee-bo.* That was close but not close enough for Claire, who was very very fussy when it came to saying the names of her horses. The *Tee* in Tibeau was long, the *bo* was short and clipped. It would have to be said just so, or Claire would be disappointed. She thought about Little Beau, rejected that, and finally settled on the following.

"... Little Albert."

The Sergeant looked confused by all this, as did the Captain. Both thought Black Bull and Lightning were two fine names for two fine horses, certainly a lot finer than Good Albert and Little Albert. Those were the names of milkwagon horses. But this girl had come a thousand miles for these two horses and McDermott was not about to argue with her. Their very lives now depended on her.

"Claire," said the Sergeant, breaking into a smile, "ya can call them horses whatever ya damn well please. Fine by us. You two just be on yer high horses 'fore the crack o' dawn."

———

There was much to do before Claire would allow herself a few hours of sleep. She had to pack what she would need, she had some medical advice for the Sergeant, she had to write a letter home, and she had to make things right with Moses. It was that last item she tackled first.

The girl hoped that her eyes would communicate as well as her hands. Claire told Moses about her family back in

L'Ange-Gardien, about Tip Weldon and the sale of Tibeau
and Beau Albert. She described her journey in the wagon,
the horses' brush with Huntley, her hope that masquerading
as a deaf boy would get her into the Union army. Moses
understood everything she said, and more, and he especially
liked the moment in the story when Albert tossed Huntley
through the fence.

Forgive me? she asked of Moses. Again, Claire made the
sign of forgiveness, her two hands washing away imagined
dirt.

Maybe, he signed, his right hand turning on its wrist, up
and down. But he was smiling as he made the sign, and Claire
cuffed him on the head knowing full well that he was teasing
her.

Then she packed her satchel. Two canteens of water, a half
loaf of bread, some slices of salted pork, hardtack biscuits and
a small tin of chocolate that the Sergeant had miraculously
found for her. Moses packed a similar bag, then the two of
them located Albert and Tibeau and gave them as much grain
as they could safely devour. Claire had a keen sense for what
amount was right. Too little grain and they risked their horses
running out of fuel; too much and they would be riding
bloated pumpkins in a race where speed and stamina counted
for everything.

At one point, Claire tapped Moses on the shoulder and
then pointed to Beau Albert. *Trust him,* she signed to Moses.
(Her hands closed tightly around an invisible object.) Then
she signed further: *He will jump anything you ask him to. Just
grab his mane and hold on.*

Claire was clearly worried about Moses. He had become a
decent rider, but she had no idea what lay between the river

and Lawrenceburg and whether Moses was ready for a mad dash of fifty miles. On the other hand, she told herself, Albert would look after him. She hoped so.

———∞∞∞———

Later, the Sergeant had a question for Claire. "Where'd ya get that gun?" he wanted to know as he gave Claire the letter from Captain Dilger and glanced at her waist. Claire had to explain about Huntley. McDermott only nodded in response, though one eyebrow arched as she told the tale. There was more than met the eye, the Sergeant was thinking, to this Claire Vigere.

The Sergeant carefully removed the gun from its holster and gave its new owner a quick lesson in its use. Claire had never held a gun in her life and she hoped she would never have to use it.

"Do you mind," asked Claire, "if I see your hand?"

McDermott was about to drop his hand into a hot kettle for another round of cleansing. He held up his poor paw, still swollen from the sabre cut. The wound ran across the top of his right hand, from the thumb all the way back to the wrist. The cut was deep but the flesh looked clean, almost bleached.

"I was wondering," said Claire, "if someone shouldn't sew up that wound. It looks good right now. I've doctored horses with worse than that. What do you say?"

Claire wanted to pay the Sergeant back in some way for all he had done for Clint, the deaf boy he had taken in almost like a son. And McDermott seemed instinctively to understand her need. When he nodded, Claire reached into her satchel and produced a needle and thick black thread, which she then dropped into the boiling water.

Maybe McDermott's grandma was like her own grand-mother: maybe she knew a thing or two. Claire waited till she thought the needle and thread were boiled free of any impurities, then she tossed the water and let her instruments cool.

"This might tickle," she warned the Sergeant.

"Get on with it," he said, and did *not* look away as some might have. He took a real interest in Claire's stitching and even admired her work aloud. "Damn fine!" he said, though he had her redo the final stitch—said it was off "just a titch." If he felt any pain, he ignored it. When the sewing was done, Claire once more reached into her satchel and found a small jar of ointment, as yellow as the morning sun. "It's my grand-father's recipe," she explained before gently applying the stuff on and all around the stitching. "I figure," said Claire, "what works for horses will work for grumpy old soldiers, too."

"Let's hope," said McDermott. Then he looked her in the eye, and, with his eyes alone, sent her his thanks.

———

Finally, there was the letter home. Claire thought of all the soldiers who had sat around campfires the night before the battle writing letters. Many of those soldiers were across the river now, captured, or "fallen" as the war memorials would later describe them. The letters they wrote would offer their wives and sweethearts, family and friends, one final contact.

Claire was keenly aware of that fact as she set out to write her letter home. She got out the Krieghoff book and flipped the pages for several minutes before finally settling on a paint-ing called *Shooting the Rapids*. It showed someone, an Indian most likely, running whitewater rapids in an empty canoe. Claire guessed that the man had earlier portaged his gear downriver so nothing would be lost if he tipped. The painter had chosen early fall to paint his scene, for the trees were dappled in reds and yellows. But the overwhelming sense was of the speed of that river, and the tension in the man's body as he tried to control his canoe. He looked to be flying down that river, or maybe the wind was in his face, for his hair was streaming behind him.

Claire ripped the painting from the book, and wrote this note.

> *Dear family:*
>
> *I'm coming home soon, at least, I hope so. You should know that I am in the company of horses I adore. I am happy, I eat well. It saddens, me, though, to think that I am the cause of your pain. I pray you can forgive me. And if I have forgotten to say it before now, I say it now. I love you all, every one of you, very much.*
>
> *Claire*

Claire gave the letter to McDermott and asked him to drop it in the regimental mailbag, but he gave it right back to her.

"Mail service is better out of Lawrenceburg," he said. "It's kinda slow here by the Tennessee River. And if the Rebs ever get a hold of ya, they'll be a while figurin' out yer letter home, in French and all. They'll be scratchin' their heads, thinkin' yer a spy and the French is some kinda code."

Then he got serious again. "Good luck, Claire," he said. "I'm guessin' Nathan Bedford Forrest will figure we'll send riders to Lawrenceburg for help, and he will send his quickest horses to try and intercept you two somewhere along the

road. And even if he don't, there might be Rebs on that road
anyway. All I can tell ya is, you might be in a horse race and
not know it. So ride like the wind, okay? And don't worry,
you can't get lost. The road leads straight into town."

Then he turned to Moses, got out a pad and wrote,
"Moses, don't fall off yer dam horse, OK?" Moses laughed
and gave the Sergeant the thumbs-up. McDermott thought
that Moses looked game for this adventure, but he could see
worry on that face, too. As for Claire, she looked like a jockey
riding the favourite on a Kentucky racetrack—she looked
calm, happy, even cocky.

McDermott rubbed the head of each horse, then stepped
aside. And they were off. The two riders galloped down the
road, Tibeau in the lead with Albert right on his tail, heading
east towards the rising sun.

"Godspeed," he said to himself as Moses and Claire, Beau
Albert and Tibeau disappeared from view. They were the
words his grandmother—the one who cleansed wounds in salt
water—had always said when he left her home in Vermont.
"Godspeed," that old blessing bestowed on travellers, was
often heard in Vermont, just as it was in Canada East—right
across the border. Ambrose Vigere used it, and so did Gramma
McDermott.

The Sergeant listened keenly to the thunder of hooves and
he hoped he would hear that same thunder again very soon.
Then he went to his tent and selected his rifle, the one with *DM*
carved into the wooden stock, from the tripod of rifles stacked
by the entrance. He joined the other men tucked in behind logs
and rocks on the banks of the Tennessee, waiting to see what
the day—and Nathan Bedford Forrest—would bring.

CHAPTER 15

Godspeed

Every now and then, Claire would look back to make sure Moses and Albert were still there. Tibeau, too, would sometimes look back at Claire as if to say, *You still with me?* "*Me voici,*" she would reply. "I'm still here, don't you worry." Tibeau was enjoying himself and had settled into that long, rolling gallop of his. He was eating up the miles on the dusty road to Lawrenceburg.

Though not built for the sprint, Albert was too proud to be left behind. He was not about to let this sassy young colt get away from him. For miles, they flew along the road at an easy clip, the taller black horse in the lead, his wider black sire right on his tail.

The two young blue-coated riders had put their hats in their pockets, safe from the wind of their own making. Moses was copying Claire, seat just out of the saddle, hunched over the horse's neck like a jockey, the wind in his eyes, hands pumping in rhythm with the horse's head. The sun had risen over the trees, the air was clear and cool, and they were well on their way. It seemed a great adventure, and whenever Claire looked back at Moses, he wore the same smile she did. Had there

243

been no Rebs, no danger, no war, this would have been a perfect ride.

Claire had to resist the temptation to forget about danger, to relax her vigilance. She lived for gallops like this. The road was straight and flat, the surface good and, so far, to be trusted. Claire loved how Tibeau flowed, how his black mane rose and fell, rose and fell. How his head dipped forward in rhythm, how he would periodically change his leads and find new energy from that simple act. Sometimes she would look over the side just for the thrill of seeing his legs in a black blur.

And she would talk to him: *"C'est ça, mon vieux. C'est ça."*

But this was no Saturday morning ride. This was a dash to save their lives, and the lives of McDermott and all the men back at the river. This was also a test of Claire's horsemanship. She would have to make critical decisions about pace, when and where to rest, for how long.

As they sped along the road, Claire thought of Ambrose. "Listen to your horse," he would say. "He has a voice too."

Tibeau was still fairly fresh half an hour into their dash, but Claire could see that Albert was starting to labour. They had eased off the pace, from slow gallop to slow canter. But Albert's eyes had gone a little wide, his head was dipping lower as he strained to keep up with Tibeau. Had Claire asked both horses to trot all day, she knew who would have won that battle—the gelding, hands down. But this was a sprint, and Tibeau had the long legs and the wind, the youth and the blood for it.

Claire made a sign to Moses to slow down. They went into a trot, and, after a bit, a walk. Even Tibeau seemed grateful for the chance to catch his breath. The maximum speed of a racehorse is about forty miles an hour (though the Quarter horse can hit fifty miles an hour), and had the two horses been able to maintain that kind of speed, they would have been at Lawrenceburg in under two hours. But, of course, no horse on earth could maintain such a pace.

Claire knew that a fit horse could go thirty miles day after day—mostly in a walk, with lots of trotting and some cantering. Clearly, she was asking a lot of her horses. Going too slow might mean that help would come too late to save McDermott and the men who remained of the 1st Massachusetts and the other regiments. Going too fast risked her horses coming up lame, or worse.

The horses were walking alongside each other now, no more than a foot apart. Both were fit, though there was a white lather showing clearly on the black skin of their shoulders, and both were wet from their long gallop. Claire was of a mind to keep them in this brisk walk for at least another ten minutes while they gathered their strength.

She caught the eye of Moses. Claire gave him the thumbs-up, but raised her eyebrows at the same time. *You okay?* she was asking him. He gave her the same sign in return, but Claire could see fatigue in his eyes. Even their long march south and many days in the saddle had not prepared them for sprints like these. The strain on the legs and back from riding up off the saddle would challenge any rider, and Moses had nowhere near Claire's time and miles on horseback. Even Claire felt a bit rubbery in her legs.

And then she remembered the locket. She had almost forgotten it, the little insurance she had brought—to be used if necessary. Moses looked as though he badly needed a boost, so Claire reached into her pocket and felt the smooth maple wood of the locket that Ambrose had made her years ago. The one he had filled with frog bones to teach her the lesson that horsemanship lay in her hands and not in charms. Claire legged Tibeau closer to Albert and handed Moses the wooden locket with the leather string looped through.

Put it around your neck, she signed to him. *It's a gift from my grandfather and it will bring anyone who wears it good luck and strength on a horse.*

Moses looked pleased, even grateful. His own grandfather had taught him to put faith in charms and potions, and he accepted—immediately and without reservation—the magical powers of the locket. He solemnly placed it around his neck, and immediately his back got straighter. Then the two riders set their horses into a lively trot and pressed on.

The road to Lawrenceburg was a desolate stretch, and what few farms they saw along the way were either abandoned or burnt out. On the sides of the road, here and there, were fortifications. Claire could see where the Rebels had dug in behind walls of felled trees, the spaces between and around them filled in with earth and mud. "This country is one big fort," the Sergeant used to say as they'd made their way south.

They were rounding a long bend in the road when both horses raised their heads a little. Moses seemed not to notice the change in their manner, but Claire certainly did. She did not like the quiet that had fallen over the thick undergrowth and forest on either side, as if the birds had fled the scene or been stilled into silence. As they walked on, she noticed, too, that on either side of the road, brush and twigs and branches had been piled high—too high for a horse to leap, too thick to charge through. Claire felt they were being watched, and every bone in her body was saying, *This is a trap! Go back and go around this stretch.* It was while she was deciding whether or not to heed this advice that Claire saw it. That thing, a hundred yards down the road, that now blocked their path.

It was what soldiers in the Civil War on both sides called a *"chevaux-de-frise."* Literally, the French words meant "horses of Friesland." The Sergeant had spent the better part of one evening back in Pennsylvania explaining to Clint and to Moses—by illustration and words on the pad—what a *chevaux-de-frise* was and where it came from. It seemed that in 1594, an army had laid siege to a town called Groningen in the Dutch province of Friesland. (Claire's interest had perked up when she saw the Sergeant write down "Friesland," for she knew that the first horses to come to New France in the mid-seventeenth century had Friesian blood in them.) The town of Groningen had no cavalry in 1594, so its defenders made something out of wood meant to stop horses.

Imagine a log, maybe a foot thick and ninety feet long. Now imagine carpenters hand-drilling holes in that log—holes as wide as your hand and a foot apart. Into those holes, they would drop eight-foot-long poles sharpened like pencils at both ends. Someone looking from the side would have seen a long row of interlocking X-shaped spikes. A horse coming upon such a thing would have seen a long row of spears rising five feet into the air and pointed at his heart. A horse attempting to leap the menacing obstacle would first have to manage the five-foot height, and then the six-foot expanse between the two rows of spikes. And if the first row of spikes did not grab the brave or foolhardy horse, the second row surely would. Most horses, of course, refused to go near the thing. The *chevaux-de-frise* would later give way to its modern counterpart: barbed wire.

And while the *chevaux-de-frise* could always be burned or removed, any soldiers attempting to destroy the barrier came under fire from defending soldiers. The barrier was more of a nuisance than anything; it was a stalling tactic, and variations of the *chevaux-de-frise* had been used in war for many centuries. Attackers having to deal with barriers like this would have had to endure through the ages a terrible rain— first from spears and arrows, then from pistols and rifles, and later from cannon and machine guns.

Claire had looked at the Sergeant's crude drawing of a *chevaux-de-frise* that night by the fire and likened it to a cruel comb. Now one of those cruel combs lay on the road, as wide as the road, and the brush on either side meant there was no going round it. They would have to turn back.

And the second they turned their horses, Moses and Claire saw that the road had filled in with Rebels. A dozen grey-coated men stood there, easy and relaxed, their rifles pointed down, grins on their faces. A tall officer with a neat beard stepped forward, moving with great dignity. Claire wondered if it was Nathan Bedford Forrest himself.

For a fleeting moment, Claire wished she had brought Huntley's gun and not left it back at the river to lighten Tibeau's load. But no, she thought, she had no desire to use it, and wearing the thing might simply have given these soldiers an excuse to shoot them both.

"G'day boys," the officer said, and he actually saluted them in a loose way. His voice was deep and southern and he spoke very, very slowly, giving every word its due. "I'll take what ya got in them satchels. And I wouldn't try boltin' past us. You'd be shot 'fore ya got ten yards."

Then he held out his hand and waited for Claire and Moses

to hand over the satchels. But that was not what Claire did. She turned Tibeau and started galloping for the *chevaux-de-frise*, but she held her horse back, giving time for Albert and Moses to catch up.

The southern officer, and it *was* General Nathan Bedford Forrest, just held up his right hand when his men drew a bead on the two boy soldiers in northern uniforms. Part of him was curious to see what would happen, and he did not want a bullet getting in the way of this rapidly unfolding drama. He was himself a gifted horseman and he was certain those horses would stop at the *chevaux-de-frise* if the boys dared to jump it. The boys would come off in a hurry or be impaled on one of those spikes. There was only the slimmest chance that one horse would try that awful fence, with awful results if he failed to clear the height. That both horses would try it was even more unlikely, the southern general thought—so unlikely he would have bet his life against it.

Still, Claire had noticed something about this particular *chevaux-de-frise*. Rains had softened the road on one side, the right side, and one entire section of the barrier there dipped low. Instead of a five-foot-high mass of porcupine's quills, there was a four-foot-high mass. The thing was still formidable, could still spill the blood of both horse and rider, and a horse leaping it had to manage both the four-foot height and the six-foot expanse. But Claire thought this was a weak spot in the defence, one they had a shot at exploiting.

Those few seconds as they sped towards the *chevaux-de-frise* went by in a heartbeat. She looked over at Moses and she could see the terror written on his face. She knew her own face had that same look. It was pure instinct that guided her now. And she hoped and prayed her instincts were good.

Every stride took them closer to the points of that cruel comb, the white, sharp ends of the logs in bright contrast to the grey of the bark. The horses were neck and neck, pounding down that road in the bright light of mid-morning. Claire had a notion (it came and went in the blink of an eye) to let Beau Albert go ahead. He was the better, more experienced jumper; Tibeau would almost surely follow him. But then she thought of Moses. Would he lose heart if asked to go first? Would his faintness of heart be passed on to Albert? No, they would take the comb together. At least, they would try to.

Ten yards from the right side of that menacing-looking fence, Tibeau abruptly altered the course of things. He stopped, and only luck and a quick grab for his mane spared Claire a tumble in the dirt. Albert likewise pulled up short when Tibeau uttered his loud and definite *No!* to that nasty-looking obstacle. The young horse was not merely testing his rider's resolve, as horses will do when faced with high fences. He was saying, *Are you out of your mind?*

Claire could hear laughter behind her and she could see the general and his men casually walking towards them up the road. Cats closing in on cornered rats. They had expected a show, maybe a gruesome show, and now that chance had passed and they would have those satchels.

Claire gritted her teeth, resisting an urge to give Tibeau a slap with her reins. That would accomplish nothing and she knew it. She backed him up quickly, maybe five steps, to let him know she did not approve of him digging in his heels like that and that she expected better of him. Now she looked at Moses and nodded with her eyes and head back towards the Rebels. *Follow me,* she was saying.

Claire sent Tibeau off in another gallop, this time towards

the men on the road. They set their rifles on their shoulders and took aim at these two upstart boys in blue who looked to be trying a drive past them. Then Claire just as suddenly turned and headed back towards the *chevaux-de-frise,* again holding Tibeau back slightly so Albert and Moses could catch up with her. Once more they were sprinting for the low side of those spikes.

Claire could hear rifle fire behind her. That casual manner had left the Rebels and she could hear the general shouting repeatedly, "Fire! Fire!"

"Trust your horse," Claire had said to Moses when they'd started off on this long, fast ride. They would both have to trust their horses. If either Albert or Tibeau were to jump too early, they would fail to clear that second row of spikes. If they jumped too late, the first row of spikes would catch them in the chest. And if either horse balked at the last moment, the rider would be the one to suffer.

But that was not what Claire was thinking about. She saw all of them, in her mind's eye, soaring over those spikes. Clearing them handily, as if a guardian angel held each rider in her arms.

A girl who loves horses is fearless with horses. If she falls off, she gets back on. She holds no grudges, but forgives and forgets. All this the horse knows, and loves the girl for it. The girl is drawn to the horse's eyes—among the largest in the animal kingdom. The girl loves the horse for his beauty and grace and power, and, above all, for the companionship the horse bestows on her. It is why a girl who loves horses would just as soon sleep in a stall as in a bed.

Claire was just such a girl, and she did not dwell on dark outcomes. She believed in her horses, and that faith gave her, gave them, wings—like Pegasus, the white, winged horse of Greek myth.

For all that, the moment of truth at the *chevaux-de-frise* was not quite like Claire's fantasy. Oh, they cleared the spikes all right. Both horses, spurred on by the rifle fire behind them, left the ground at precisely the same moment. Asked about it after the war, Nathan Bedford Forrest would say it was one of the most beautiful things he had ever seen. "It was like they was twins," he would tell a reporter for a newspaper in Memphis. "Two fine black horses, one stout and one fine, flying with nary an inch between them in every way. Them boys riding them had gumption and grit and my hat goes off to them. But it's the horses I will not soon forget."

"Them boys" landed with little in the way of grace. Claire came down the better of the two, for she had leapt such a height before. But Tibeau jumped so high to avoid those spikes that he lost balance in the air, his nose dropped low and to the right when he touched down, and when Claire landed it was not with her usual soft touch. She was yanked forward and her nose met Tibeau's hard head when it rose.

For Moses, jumping was altogether new, and when Beau Albert leapt into the air, the horse took his rider by surprise. A more experienced rider would have gone with the horse's motion, anticipated the moment of liftoff, used his hands and crouch to help. Moses tried, but his timing was a second late, and so Albert left his rider behind him. Where Claire kept her crouch and hugged Tibeau's neck, Moses was left back in the tack, his arms outstretched, trying desperately to catch up to the horse beneath him. He never did catch up. And he was ill equipped for the hard landing, when about 1,100 pounds of horse hit that dirt road with his front hooves, and then his back hooves. Moses pitched forward violently and slid off Albert's right side.

It was a hard landing, though Moses did just what he should have. He rose in an instant, clutching his right arm, for he knew that he had to get back up on that horse in a hurry or the Rebs running towards them would soon pick them both off. Albert, bless him, stood stock-still while Moses rather inelegantly climbed back on. And they were off once more: Moses with his sprained right arm, Claire with blood flowing freely from her battered nose. But the two of them were giddy and relieved, and the horses found a gear they never knew they possessed.

The rest of the way was kinder to the four. Any soldiers in their path seemed to have vanished into the woods, or maybe there were none at all. It was as if the journey had already posed its greatest challenge—the southern general and his spiked wooden horse. And, having met the challenge and faced it down, the riders and their horses were rewarded with a free and clear path.

Out of caution and concern for the well-being of their horses, Claire and Moses settled into a trot. They let Beau Albert set the pace, and he fell into that all-day trot of his. This pace pleased him mightily and he looked almost haughty as he moved down that road. A farmer seeing him from the roadside might have said, admiringly, "Now *there's* a flashy horse."

As for Tibeau, he was less pleased. He would launch into a canter, and Claire would restrain him. Albert would match the canter, and then it was the turn of Moses to restrain. Both riders handled the job nicely.

Moses had gained confidence from the business with the spikes, and from the maple locket, too. And though Albert several times tested his will, Moses passed the exam. It is what a horse, any horse, wants after all: the knowledge and the security that the rider on his back is fair and skilled and kind. That the rider is *in charge* but not inclined to abuse his power. And so, after some discussion, Albert and Tibeau, sire and son, found a pace they could agree on and all undertook the long trot to Lawrenceburg.

Moses and Claire were bruised and battered, but they were alive. Moses's arm ached and was swollen at the elbow, but what was a little pain? Claire put a handkerchief to her blood-ied nose and eventually the flow stopped, though her blue coat now wore a proud red badge.

At the outskirts of the town, they were met by friendly forces. Though *friendly* did not quite describe the way in which they were greeted. Claire had expected open arms, grat-itude for their huge effort, a welcome at least before the boys in blue rode off to rescue their own.

That was not what happened. The sentries on the road were rude and skeptical. While three soldiers trained rifles on Moses and Claire, a fourth did the talking. The talker was clean-shaven, widely built and had a foot-long knife tucked in a scabbard on one side of his belt and a pistol jammed in the other side. Claire thought he looked grim, as if the whole world had been lying to him for years, and along had come yet another pair of liars.

"Off your horses. Real slow, everything slow. My boys are trigger-happy. Road's crawlin' with Reb spies and we ain't so impressed any more with blue uniforms."

Claire was almost stunned into silence. Then she got angry.

"Listen, there are regiments being attacked back at the Tennessee River and I'm carrying a disp—"

"Save it for the officers, boy," grim-talker said, cutting her off. "Follow these men."

Two soldiers led Claire and Moses, who in turn led Beau Albert and Tibeau, towards a wide field filled with white tents. "Nice horses," said one of the soldiers leading them. He was not infected with grim-talker's sour manner.

"Listen," said Claire. "These horses have ridden hard and long. They need water and hay. Can we do that first?"

"Sure," said the soldier.

Claire looked more closely at him. He was perhaps a year older than she was. The boy looked embarrassed to be associated with anything so unkind, so plainly discourteous, as war. He led them to a picket and gave both horses a spot to themselves, with buckets of water and several sheaves of hay. It did Moses and Claire good to see their sweaty horses with their saddles off, vigorously shaking off the dust, tucking into their food, blowing and whinnying loudly—to let every horse in the neighbourhood know that two new lords had arrived.

At the officers' tent, Claire and Moses got only a little more warmth. General John Geary hardly looked up from his map when they were presented to him. Well at least, thought Claire, he wasn't pointing a gun at them. He was, in Claire's opinion, a handsome man. He wore a high blue hat pinned up on one side, with a yellow cloth bugle sewn into the front. His blue coat dropped all the way to his knees. The General continued to study his map, ignoring them. Finally, Claire spoke. She was still angry but she would try for a diplomatic beginning.

"Sir, I'd be grateful if you listened to our story."

Now the General glanced up. He wore a look somewhere between curiosity and irritation. Who *was* this young pup?

"General, sir," she began, and, as quickly as she could, she described the situation at the Tennessee River, their hard ride, and then she reached into her satchel for the dispatch from Captain Dilger.

"Hmmmmm," General Geary said as he read it. "Do you have any idea," he asked Claire, "how many such 'dispatches' come through here in a day, Private? The Rebs would love for us to go gallivantin' all over the country, into their traps and the path of their cannon." And he handed Claire back her dispatch. "Dismissed," was all he said, and he went back to his map.

"Sir," said Claire, and now she was angry again. "Those men will die back there while you read your damn map!" It was something the Sergeant would have said, but *she* had said it, and loudly.

Anger flashed in the General's eyes. But, unlike Claire, he was good at containing his rage. "Just before I strap you in chains, boy, I'd like to know your name."

"I'm *not* a boy," said Claire, fighting back tears and failing. "I am Claire Vigere, I live in Canada East, I followed my horses in Tip Weldon's wagon and now I'm sorry I ever left home. *Merde!*" she shouted. *"Merde!"*

Moses went to her, put his arm around her and held her in his arms. He had no idea, of course, what had been said, but he knew that their plans for rescuing the Sergeant and the men of the 1st Massachusetts had completely fallen apart.

"Did you say Tip Weldon?" the General asked her. "Captain Tip Weldon?"

Claire nodded.

Now the General was letting the questions fly: "What does Tip Weldon look like?" "How many horses did he buy that time in Canada?" "What's the name of his horse-breaker?" "When, exactly, did you leave Canada and when did you last see Captain Weldon?" "What route did they take from Canada to get here?" "You say you're French, let's hear some." "What about your friend here? Why isn't he talking?" "You seem to know his sign language—show me some more."

The General grilled her for half an hour. It was a test. And when it was over, when it was clear to Claire that she had passed, the General was a changed man. Full of apology, full of warmth and charm.

The General, you see, knew Tip Weldon. Knew him very well. The two had been students together at West Point, the big military academy in Maryland. They had seen each other just weeks before, at Giesboro Point in Washington. There were huge army stables there. It was where horses gathered from all over the northern states and Canada were issued to regiments in need of them. Giesboro was the warhorse capital of the northern army. And it was there, over dinner, that Captain Weldon had told his friend General Geary the astonishing tale of Claire Vigere. Had the General *not* heard the tale, Claire and Moses would have landed in a military prison as suspected Rebel spies.

"You must be hungry, soldier," Geary said to her. "You two sit here. I'll have some food brought to you." And then he was off.

The food that soon came was a general's fare: fried chicken that even Moses admired; new potatoes, boiled, with lots of butter; fresh peas; fresh milk; apple pie for dessert. Moses kept signing to her, wanting to know what the heck she had

said to change things. *Later,* signed Claire, who was intent
on her meal.

She had just eaten her last bite of that extraordinary pie
when more officers arrived. More questions. The number of
men left in the 1st Massachusetts and the other regiments?
The size of the bridge? How many cannons and ammunition
wagons left? Number of horses? Any sense of the size of the
enemy forces? If they thought they had seen Nathan Bedford
Forrest, what did he look like?

Finally, Claire approached General Geary and said, "Please,
let's just go. My sergeant is back there and every second
wasted is precious."

"I know, Claire," said the General. "And I wish the army
moved faster than it does. I will make every effort. But, you're
coming with us?"

"Oh yes," she said, smiling. "Sarge is expecting us."

The rescue was far less eventful than anticipated, and both
rescuers and rescued were glad of that fact. The several
regiments under General Geary's command encountered no
opposition along the way, and even the *chevaux-de-frise* had
been removed from the road. The Rebs, no doubt, had hauled
it away and given it a new job elsewhere. It was as if the
spiked wooden horse had never been there. But as they passed
the place, Claire could see blood on the road. Her nose had
marked the spot, and she got a smile from Moses when she
pointed to it.

Geary's regiments walked and trotted the whole way, and
when they got close to the Tennessee, the General let loose his
bugler as they cantered into the camp by the river. Claire

wished that Moses could have heard that beautiful sound, or the *"Yeehaw!"* that went up in response. There was no mistaking the Sergeant's voice.

There were hugs all around, from Sergeant McDermott (who proudly displayed the clean pink scar forming on his hand) and Captain Dilger ("Vell done, vell done," he kept saying). Both wanted to hear of their ride on the road to Lawrenceburg, and it was a story that Claire would tell often. She had some of her grandfather's flair for a tale well told.

And if General Geary and his fellow generals were exceedingly grateful for what Claire and Moses had done, they had reason to be. The two grooms had not only saved what remained of the 1st Massachusetts and the other regiments, as well as their precious ammunition wagons and cannons (which otherwise would have fallen into the hands of Nathan Bedford Forrest), but Claire herself had done something far more important. She had given them all a story to tell among themselves.

———— ✦ ————

A newspaper sent its best reporter and a photographer to track Claire down in Tennessee. The photo in the paper showed her, still in uniform but with her hat off and smiling broadly. She was standing between Albert and Tibeau, each saddled and brushed and groomed as if for a show. Someone behind the photographer must have tossed leaves into the air to catch their attention: both horses had that alert, eyes-forward, ears-cocked look.

Claire's story would be told in newspapers all over the North, not always correctly, and not without dashes of wild invention. The reporters, or their editors, simply could not resist making her braver, taller, smarter, prettier than she really was. Tibeau and Beau Albert would similarly be stretched into heroic poses, as would Moses—the deaf former slave who learned to ride well enough that even a *chevaux-de-frise* could not keep him from his role in the daring rescue mission. But it would be Claire Vigere who would star in every reporter's front-page story.

The Clint/Claire story brought some warmth to a war badly in need of it.

The grateful army of the North relieved Claire and Moses, Tibeau and Beau Albert, of further duty. The horses were hers now; no more hard treks for them, no private's uniform for her. The war would be over soon, in any case. By the following spring, the nation had had enough of fighting with itself, of brothers slaughtering brothers, of bummers and lawlessness, of all the dead and the horribly wounded.

Moses decided to stay with the Sergeant until the war was over, then he planned to go south and look for his family. He and Claire parted reluctantly and with great sadness. She had taught him a lot—about horses, riding, horse-doctoring. But Moses had returned the favour: he had given her a new and silent language, a whole new way of seeing the world.

She bade him adieu as he had taught her—hand to mouth and out again, as if blowing a kiss. Still wearing the maple locket around his neck—Claire had insisted he keep it—Moses stood on the platform as Claire's train pulled away. He returned her farewell sign, and then he made another sign— two hands clasped, palm on palm. *Marry me?* he was asking her, but the huge grin on his face said he was kidding. The train slowly picked up speed, spewing steam with every stroke of the engine and every *chug chug-chug chug-chug-chug* while

Claire returned her friend's grin. The two held each other in sight until each disappeared from view.

Claire was certain she would cross paths with Moses Odell again, and she was right. But that is another story.

———

Claire's journey north was nothing like her trek south, though each trip had one thing in common: the passenger had gone some two thousand miles and paid nothing. Now she was heading home on a train—the army had agreed to pay for her passage and that of her horses. The Sergeant had put her in the company of an aged corporal named Sam Wilburforce. A blacksmith from Maine, he had lost the use of one eye in the battle by the Tennessee River. Sam's right eye, thought Claire, looked every bit as good, and just as brown, as the left. But the eye was dead, and the army had no use for a one-eyed soldier. And since Sam was a trustworthy sort who was more or less going her way, he was charged with getting her—and her horses—as close to home as he could.

They stopped for a time at Giesboro Point in Washington, where horses were still being gathered in these last months of the war. Claire would come back this way one day. She had plans for her horses, plans that would take her south once again.

That was in part because of a chance encounter just days before reaching Giesboro Point. On her way through Kentucky, in a tiny place called Beaver Dam, Claire had got off the train to stretch her legs. On the platform she met a horse trainer named Hank Marquette who seemed to know a great deal about her and her horses. When he timidly asked if he could see them, she took him to a boxcar at the rear of the train where Beau

Albert and Tibeau were enjoying their hay and the deluxe rolling accommodation.

Marquette walked around the two horses as though he were admiring sculptures in a gallery. He said nothing as he ran his hands over every inch of them and picked up their feet, looked at their teeth and, for the longest time, into their eyes. Marquette thought Beau Albert would make a wonderful racing trotter and he knew just the tracks to bring him to. Tibeau, he thought, had a great future as a stud and racehorse and he knew just the trainer to bring him along: one Hank Marquette.

Hank Marquette was a red-haired, blue-eyed Cajun, a French speaker from New Orleans. He was poor as a church mouse and as shy as one, but he knew horses. Better yet, he was honest. Were he a horse, Claire would have remarked on his "kind eye." Claire and Hank shook hands, exchanged addresses. Their paths, too, would cross again.

Finally, at Giesboro Point, she ran into two men who were, each in his own way, familiar to Claire. The first was Tip Weldon, the tall, imposing man whose wagon cupboard had been Claire's transportation into Vermont and on into the war. That trip seemed a long, long time ago.

Corporal Sam Wilburforce and Private Claire Vigere had been walking on a Washington street, bent on a modest hotel restaurant that had been recommended to them, when Claire spotted the Captain, who had paused—no surprise—to admire a carriage horse hitched to a post.

The Captain was overjoyed to see her, but not surprised. The army had forewarned him that Claire would be in Giesboro, and when. He invited Claire out for a dinner to celebrate her adventure and the fact that both she and her horses had survived the war. The Corporal was invited to join them, but he declined and told Claire later that he would not have felt comfortable with a captain watching the peas fall off his fork. Sam arranged to meet Claire back at the stables later.

"You look well," the Captain told Claire in the hotel restaurant, the best that Washington had to offer in the summer of 1864.

Claire's hair had grown out, and though short hair on young women was not the fashion then it seemed the perfect frame for her face. She wore to the dinner her Union army uniform, cleaned and pressed in a manner that would have made the Sergeant proud. One added touch was a fine pair of dark-brown leather boots she had bought with her army wage of a dollar a day (of which she had otherwise spent not a penny). Claire was only days from turning fourteen, but she carried herself like someone much older. She was a striking young woman in uniform in the company of men, who noticed her.

When they were nearing the end of the meal, Tip reached up with his napkin to dab his lips and he said, "I've decided not to press charges against you, Claire."

She frowned. She had no idea what he was talking about.

"Theft," he said, trying not to smile but doing a poor job of it. "That little matter on Lake Champlain—the stolen bread and ham, and the dollar coin from that poor, confused wrangler! And especially the goatskin of rum!!!!" Finally the Captain burst out laughing, and so did Claire as it all came back to her.

"I had such a headache in the morning," she groaned.

Then the Captain switched the topic of conversation. "Ambrose will be glad to see you when you get home. He's missed you more than I can say."

With those words, Claire felt a great wave of emotion come over her. Everything ran together: her affection for this man, an almost physical attraction that was new and that she had no words for. Her longing to speak French, to sleep in her own bed, to fight with her brothers, to hug every Vigere. Her sadness at some of the losses she had endured on this journey: loss of innocence, certainly, for certain memories—of Huntley, of men lost in war, of horses lost in war—still haunted her. All this time, she had held herself in check. Claire had been a runaway girl for almost two hundred days, she had been up on a stage cast as a deaf boy in a soldier's blue uniform. Now the play was over and she was exhausted. It took all her resolve not to go to the Captain and throw her arms around him and let the tears run.

Tip Weldon saw it coming, though, and he shifted gears yet again to spare them both.

"That day in the round pen in Williamstown—after Beau Albert bucked off Huntley and you and Albert jumped that five-foot fence? You must have wondered if I had recognized you from Missisquoi Bay."

"Yes," replied Claire. "I was terrified that you would remember me. Did you?"

"Maybe," he said with a smile, and, at this, Claire dipped her fingers in her water glass and playfully tossed a few drops his way. Tip Weldon pretended to cower under the spray and used his napkin as a towel.

"There's someone else here tonight who is dying to meet you," he said. "Shall I bring him over?"

Claire nodded.

Tip Weldon brought back to their table a tall, dignified man whose clothes cried out for an iron.

"I hear," he said as he took Claire's hand, "you've been ripping pages from my books." Then he bowed low, still with her hand in his, said, *"Enchanté, mademoiselle,"* and kissed the top of her hand as if she were a princess and he a diplomat from some faraway land. "Krieghoff. Cornelius Krieghoff."

Claire's mouth opened ever so slightly, and the tall man became, before her eyes, a little bit taller. He had been invited by the Union army to paint battle scenes and portraits of generals standing proudly in front of their tents or soldiers posed leaning against trees. Krieghoff seemed weary at the very thought of it. In fact, his health was not good. Claire was delighted to meet him, but she kept staring at his wild and curly hair, which seemed to have a life of its own and to fly from the top and sides of his head. The hair was receding, too, and his long, wide expanse of forehead gave him the look of someone whose brain had begun to grow and whose head was expanding to make room for it.

"It's work," Krieghoff said of the war art, and he shrugged his shoulders. "What I really want to paint," he told Claire, "is you."

Cornelius Krieghoff had come to know her story, of course, after meeting Tip Weldon and Ambrose Vigere at the auberge in Farnham. Krieghoff had also seen the newspaper photograph of Claire and the two horses, and he thought the image failed to do justice to her bold adventure. He had made inquiries through his many contacts in the army, learned of Claire's plans and arranged to be in Giesboro when she was. The painter had gone to what he called "a great deal of trouble" to find the girl he was convinced would be the subject for a great painting. A painting that would make him famous, end his money troubles and secure his reputation forever. His brown eyes were flashing now, and his intensity was beginning to make Claire uncomfortable.

"All my life," the painter said, sounding sad, "I have done landscapes—because that's what people wanted. Or portraits—because that's what I was paid to do. I have been looking all this time for a truly worthy subject for a painting. A painting that will revive my passion for art. A painting to tell a great story, one that will have a life long after I'm gone. Well, I have found my subject. It's you, my dear. It's you."

Krieghoff moved closer to her, put his arm around her chair and began to describe in great detail the painting he envisioned. His voice got softer, as if he were telling her a secret that no one in the hotel should hear. Claire looked over at Tip Weldon, a plea for help. He gave her just a hint of a smile, for the Captain had great confidence in Claire. She had handled all sorts of adversity by herself, and now she would learn to handle this new thing: men taken by her and by her tale.

Like a man possessed, Krieghoff talked about the work of art he had in mind, a series of three paintings to be set alongside one another. And though each frame would be tall and rectangular, each painting would be oval-shaped—the shape, more or less, of an egg on its end. The first painting, on the left, would capture Claire as the village girl. The second, in the middle, would be of Claire as boy soldier. The third, on the right, would show her as a young woman.

And it was this third painting that he was most anxious to describe. The horses, Tibeau and Albert, would be loose on either side of her. The horses would have their heads lowered, near hers, as if they were all somehow connected by blood.

"The bond between the girl and these horses—that's what I'm after," said Krieghoff, beaming now.

It would be summer, they would be in a field, with the Vigere cabin and barns in the distance. "The girl/woman (that's how Krieghoff put it) would be on the ground, stretched out, like Eve in the Garden of Eden." Her naked-ness, the painter assured both Tip Weldon and Claire Vigere, and he looked to one and then the other, would be discreet. "Branches and leaves in the foreground, as well as her long hair," he said, "would, of course, shield her modesty ..."

Claire rose slowly from the table before he could finish his sentence, and both men rose when she did. What she really felt like doing was laughing, one of those loud belly laughs where you bend over and gasp for air. And she wished Moses were there so she could sign to him the silly Garden of Eden scene that this painter had in mind. She liked Krieghoff, liked his enthusiasm and very much liked his art, but some ideas needed to be mocked, and this was one of them.

Claire's time in the military had taught her the value of the hasty retreat. Which is what she now did. With dignity, she thanked Monsieur Krieghoff for his interest and Captain Weldon for the fine meal. Claire shook the painter's hand and thanked him sincerely for his book of paintings. "When I was far from home," she told him, "those scenes gave me more comfort than I can say. I looked at your book every day for the six months I was away. *Merci beaucoup, monsieur.*" Then she turned to the Captain and offered him a warm embrace, which he returned in kind. "Thanks for the ride," she whis-pered in his ear, then stepped back and saluted him.

Claire bade them both adieu. In her mind she was already on a train heading north, watching the birches and the pines and the oaks roll by, hearing and feeling the rhythm of the coach on the steel rails. Claire had never been on a train before boarding one in Tennessee, and she loved it. That rocking motion and the sounds of the rails *(ther-thu ther-thu ther-thu)* had put her into a sweet sleep, and she was looking forward to another one.

—⊶⊷—

Claire dreamed all the way home of Magrette's cooking, of all that was good and familiar about the Vigere clan and the old village of L'Ange-Gardien. Somewhere before the Canadian border, the train stopped and Corporal Wilburforce gave Claire a lazy salute and stepped off the train. His home in the Blue Mountains of Maine, just east of Sherbrooke, was close now. Coach and horse would take him the rest of the way. For the one-eyed, brown-eyed soldier, the war was finally over.

The Corporal had hardly uttered two words in all their time together, but Claire would miss him nonetheless. Travelling with such a quiet man was like travelling with Moses. And that was all right, for she had acquired an appetite for silence.

The train continued chugging north in the early-morning light, black smoke spilling from its massive black stack. Claire had the compartment all to herself, and she stretched out on the seat and dozed as the train beat out its rhythm on the tracks.

—⊶⊷—

Ther-thu ther-thu ther-thu …

By the time Claire, Beau Albert and Tibeau arrived at the Canadian border, the landscape had not changed much, but the names of towns had. St. Albans, Swanton and Highgate

Springs in Vermont had given way to names in Canada East that Claire well knew: Saint Armand, Bedford and Farnham.

Many miles from the village of L'Ange-Gardien, she spotted in the distance the dark outline of familiar hills. Mount St. Gregoire and Rougemont to the west. Yamaska to the north. Bromont to the northeast. The land around the village was flat, so you could always see the high hills and mountains, some near and some far, and she looked on them as old friends.

At the station in the centre of the village, Claire led the horses down the ramp and off the train. It was not much past dawn, and no one was about. She saddled Tibeau, who sniffed the air and issued a loud whinny. The young horse knew he was home, and that an answering call would come soon enough. Even Beau Albert—always willing to stand patiently when asked—danced in anticipation as Claire fixed a halter and lead rope on him.

"Attends, attends," she told him. "Hold your horses."

At last he fell in behind Claire and Tibeau as they took the road to home. Past the general store and the church—both made of the same fieldstone. She had been eleven years old when that church was constructed, and the store had been built using stone left over from that massive undertaking. Now store and church were sister buildings. Claire remembered how the men of the village had dug a great pit and tossed in—every day for weeks prior to construction—rocks almost the size of horses' heads. The stones they had cursed in the fields had been given a new and sacred duty as building material.

Even then she had been amazed at the colours of the stone. All shades of brown and grey, rust and black and pink, some of the rock streaked with pale lines. Time lines.

She could not have known that all of the stone had long ago been underwater on the bottom of an ancient sea.

Claire had a favourite stone among the hundreds used in the building of the Church of the Guardian Angel. The rock was on the west face, midway down. Not rounded like most of the others, this one was more rectangular and was distinguished by its polished grey surface and a black marking that looked for all the world like a king's crown. The kind of crown, Claire thought when she had first spotted it, that branded the horses sent by the King of France in the 1600s. This was a stone you wanted to touch. When she was eleven, Claire was tall enough to reach up and touch that stone, and she had often rubbed it for good luck after Sunday Mass.

Now she looked to her right as she rode past and thought of rubbing the stone once more, but the horses seemed anxious for home. Besides, she already had luck. Luck or God or fate, and maybe all three, had gotten her and her horses through a terrible war. To ask for yet more luck seemed almost greedy, Claire thought.

The closer they got to the Vigere farm, the more wound up the horses became. Claire could hear Minon and the others calling, and Beau Albert and Tibeau were keenly answering. Pure instinct guided Claire now. She leapt off Tibeau, put up his stirrups and knotted his reins, then removed the rope from Albert and let the two horses race for home. She herself would walk the final steps to the cabin.

⎯⎯⎯⎯✦⎯⎯⎯⎯

At the cabin, Ambrose was up as usual. The sun was just rising and he was down in the root cellar making it ready for the harvest. This day he was building shelves, which he hoped would groan in a few months under the weight of apples and carrots and Magrette's preserves. When he heard a loud rumble outside, Ambrose thought at first it was thunder heralding a storm. But when he raised his head up out of the cellar, he heard the hooves and then saw a blessed sight. Beau Albert and Tibeau, neck and neck, running his way.

Ambrose climbed outside in a hurry and stood waiting. He thought they were running towards him, but he should have known better. The old horseman did know better, but the joy of seeing those horses again had clouded his judgment. Of course they ran by him, like water around a boulder in a fast-moving creek. The horses would seek him out in a minute, but first they had to greet Minon and all the other horses. The horses would breathe each other in, and remember. Ambrose would have to wait his turn.

Now he hoped, hoped against hope, that where the horses were, Claire was, too. He waited, and looked down the road, for what seemed an eternity. Then he saw her. And when he did he dropped to the ground onto his knees and wept like a child. That was how they embraced. The old man on his knees, his head at his granddaughter's belly, his arms at his side, the young girl kissing the red hat on his head.

They said nothing for the longest time, and finally Claire, too, dropped to her knees and looked into her grandfather's very wet, very blue eyes. She was crying too, and she was already planning a long hack with him through the woods with Beau Albert and Tibeau. She would tell *Père-père* on the trail, she promised, story after story of all that she had seen and done, and of her great plans for her two black horses in days to come.

"*Ben*," the old man said. "*Ben oui.*"

Then Claire stood up and helped the old man to his feet. She ran her left arm through the crook of his right arm and launched into a little jig, which her grandfather picked up on in an instant. She led him left, then he led her right, and that's how they made their way to the Vigere cabin. Not in a walk, not in a run, but in a silent, gingery, zigzag dance.

AUTHOR'S NOTE

As far as I know, Claire Vigere and her family never existed, but the poverty of *habitants* in the nineteenth century was very real. The scene early in *The Horse's Shadow* describing the Charette family being evicted was repeated countless times.

Between 1850, when the fictional Claire was born, and the end of that century, some 500,000 men, women and children left what we now call Quebec. Given the tiny population, the numbers are shocking. Today, we would call such people refugees. In those days, they were just the wandering poor.

In the year that Claire was born, a farm labourer around L'Ange-Gardien earned a dollar a day; live-in help got even less. Butter was only twenty-two cents a pound at the village store and eggs were just twelve cents a dozen, but cents were hard to come by. I have all these figures thanks to a remarkable book called *La Petite Histoire de L'Ange-Gardien,* published in 1981 by dedicated amateur historians in the village.

Captain Tip Weldon did not exist either (at least I don't think so), but there was indeed a massive sell-off of Canadian horses to American horse-buyers at the time of the Civil War. It has been estimated that the war used up millions of horses. Many of Canada East's finest stallions and mares went south— some across the frozen Lake Champlain, much as I have described it—never to return. Only years later did breeders realize the damage done to the bloodlines and the value of a heritage horse they had all come to take for granted. And yes, the *habitants* did race their horses on frozen rivers, ponds and lakes—including Missisquoi Bay.

There were some 150,000 Canadian horses in Canada East and Canada West in the 1850s, and they enjoyed a reputation as the finest all-purpose horse on the continent. But by the end of that century, it was hard to find any pureblood Canadian horses on this side of the border. The war, sales to the carriage trade and breeders below the border, cross-breeding: all just about destroyed the breed, until the government set about reviving Canada's national horse. (The history of the Canadian horse forms part of my book *Little Horse of Iron*.)

The terms "Canada East" and "Canada West" might seem unfamiliar to some readers. Certainly Ambrose Vigere would have found the phrases strange: when he was a boy, there was only Upper Canada (Ontario) and Lower Canada (Quebec). In 1841, they were renamed Canada West and Canada East, but the designation was short-lived. In 1867, Canada was born.

Moses Odell is another imagined character, but what is factual is his use of sign language. The nineteenth century was the golden age of Sign. Alexander Graham Bell (1847–1922) launched a campaign to get the deaf to speak, and many deaf people are grateful for what he did to bridge the gap between the hearing and the deaf. But others among the deaf wish he had not bothered and argue that Sign is the true and natural language of the deaf.

As for the names of some of the soldiers in Claire's war, I am grateful to Bruce Catton's book, *The Army of the Potomac Trilogy*, that classic account of the Civil War published in

1951. Nathan Forrest existed, and military strategists of the First World War and the Second World War were still studying his great victory at Brice's Crossroads. Some called it "the perfect battle." And there *was* a massacre of black soldiers at Fort Pillow.

There was, indeed, a courageous German soldier nicknamed "Leatherbreeches" (Hubert Dilger) fighting on the northern side. There was a Major Pennock Huey and a General John Geary. There was even a Sergeant Daniel McDermott, who fought with the 7th Wisconsin. But real though the names are, their characters are mostly invented. The women in the war—"Mother" Bickerdyke and Annie Etheridge—existed much as I describe them.

By the end of the Civil War, the dead on both sides numbered 620,000, with just as many wounded—not to mention all the civilian dead, who were never counted. Those losses were greater in number than the casualties sustained by the United States in both World Wars, the Korean War and the Vietnam War combined.

The Civil War was not so long ago, really. A girl born today could have had a great-grandfather who fought in that war. That is how history should be measured: in lives lived.

Finally, there was a painter named Cornelius Krieghoff and he appears in *The Horse's Shadow* much as he was in Claire's time. Krieghoff died just six years after the Civil War ended, and his obsession with a thirteen-year-old girl playing boy soldier is entirely my invention. This book owes a great deal to the man and to his art. Any reader who wants to see the several Krieghoff paintings described in the novel will find them, in splendid colour, in *Krieghoff: Images of Canada*, by Dennis Reid.

ACKNOWLEDGMENTS

Thanks to: Norah Brown, Daphne Maclean, Colleen Revell, Diana Wyatt and Silver Smith Wyatt—stablemates at the Cataraqui Equestrian Centre near Kingston, Ontario. All read an early manuscript and kindly offered counsel and encouragement. Kathi Bayly, Ulrike Bender, Claudine Carpenter, Maureen Garvie and Elva McGaughey likewise. The thirty-one horses at the stable, meanwhile, continue to educate me on matters of herd dynamics and the many shades of equine personality.

Père Léo Lemay, for the gift of *La Petite Histoire de L'Ange-Gardien,* the tour of the church, and the stories. Frances Itani, for the gracious loan of *The Sign Language: A Manual of Signs,* published in 1910. Patricia Cooper, for introducing me to the Canadian horse some seven years ago and setting me on this course. Editor Diane Turbide, for setting the bar high, and copy editor Catherine Marjoribanks, for the fine fine-tuning.

And, finally, my thanks to Saroma Dark Fox Dali, my rugged Canadian horse who has taught me so much about his kind and whose spirit guided this novel from start to finish.